WHERE I WAS
PLANTED

D1255211

WHERE I WAS PLANTED

Heather Norman Smith

AMBASSADOR INTERNATIONAL
GREENVILLE, SOUTH CAROLINA & BELFAST, NORTHERN IRELAND
www.ambassador-international.com

Where I Was Planted

© 2019 by Heather Norman Smith

All rights reserved

ISBN: 978-1-62020-907-3
eISBN: 978-1-62020-920-2

No part of this publication may be reproduced, distributed, or transmitted in any form or by any means, including photocopying, recording, or other electronic or mechanical methods, without the prior written permission of the publisher, except in the case of brief quotations embodied in critical reviews and certain other noncommercial uses permitted by copyright law. For permission requests, contact the publisher using the information below.

This is a work of fiction. Names, characters, and incidents are all products of the author's imagination or are used for fictional purposes. Any resemblance to actual events or persons, living or dead, is entirely coincidental. Any mentioned brand names, places, and trademarks remain the property of their respective owners, bear no association with the author or the publisher, and are used for fictional purposes only.

Scripture taken from the New King James Version®. Copyright © 1982 by Thomas Nelson. Used by permission. All rights reserved.

Cover Design & Typesetting by Hannah Nichols
Ebook Conversion by Anna Riebe Raats
Edited by Katie Cruice Smith

AMBASSADOR INTERNATIONAL
Emerald House
411 University Ridge, Suite B14
Greenville, SC 29601, USA
www.ambassador-international.com

AMBASSADOR BOOKS
The Mount
2 Woodstock Link
Belfast, BT6 8DD, Northern Ireland, UK
www.ambassadormedia.co.uk

The colophon is a trademark of Ambassador, a Christian publishing company.

That he would grant you, according to the riches of his glory, to be strengthened with might by his Spirit in the inner man;

That Christ may dwell in your hearts by faith; that ye, being rooted and grounded in love,

May be able to comprehend with all saints what is the breadth, and length, and depth, and height;

And to know the love of Christ, which passeth knowledge, that ye might be filled with all the fulness of God.

Now unto him that is able to do exceeding abundantly above all that we ask or think, according to the power that worketh in us,

Unto him be glory in the church by Christ Jesus throughout all ages, world without end. Amen.

Ephesians 3:16-21

Chapter One

WEEDS

I'VE SPENT A LOT OF time thinking about weeds. Not just the dandelion and chickweed that pops up uninvited in people's vegetable gardens. I'm talking about the kind of weeds that squeeze themselves up through the tiniest of cracks in sidewalks, and in roads and parking lots, and in little crevices in rocks. They're unattractive to most people, but I think these plants are remarkable. Shallow soil, short roots, and trampled on by every pair of feet that happens their way—not to mention tires. But still they manage to keep growing, or at the very least, sprout up a little and stay green. I reckon most people have never even thought about it, how special they are. But I've thought about it a lot . . . because I'm one of them.

I figured it out on a Saturday afternoon, in the early spring of my fifth-grade year, at Susie Pennywell's eleventh birthday party. I hadn't laid eyes on Bert in three days, as he came and went mostly while I was at school or asleep, so it seemed okay to go without asking his permission.

It was a long walk to Susie's house. I started out with a swift pace, determined not to be the last kid at the party. But after the first twenty minutes, it felt like my shoes were filled with lead. I shoved my hands down deep into the pockets of my denim trousers and forced my legs to work harder, step by step. *That cake's gonna be worth it, Nate. Just keep walkin'. That birthday cake will surely be worth it,* I thought.

I had never been to Susie's house before, or to any of my other classmates' houses, except for Patrick's. He was my best friend and the only person in the world I could count on, besides our teacher, Miss Gentry.

Like Patrick, Susie never picked on me about my height.

I was six inches shorter than the next shortest person in my class. My father was of normal height, and so was my mother when she was alive—as best I could recall. I had no symptoms of anything wrong with me, like a sickness. I was just little. Miss Gentry liked to say to me all the time that special things sometimes come in small packages. It did make me feel a little bit better—not because I believed what she meant about my size, but because she smiled really sweetly when she said it, her eyelashes fluttered like butterfly wings, and she patted me on the shoulder.

The name *Weenie* was born on the first day of first grade, assigned to me by a giant of a kid named Hershel West. It didn't matter that he was the dumbest kid in the county, and everybody knew it. The name stuck; and by second grade, some kids didn't even know my real name. I tried for a while in the beginning to convince kids to call me Nate, but eventually I gave up and surrendered to being Weenie. I figured there were worse things they could call me.

Some people could be real jerks about my height. Some didn't seem to care enough that I existed to give two turnips about how short I was. And there were others, a rare few, who were a real kind of nice, and they seemed to like me, little legs and all. I've learned that just about all people fit into one of those groups in general—the mean ones, the ones that don't care, and the nice ones. Susie was part of the nice group, and I had a good feeling that, even if her parents hadn't invited the whole class, she would have invited me to her party anyway.

When I got there, all the guests were in the backyard; and for a while, nobody saw me. I milled around the food and gift tables covered in pretty pink cloths, pretending to be a secret agent on an important mission. No one saw when I slipped the folded piece of notebook paper out of my shirt pocket and placed one corner of it under a fancy, wrapped box on the gift table to keep it from blowing away. It was a homemade birthday card for Susie—one that told her how pretty she was and what a nice smile she had. I had signed it from "a friend." I walked away and overheard some grown-ups debating whether or not to move the party indoors. The sky was like one giant marshmallow, with no blue to speak of.

"I think the rain's going to hold off," said a man as he looked up into the sky. He wore a tall, Red Man tobacco cap high on his head. He leaned his head back so far to inspect the clouds that he had to hold the hat to keep it from falling off.

"I hope you're right!" said a lady with thick-rimmed glasses.

I imagined the couple were double agents, working for the Kremlin.

I looked around for Patrick, but I didn't see him; so, I sat down on the cinderblock back steps of Susie's house and watched my classmates play.

The grass of the yard still looked like wintertime—dull grayish-green, dotted by crunchy brown patches. The space was bounded by tall trees, and it was mostly flat, except for a mound of earth in one corner, which begged for someone to climb it. All the boys grouped together on top of that hill, and all the girls stood in a group in the middle of the yard; and the two groups pretended not to notice each other for the first ten minutes of the party. The air had a strong chill, but none of the kids seemed to care. It was balmy compared to the bitter cold that had dug its claws in for all of the winter months. There was more snow in the winter of 1960 and '61 than I had ever seen before or have since.

I hugged my knees up tight to my chest and wrapped the plaid, flannel shirt that I wore for a jacket around all of me. A thin woman with giant hair and kind eyes walked over to me and placed a Dixie cup of red Kool-Aid in my hand.

"Thank you, ma'am," I said to her.

"You're certainly welcome! I don't believe I know your name." Her voice was high-pitched and floaty.

"I'm Nate Dooley, ma'am."

"Well, it's nice to meet you, Nate. I'm Susie's mother, Mrs. Pennywell. Do you live close by? I didn't see anyone drop you off. You must live close enough to walk."

"About a mile and a half, ma'am. Yes, I walked to get here."

I took a big gulp of my drink. I'd only ever had Kool-Aid at school, on special days, and that artificial blend of fruity flavors made my taste buds feel alive.

"That's quite a ways," Susie's mother said, looking concerned. "Would you like for Mr. Pennywell to drive you home when the party is over?" She placed a hand lightly on my shoulder.

"Well, I don't want to be any trouble."

"Oh, it's no trouble at all. He'll be happy to do it. We especially don't want to send you walkin' home, since it's lookin' like rain."

"Thank you, ma'am," I said. "That would be nice."

Susie saw me sitting there on the steps and bounced over, her braided pigtails bouncing off her shoulders. She flashed a big, bright, it's-my-birthday smile at me.

"Thanks for coming to my party, Nate. I hope you have a good time," she said. Her mother beamed proudly at Susie's good manners; then Susie ran off across the yard, and I yelled after her, "Thanks for inviting me!" My voice squeaked a little.

A boy in a green jacket had stopped ignoring her and was chasing her in a game of freeze tag. It looked fun, but I was still tired; and I was better off not wasting my time. Someone always tagged me first, and I had to stand frozen for an uncomfortably long span.

The first party game was a sack race. I tried it, only because Susie asked me to, but I did as badly as I expected I would. The sack was too tall, so I either had to hold it up to my eyeballs or let it bunch around my feet, which made jumping tricky.

The kids lined up for horseshoes next, and I was last on my team. When it was finally my turn to toss, the heavy shoe landed two feet in front of the stake—the third worst throw of the game, better than only two of the girls. *Always too short*, I thought. I stayed in line but passed on my final turn.

The most exciting thing about the party, even better than seeing Susie, was the cake. All the kids gathered around the long food table, and we sang "Happy Birthday" as Susie's mother brought out three layers of fluffy strawberry goodness covered in creamy, sweet, homemade frosting. She walked slowly, holding the cake stand out in front of her by the glass pedestal. It reminded me of the picture in my Bible storybook of the wise men presenting their special gifts to the baby Jesus.

With eleven white candles aglow on top, the cake looked like something out of a magazine. But it was more than pretty. It tasted like something out of a dream, and it was just about the highlight of

the entire month of March for me. There was even enough of it for
everyone to have two pieces.

As much as I enjoyed that delicious dessert, it wasn't a birthday cake
that caused me to see the differences between Susie's life and mine.
It wasn't the fact that Susie always had friends swarming around her,
while people tended to avoid me as if I smelled bad, although I was almost certain I didn't. It wasn't even because she called her father *Daddy*,
while I had always called mine by his first name. It was what I saw her
father *do* that helped put my circumstances into the right perspective.

Right after birthday cake, when bellies were still too full, the
kids divided into teams again for a relay race to the edge of the yard
and back. I sat out, still savoring the strawberry taste in my mouth,
and I ended up with a front-row seat to see Hershel stick out his
stinky, clunky foot and trip Susie at the start of her turn. Susie's
father saw it, too, and immediately, the veins in his neck popped
out. The blue lines looked like the rivers of the Smokies on a map
in our classroom.

Mr. Pennywell scooped Susie up off the ground and gave her
a two-armed, swallow-you-up kind of hug. She looked fine to me,
but maybe a little dazed from how suddenly she had gone down.
He checked her all over and made sure she wasn't hurt. He stooped
down to look her straight in the eyes, to see if there were any tears.
He helped brush the dirt off her plaid dress. Right there in front of
me and everybody else, her father turned an invisible emotion into
something I could see with my own two eyes.

After he made sure his daughter was okay, I could tell it took every
bit of Christian goodness he possessed not to lay Hershel out right
there in his backyard. He did give him a tongue-lashing, though, with

everybody watching, and I think he made Hershel wish he had laid him out instead.

"I . . . I'm . . . sorry, sir," big ole Hershel blabbered like a baby, as Mr. Pennywell stood over him with his pointer finger almost touching Hershel's nose. "I . . . I . . . wasn't tryin' to hurt nobody."

"Well, you sure better be glad she's not hurt, or I'd be takin' it up with your father! It would serve you well to learn some manners! What were you thinkin'?" Susie's father put away his pointer finger and was almost nose-to-nose with Hershel, who was trying his best not to cry.

The scene was outstanding. Susie's father came to her defense, like a knight in shining armor against a fairytale dragon. He stood up for her, and it seemed like a perfectly natural thing for him to do. And I wondered why I hadn't seen the way of things before.

I couldn't remember a time that I needed defending when Bert was around. The fact was, he wasn't around very much. But I knew that if he ever did see an injustice toward me, like the one Susie suffered, he wouldn't react like Susie's father. I just knew it. And for the first time, I understood that life with the man I knew as my father was not the standard. I searched the faces of the other kids, trying to see if the light bulb had gone off for anybody other than me. I didn't even notice the falling rain that made big wet circles on Susie's card on the gift table.

Maybe it's just that way with fathers and daughters, I tried to reason, but it felt like I was lying to myself.

I had always been content at home, and until Susie's party, I didn't know I had reason not to be. I had food and clothes and a bed to sleep in. And Bert never beat me, not even once. But I was invisible.

My father worked a lot, I guessed, sometimes during the day and other times at night; but I didn't even know what he did for a job. He once told me that I should save my breath instead of asking questions. "If I want you to know something, I'll tell you," he would say. So, most of what I knew about him, I gained through observation and deduction. I assumed that when he looked tired, he had been working. And certain smells were hints. Sometimes smoky, other times greasy, the tired look and the smells usually went together.

I didn't think much about what Bert did when he was away from our house. I just knew he wasn't there, and I tended to make the most of having the place all to myself.

In the evenings, I listened to *Gunsmoke* on the radio. And I read a lot, mostly books I brought home from school. When she finished with them, Miss Gentry gave me all her personal copies of the *National Geographic Magazine* to keep because I loved them, and because she was just nice—the nicest person I knew. I read those over and over, and I lost myself in the pages every time.

Based on what I knew of the world up to that point, my life didn't seem so bad, especially compared to some of the stories in my magazines, about real people who lived right out in the wild. But what Susie's father did shook me up. I understood how things were supposed to be. And had it not been for the delicious cake, I would have almost regretted going to the party at all because of how much it changed me.

Like in my big Bible storybook, where Adam and Eve sinned and suddenly realized they were naked—that's how I felt. Seeing Susie's father act like he did opened my eyes, and then I couldn't see anything else for a while, except how wrong things were at my house.

I didn't put it together about the weed right then. I made that observation a few weeks later on a Saturday morning on the way to meet Patrick. We had plans to hunt for glass bottles at the dump site down Higgins Road.

The dump had mostly old tires and broken toilets and other things that people dropped off there when they didn't know what else to do with them. But sometimes, we would find a few bottles we could turn in for a two-cent refund in town and then buy bubble gum.

I took my time walking, saving my energy for bottle-hunting. I passed a handful of houses, and a few people called to me from their front porch or garden or yard.

"Hey there, Nate!"

"Hello, Nate!"

"What's up, Nate?"

It was nice to hear my name.

Some neighbors I knew, just from my normal walks. Others I didn't know at all. Yet, everyone knew my name. I figured they all had heard about the poor boy who lost his mama and lived with a father who wasn't around very much. Either way, I smiled and waved back. It felt good to know I wasn't completely alone in those hills.

My walk to meet Patrick took me a long way down my gravel road, then across the paved road that led to town, then to the dirt road that led to the dump. Just before my feet hit the hardness of the highway, I noticed a puny weed, about five inches tall, growing in the asphalt. It was right in the center of a lane, between the white and yellow lines, and a beam of sunlight fell on it like a spotlight. The crack in the road was so impossibly small, the plant looked as if it were growing straight through the hardtop, like some sort of magic trick.

It was such an ordinary, every-day sight; but on that day, it stood out to me how a living thing can survive in less-than-ideal circumstances. And I couldn't quit thinking about that thing, growing up where it wasn't supposed to be, but too inconsequential for someone to come along and pluck it up. I stared at it, focused on its sad-looking leaves. The stem looked strong, but I wondered if it would grow better if it had the chance to live in good, deep soil.

There was no way to move it. If I tried, I would break it off above the root, and it would die. But it was just a weed.

I tried to explain it to Patrick when we met up, the things that seeing that weed had made me feel. We talked while sifting through old junk, trying not to get our hands cut on rusty metal.

"What do you mean, Nate? You're nowhere near as small as a weed," he said. He lifted the corner of a soiled, water-logged mattress to check for bottles we might have missed before.

"I don't mean I'm little like a weed. I just mean that sometimes I think . . . never mind." It was too much for little boys to talk about.

I looked at my distorted, disappointed reflection in the bottom part of a grime-covered window of an old car with no tires. The winter hadn't stolen my tan. I was still golden-skinned heading into the spring. I stood there squinty-eyed as the sun bounced off the glass and onto my face. *Never mind*, I instructed myself.

I really didn't want to burden him with the new knowledge that had troubled me, so I let it go. Patrick's situation wasn't exactly the standard either, since his stepfather was an alcoholic and could go from tolerable to not in two seconds. But Patrick wasn't ready to hear it. After all, we were only ten years old. He still had plenty of time to figure out he was a weed in the road. I had just figured it out a little early.

Chapter Two

FIGURING THINGS OUT

"NATE, DEAR."

She spoke softly, but it still startled me. Miss Gentry had squatted down on the right side of my desk, the second from the back in the middle row of five in the classroom.

"Your mind is somewhere else, isn't it?" she whispered.

The rest of the class was heads down on their arithmetic work, while my pencil hadn't yet touched the paper. She had caught me in a daydream, thinking about ways I might change my situation.

"I'm sorry, Miss Gentry," I said, with my eyes fixed on the shoelaces of my canvas sneakers.

"You've seemed very distracted lately."

"I know." I looked up and around to see if the other kids were watching. I locked eyes with a couple of people in the row to my left; then those nosy kids pretended to get back to work, like they were minding their own business. From what I could tell, everyone else was actually working.

"Nate, I want you to know that I'm here for you if there's anything you need to talk about. For now, I need you to focus on your work please." Her voice was like honey.

I wanted to talk to her. I wanted to explain why I was so distracted, but it was too hard.

"Yes, ma'am," I said.

For weeks after Susie's party, I had pondered what I should do with my new knowledge. I thought about leaving Copper Creek, just picking up and making a new life for myself somewhere else. I didn't necessarily want to look for something better. I just figured it wouldn't matter to Bert if I left, so I might as well go. Simple as that.

The books my teacher gave me had stories of amazing places that I wanted to see, that I felt destined to see some day. One of them had a feature on Central Park in New York with a two-page color photograph taken from seventy stories high on top of the RCA building. The scene in the picture stretched for miles and showed building after building that reached way into the sky, and the Hudson River in the distance. The picture was of happy-looking people on the observation deck of the skyscraper, looking out into the big city. It was interesting to think about what a person can see when they have the right vantage point.

My daydreams weren't all selfish, though. Our new president had challenged all of us. He told us to ask ourselves what we could do for our country. Those words played in my mind a lot. Wherever I wound up, I wanted to find a way to make it a better place. *Surely, I can do whatever I set my mind to. All I need to do is work hard,* I often thought.

That afternoon I talked to Patrick about it as we walked home from where the school bus dropped us off at the end of Pecan Lane. It was mid-April; and if I hadn't known it by the calendar, the columbine and milkweed in bloom would have told me so. The air felt warmer than normal for that time of year in the High Country.

"Where would you go?" he said, when I brought up the idea of leaving.

"I could hop on a train and just see where it takes me." I paused for a second, as I tried to figure out in my head whether train-hopping was the same thing as stealing. Stealing was number seven in the picture of Moses' stone tablet in my Bible storybook. But I decided it wasn't the same thing.

"Who knows, I might get to see the Grand Canyon. Or I could end up in New York or New Orleans or New Mexico! Anywhere *new* would be okay," I said, cracking a smile.

"Nate, I don't think you wanna do that." He looked serious. "What if you decide you wanna come home, and then you don't know which train to get on to bring you back? I'd never see you again."

"I guess you're right," I said. I shifted the weight of my school bag on my shoulder. "I don't want to leave for good."

I wanted to see the world, but I loved my mountains, too. And it meant a whole lot that at least Patrick would miss me. I would miss him, too. And Miss Gentry.

"Wouldn't it be fun to take off just for the summer, though, Patrick?" I asked, reaching up to give him a slap on the back. "We could be like Robin Hood and Little John. We could travel all over and find people who need our help along the way. See some sights and do good at the same time." It made me feel big thinking about it.

"I guess. But they stole from the rich." He shot me a wary look, and I saw the stone tablet in my mind again.

"Well, okay, maybe not like those guys, but we could still help people somehow. We'd just have to figure out ways to do it."

I wanted to make a difference, and I wanted to see what else was out there, to touch it, and taste it, and smell it, like I couldn't do in the pages of my magazines. Not forever, but for a while.

"I don't know, Nate. Just promise me you won't take off without telling me. And if you do take a trip, you have to let me know when you plan on coming back."

Patrick had been my friend all through school. He was a good listener, and I tended to unload my thoughts on him, since I spent much of my time at home alone. Patrick didn't think it was strange that I had memorized all the state capitals and the names of all the Great Lakes or that I knew that the Panama Canal was forty-eight miles long.

We had a special kind of partnership. He wasn't a great student, so I helped him with his homework when I could. And since kids at school liked him, on account of he was a good-looking kid and the fastest runner in the fifth grade, he was usually able to shut them up when they started picking on me about my size.

What he said about coming back if I left made me think of the story in my book about a son that left home. The book called him a prodigal, although I didn't really know what that meant. When the prodigal came back home, his dad threw a big party for him.

Patrick and I trudged along, and I imagined myself in the story. I daydreamed about leaving, having a grand adventure for a few months, then coming home on that same gravel road, to a big, fancy party. It wasn't realistic. *Bert might throw a party when I leave, but not when I come back*, I thought.

The Bible storybook was my most prized possession. It was a gift from my mama right before she died. I think she ordered it out of a catalog, and I guessed it cost more money than she could afford to pay, which meant she had a good reason for buying it.

I was four when she died—just old enough to have a few random memories of her, but still too young to remember much. I had a black and white photograph of her, and I kept it in the Bible storybook. Before I could read, I would flip through the book, look at the pictures on the glossy pages, and make up stories to match the scene. I told the stories to her photograph, just like she was really there. Her image was better company than Bert.

When I learned to read, I discovered she had left instructions for me as an inscription in the front of the book.

Keep these stories in your heart, my son. They are true and will teach you everything you need to know about life. Remember that even though your mama can't be with you, Jesus is. I love you always—Mama.

The doctor suspected cancer when my mama was pregnant with the girl. They couldn't confirm it until after the baby was born, and by then, there wasn't much they could do. The girl was six months old when Mama died.

The girl had a name, but I always just called her *girl*. I figured out later that the new baby wasn't the reason Mama got sick; but I wasn't so sure back then, so I didn't like the girl very much when she was still around. Bert kept her for a little while, but then he gave her away. A baby was too much for him, I think. I was a little easier, I guess, so I got to stay. Sometimes I wished he would have sent me away with Colleen. That was the girl's name. Somewhere along the way, I learned that her name actually means *girl*.

Patrick and I parted ways when we got to his road. I continued slowly toward my house, lost in thought about places I could visit. I shuffled my feet on the gravel road, making clouds of dust in the air and watching the dirt drift away into nothing. *It wouldn't be running away*, I thought. *I won't have to run because nobody will be coming after me.*

Bert proved me right that very same day. When I got to my house, he was gone. He had left me like a worn-out tire at the dump on Higgins Road.

I found my first clue after I finished my afternoon snack. When I went to the bathroom, his toothbrush wasn't in the white plastic holder it normally shared with mine. I opened the mirrored cabinet over the sink to find that his razor was missing, too. Tiptoeing for no obvious reason, I went into Bert's room. I opened the louvered closet door as if something might jump out and scare me. My brow crinkled at the sight of an empty clothes rod, and even though it felt wrong, I opened each of his dresser drawers, too. I kept each drawer open only long enough to see that none of Bert's clothes were still in them; then I pushed them back in as fast as I could.

I went and stood in the middle of the living room that opened straight into the kitchen, and I slowly turned in a circle two full times. Besides Bert's missing things, everything else in the house was just as I had left it when I walked out the door to go to school that morning.

I didn't cry or panic when I found out Bert was gone. It felt like the spots of color you see hazing over your vision when you come indoors after playing in the bright snow all day. After my brain adjusted to the situation, I still wasn't upset, but I wasn't exactly relieved either.

The peacefulness of the backyard called to me, so I went, barely picking up my feet as I walked. I laid down in the hammock I had made out of an old bedsheet, then put my hands underneath my head and breathed one long, slow breath in for as long as I could suck in air. I let it out in a hard, single blow. The hammock was my favorite place to think. If I was really alone, I was going to have to be smart. I needed a plan.

For thirty minutes, I brainstormed under the Carolina blue sky, then I made my way, with lighter footsteps, back inside the square, two-bedroom house. I sat down in the kitchen with a notepad and pencil, to make a list of all the things I needed to do. The first thing I put down on the list was *get food for myself.* I jumped down from my chair, got a stool, then climbed up to inspect the cupboards.

I could hardly believe my eyes when I opened the cupboard and saw it full of food. At least fifty cans of pork and beans stared me in the face. And the can opener sat right inside the cupboard for me, too. It was quail and manna in the wilderness, like in my book, although I didn't think it would last me as long.

It was pretty decent of old Bert. *If you're gonna abandon a kid,* I thought, *I guess the very least you can do is to make sure they have some-thing to eat for a while.* And that wasn't all. Besides the pork and beans and the food that was already in our refrigerator and pantry, Bert had stocked enough canned peaches and green beans to last me a long time, too. *He must care at least a little to make sure I have a fruit and a green vegetable. Surely, he does.*

It occurred to me that all that food also meant Bert didn't expect me to tell anyone he was gone. And he was right. I didn't see any reason for it. If I told a neighbor or my teacher, there was no telling where I would end up. *They might stick me with somebody like Patrick's stepfather,* I thought. I decided that staying in my own house, with my own things, just like usual, was a better option. *At least until I get my trip planned for the summer, and I can head out.*

Going back to my list-making, I couldn't think of anything else I needed that I didn't already have or couldn't get easily. I had plenty of clothes, and there was plenty of soap in the house. It seemed like, for a short while, the only thing I might need money for was toilet paper and toothpaste, and those wouldn't be running out soon either.

I leaned back in the kitchen chair and felt the pride pull my mouth into a big grin. *I can do this,* I thought. *I can stay here on my own just fine until I make up my mind to do something else.*

The sound of truck tires on gravel made me sit up straight. Through the kitchen window, I saw a bucket truck with three familiar letters on it—TVA—roll past my house.

I didn't know what the letters stood for, but I had seen trucks like it lift men up high to work on the black cables that carried electricity into people's houses. Mountain folk cherished those lines. We understood how much work it took to have electricity. Setting poles and running lines for miles was no easy task on flat ground, much less in the high country, where the land was more uncooperative and the distance between houses was sometimes far.

As if an electric wave carried the information to my brain, I knew another thing I needed. I added *pay power bill* to the list.

The last task had me stumped. Even if I could figure out how to get the money, I didn't know how I was going to make the payment every month; I didn't know where the power company office was; and I didn't know if they would accept money from a kid without any questions asked. I decided to push the questions out of my mind until the morning.

With a new sense of independence, I climbed back onto the counter and took a can of pork and beans from the cupboard. With my knees on the gold-colored Formica, I opened the can with only five turns of the crank. I climbed down, careful not to drop my dinner, then flipped on the radio, sat at the kitchen table alone, and ate my evening meal a little early, straight out of the can.

Chapter Three

THE POWER COMPANY

THE DAY AFTER BERT LEFT, I hatched a plan. Sometime between recess and Miss Gentry's afternoon science lesson on states of matter, I made up my mind to take care of the power bill myself.

Instead of taking the bus home after school, I hitched a ride from a familiar stranger, my preferred mode of transportation. The power company office would have been a short walk from my school, only I didn't know exactly which building in the long row of stores and offices on Main Street it was. Asking for a ride got me delivered to the right place, so I didn't have to hunt for it.

Nameless Man in a Cowboy Hat gave one short nod and half a smile as I thanked him for the ride and jumped down from the pickup truck. I stood on the sidewalk, facing the squatty brick building, and I took a moment to gather myself. I untwisted the galluses of my overalls and made sure my blue-and-white-striped t-shirt was tucked in neatly. I straightened my baseball cap, too; then I decided to carry it in my hand instead. I dropped my dirty school satchel on the steps outside; then I took a deep breath and let my little legs carry me into the office, channeling the confidence of a grown man just taking care of his normal, grown-man responsibilities.

I walked casually up to the bill-pay counter. It made me feel like Esther, from my book, when she called for an audience with the king. Like the queen, I had no way to know what the outcome would be. In my case, it might mean the authorities would find out about me being alone and cart me off to live in an orphanage. But there was no way around it. I didn't want to wind up using candles at home if I could help it. My magazines had articles about different parts of the world that lacked electricity. People managed just fine in remote places without modern conveniences, but I assumed that's just because they were used to living that way. I wasn't.

There were no other customers around, and I was glad for that. I stood at the tall, white, wood counter, with its decorative molding and dark-stained top, and immediately, I had a problem. The counter was too tall for me to see over, which meant the guy behind it couldn't see me either.

I took a few steps back until I could see the man's face. *Hrhmm.* I cleared my throat. No response. I cleared it more loudly, with a phlegmy, grown-man sound. *HHHRRHMmmm.* The pretend coughing made me choke, and I started coughing for real. I slapped at my chest, trying to beat the cough out of me, but it kept coming.

As I stood there hacking, my face blushed from lack of oxygen and embarrassment, the employee stood up from his stool and leaned over the counter. Looking down at me with a curious grin mixed with concern, he stuck out his hand and offered me a red hard candy to help calm my throat. I guessed there was a dish of them on his desk, but I couldn't see it.

I took the cinnamon candy from the man's hand and popped it into my mouth, then smiled sheepishly to say thank you, trying not to choke on the candy or my nerves.

"Hello, sir. How may I help you today?" he said, as if I was any regular customer. The coughing episode ended, and I stood back up straight. The employee stayed standing so he could see me and waited patiently for my answer. It was a much better reaction to start off than I had expected.

"Well," I said, trying not to lose my nerve, "I need to know if the electric bill for my home has been paid, please." I tried to use my regular voice, but it came out deeper than normal without me meaning for it to.

"Certainly, sir. May I have your address and the name on the account, please?"

I gave the man my rural route address and Bert's name and waited while he looked it up in his ledger. The faded ball cap slid around and around through my fingers.

The man was young, tall, and slender, with ears only slightly too big for his head. He smiled as if his paycheck depended on how much teeth he showed, but his narrow eyes had a genuine glint in them. The biggest part of his face was from between his happy, brown eyes to the tip of his nose, but the nose didn't protrude too far like the ears. He wore a crisp, buttoned shirt and smart suspenders, and his dark, slicked-down hair parted in a perfectly straight line, far to the left side of his head. His foot tapped constantly, drumming out a lively rhythm while he searched the spiralbound book in front of him.

I looked at the man's nametag. *R. Smithson.*

I had rehearsed what I would say a thousand times. I thought about saying that my father sent me, but I couldn't lie. That was number eight on Moses' stone tablet in my book. I had decided that all I could really do was ask if the bill was paid for the month, and if not, find out how much it was and when it was due. Then I would know how much I had to try to earn.

When the man found the entry in his ledger and reported the verdict back to me, I knew for sure that Bert wasn't such a rotten scoundrel after all.

"It appears the account has been paid in advance, in the amount of thirty dollars," Mr. Smithson said.

I almost choked on the sliver of cinnamon candy left in my mouth, and I had to fight back the relief that wanted to burst out.

"Thank you," I said. "That's what I needed to know."

"Is there anything else I can help you with today, sir?"

"No. That's all." My voice squeaked a little. "Actually," I said, changing my mind, "could you please tell me how long . . . um . . . uh . . . " I didn't know how to ask what I was trying to ask.

"Based on your usage history, sir, the balance on the account should take care of the next couple of months." He studied the book again. "I'd say you're paid up until the end of June. Of course, that's just an estimate. Will that be all, sir?"

The man was still pleasant. His kindness seemed genuine, but I could tell that his *professional* voice was an act. It had a trying-too-hard kind of sound, each word articulated just a little too much. It betrayed his real accent, the same mountain drawl I knew that I, and most everybody I'd ever met, had.

"No, thank you, sir," I said, this time letting the relief show a bit.

"Okay, then. Have a nice day!"

"You too, sir," I said as I turned to leave.

The man whistled a cheerful tune as I shuffled out the door. Without thinking, I poked my head back inside the office. "Thanks for the candy," I said, and I touched my throat to sign that the candy had helped.

The man gave a big smile and a floppy-handed wave. I couldn't help but smile back, even with everything I had on my mind.

I walked out of the office and sat down on the front steps of the building, looking back and forth as cars cruised by slowly on the main drag of town. To the north and to the south, two mountain peaks loomed like bookends on a shelf. Town was the books between them.

Where on earth did Bert get the money? I thought. *And the money for all those groceries?*

As far as I could tell, we always had what we needed, but I could hardly believe there was that much to spare. I didn't know he could afford to pay the power bill in advance or why he would have done it, but then again, there were lots of things I didn't know about my father. Or myself. I lived in a thick fog, thicker than the early morning mists that settled down in the valleys all around.

Since Bert carried on a real conversation with me only once in a blue moon, I didn't get a chance to learn much from him. I didn't know anything about grandparents, or aunts, or uncles. I didn't know how my parents met or how they ended up living in our little house in Copper Creek. There were no picture albums around the house to give me clues. So much was a mystery.

Maybe he's been planning on leaving for a long time, and he's been saving up for this. Then a new thought crossed my mind. *What if he really isn't gone for good? What if he paid up the bill just long enough to keep the power on until he gets back?* I bristled at the possibility. I had already gotten used to the idea of being master of my domain. I was king of the castle. And my tiny body felt a whole lot bigger just thinking about it. I wondered if King Josiah felt the same way when he became king. He was only eight years old at the start of his reign.

I looked up and down the street from my throne there on the steps of the power company office. *This is my territory, too,* I thought.

A voice like soured buttermilk rang out from a passing car, and the words knocked me off my throne. "Hey, Weenie! Whaddaya doin' out here? You'll get stepped on down there if ya ain't careful." The last words trailed off as the car got further away, and a sixth-grade boy pulled his head back into the car. The boy's mother in the driver seat gave the back of the boy's head a swat.

I stayed there on the step, studying the storefronts. I hadn't looked twice before at some of them, and I wondered if there was more business stuff that I should know about being an adult. There was a bank, a hardware store, an appliance store, and an insurance office close by. *Should I know about insurance?* There were lots of advertisements for it in my magazine, talking about life and homes. I hoped it wasn't something I needed to know about.

I couldn't make out the names of the businesses further down the street, but I knew one of them was the Five and Dime, where most things no longer cost just a nickel or dime; and one of them was the barber shop, where a man named Marty usually cut my hair once a month. The old hotel and a big new supermarket sat at one end of the long stretch of stores and offices, and my school and the Methodist church were at the other. That one street was the heart of Copper Creek, but the lifeblood was the river that flowed just beyond my sight and the rail line that ran alongside it. The river and the rails sustained the saw mills and factories, where most people made their living.

It was a familiar place, yet so foreign. I felt like I was seeing everything for the first time. *This is your home, Nate,* I reminded myself. But I couldn't shake the feeling that I had been dropped there, like a seed carried by a bird, with no choice but to grow where I was planted, and I thought of the short roots of the weed growing in the road.

My bottom was sore from sitting on the concrete step for so long; so, I stood, picked up my satchel, shook off thoughts that were bigger than me, and headed down the sidewalk, hoping to spot a neighbor or anyone who could drive me back out into the country and at least get me close to my house. I stopped to watch television through the window of Walker's Appliance Store. He had the latest model color console on display, tuned to a news broadcast. The flashes of light and movement on the screen sucked me in.

This is what Miss Gentry was talking about in class today, I thought. I wiped the moisture from my breath off the glass with the side of my fist and backed up a little.

The images were of men carrying guns. Some wore plain clothes, and others had uniforms; and they were someplace called Bay of Pigs. In one scene, they were lying in the sand on their bellies with their rifles aimed, like they were training. The picture switched to a bearded man behind a microphone who was waving his fist in the air, and it looked like he was yelling. I watched for a while, until Mr. Walker caught me and waved me on. He didn't like loiterers outside his store.

The news story interested me because Miss Gentry had taught us it was a big deal, but at the same time, everything on television interested me because I didn't have one at home. Bert wasn't there enough to watch TV, and I figured he didn't want to spend the money on it just for me.

It's probably a good thing I don't have a TV, I thought. *It would use up money on my account with the power company faster.* I was already thinking like a grown-up.

I thought about what it would be like in my house if they did cut off the power—no lights, no radio. *Surely, I can earn enough money to pay the bill when it comes due,* I thought. *But maybe by then, I'll be tired of living by myself anyway. Maybe I'll be ready to set out on my adventure.*

In the Bible storybook, a man named Gideon asked God for an answer to a question by leaving a piece of wool on the ground overnight. He asked God to make the wool wet and the ground dry the next morning if the answer to his question was *yes.* It seemed to me that Gideon treated The Almighty like the Magic 8-Ball somebody brought to school one time, but it had worked out okay for him. Maybe I could use the electricity as my fleece.

I decided that if Bert wasn't back home by the time the lights went out, I would move on.

Chapter Four

IN NEED OF A FRIEND

WHEN I GOT HOME FROM my adventure at the power company office, there was hardly an ounce of energy left in my small body. I had to walk a mile of the way home, most of it so steep that the tops of my feet and the bottom of my legs met at a forty-five-degree angle. A large woman driving a Buick with two crying babies in the backseat stopped and picked me up, and I couldn't have been happier to stop walking. She was happy because, at least for ten minutes, I got the infants quiet by looking cross-eyed and making pig snout faces at them.

The lady set me out in my driveway, and I didn't even bother to take my satchel inside. I went straight to my favorite spot in the back-yard—the bedsheet tied between two young, but sturdy, sourwood trees. I dropped the bag of books on the ground, then dropped myself into the cradle of the sheet with the same lack of attention.

The hammock was a simple invention, yet endlessly useful. Sometimes when Patrick came over, we spread the sheet out wide and used sticks as posts to turn it into a little canopy. Sometimes, I pretended it was a boat, and I was handlining a giant marlin like in *The Old Man and the Sea,* feeling the force of the waves as I rocked back and forth in tireless battle with the marine beast. Sometimes, it was an alien spaceship, carrying me off as prisoner to some unknown planet, while I plotted my escape and return to Earth. Most days, I was just Nate taking a rest. I liked to lounge and look up at the sky between the bare branches or the white bell-shaped flowers and down-turned green leaves or the red leaves. The skyward view depended on the time of year, and every change came faster than the one before it.

Both of my short arms dangled off the sides of the makeshift hammock, and I moved one of them like a pendulum to make it swing from side to side. After only about ten back-and-forths in my cozy ride, a quick feeling of something soft and wet on one of my hands nearly made me wet my pants. I sat up fast, with the hammock still in motion, fell out, and hit the ground hard on my stomach. Before I could right myself, I felt the same softness and wetness on the back of my neck. This time, I recognized it was a tongue on my skin, and I felt a momentary panic at not knowing whose tongue it was. I flipped myself over like a click beetle and was relieved to see a friendly-looking dog standing over me, panting right in my face.

I quickly pulled myself up to a seated position in the dirt, scooting back only a little, just in case the dog's disposition changed quickly. "Where'd you come from?" I said.

The dog stepped toward me and stood on my legs with his front paws, as if to say, *"It doesn't matter. I'm here now."*

I examined the mutt. He was mostly white; but he was so dirty, it was hard to tell what shade of white he might be. I figured he didn't have an owner, or at least not a good one, because there was no collar and his fur hung down into his eyes, making it hard for the poor thing to see. The fur was matted all over, and he even had pieces of dried leaves stuck in the tangled mess, which I instinctively began trying to free and let fall to the ground.

"You look like you could use someone to take care of you, fella," I said.

I checked his paws and looked at his teeth. I didn't know what I was looking for, but I had read in a book that a dog's teeth could tell you a lot about their health. They seemed to be all there. Since he needed taking care of—and I was pretty good at taking care of myself—I decided right then and there that he was my dog.

I stroked the nasty mess of matted fur that felt like yarn, and he wagged his tail and continued panting. We were about nose-to-nose, since I still had my butt in the dirt, until he flopped down on the ground in front of me and rolled over on his back, begging me to rub his belly. I obliged, and when I stopped, he licked my hand again.

"Come on, you," I said, getting up off the ground. "Let's get you something to eat. Then we'll get you cleaned up."

The dog stayed close on my heels as if he had known me all his life, followed me as I picked my school bag off the ground, then went onto the porch and inside the house. My energy had returned. The appearance of the guest seemed like a miracle. *How'd you know to show up now?*

"A couple days ago, I wouldn't've been able to keep you," I said.

Bert wouldn't let me have a dog. I'd had the courage to ask him only once, after hearing the kids at school go on and on about *Lassie* and how brave and smart she was and how much everybody wanted a dog like Timmy Martin's. "Dog food's too expensive," Bert had answered, with a tone that I knew meant *don't ask again.*

I knew I could figure out how to afford food for my new friend, though. For the time being, I had plenty of pork and beans to share; and because he was pretty skinny, I didn't think he would be picky. I was right. I found a plastic container with a missing lid and emptied a can into it for him. The dog licked the bowl clean, making a slapping sound with his tongue as it hit the sides in search of any last bit of flavor.

The scraggly beast finished his food and water, and I filled up the bathtub. I squatted and wrapped one arm around his front end and one arm around his back end. My hands didn't come close to meeting on the other side, and I couldn't get a handle on him to lift him into the tub.

Next, I tried going over his back and locking my hand underneath his belly. He didn't fight me at all or even whimper, but the dog was much heavier than I imagined he would be, even trying to lift just his front half. After a couple of awkward attempts to hoist him in head-first, I set his paws back on the bathroom floor and sank against the wall for a moment to rest. He sat on his haunches and stared at me, his black eyes laughing at my struggle. Determined, I got up off the floor and sat on the edge of the tub.

"Come on, boy. Jump in here," I said in a sugarcoated tone, and I tapped the inside wall of the tub. The mutt immediately jumped in and stood there happily, almost mockingly. The warm water came up to his elbows and knees, and his belly fur floated on the surface. "So next time, I'll guess I'll just ask first," I said, laughing.

On my knees, I leaned over the edge, reaching to scrub him all over with the same bar of Ivory I used on myself. He enjoyed the massage as the soap lathered his fur. After the rinse, he looked a new shade of white, and the bathwater was dingy brown.

"I wonder where you came from," I said to him. He shook with his whole body, sending waterdrops flying across the bathroom. The drops covered my shirt, and some hit me in the eye. I wiped my face with my arm. "Did you have a family? Did you leave them, or did they leave you? You've been alone for a very long time, haven't you?"

I dried the dog with a towel from the tiny linen closet next to the tub; then I found a pair of scissors in a drawer in the kitchen, and I took him to the side porch for a haircut. There was just enough daylight left to get the job done; and although I didn't know the first thing about giving a dog a haircut, I went about it pretending to be a professional groomer. I pulled up sections of fur at a time, held them between my pointer finger and middle finger, and snipped across in a straight line. The dog's cooperativeness seemed too good to be true; and when I finished, I stood back and admired my handiwork with a big grin on my face. At least he could see better and didn't look like a dirty mop anymore.

I got the broom from the house and whisked the clumps of fur off the porch. The dog watched me curiously. Bert didn't like me leaving messes, and I didn't like them either. Having things left around, not neat and put in their place, made me feel jumpy on the inside. A gentle wind aided and made the white fibers float away across the yard like dandelion puffs; and in no time, the porch was clean.

There was no brush in the house, but I had a comb; and I sat on the wooden floorboards of the porch, holding pieces of hair in one hand and gently combing out tangles one at a time with the other until the sky turned dark and the mountain air became an unfriendly temperature. He sat like a statue the whole time as if he knew I was helping him.

"You're a smart dog, aren't you?" I asked.

I could see we were going to get along just fine. A friend had shown up out of nowhere when I could really use one, and I was thankful. Sitting on the couch later with my new not-quite-as-scruffy dog resting his head in my lap, I tested out names for him.

"Freddy? No. Jasper? No . . . Maybe I should name you after a place from my magazine. How about Yukon?" I dismissed that idea quickly.

"Oh, what do you think of Congo? That sounds pretty good!" The dog sat up and turned his head sideways, as if he were thinking about what he wanted me to call him. I looked him over, examining the results of his makeover. He was a good-looking dog all cleaned up. "You know, boy, I didn't do too badly at cutting your hair," I told him proudly. "Haircut! That's it! I'll call you Samson! Like in the story of Samson and Delilah."

I went to get my Bible storybook, so I could read Samson the story. He followed me to my room, where I kept the book in a long cardboard box that fit snugly under my bed.

The box was special because it was full of everything I owned that was important to me—the book with the picture of my mama tucked inside; my giant bag of marbles; my collection of *National Geographics* from Miss Gentry; some drawings I was proud of; a few certificates from school for things like winning the Fourth Grade Spelling Bee; and a ribbon for memorizing my times tables through twelve, even though everybody had gotten that one.

The bag of marbles was big because Bert had put the same thing in my stocking for the past four Christmases—a bag of marbles and a chocolate bar. I couldn't remember before that.

My magazine collection was growing, too, and was about to outgrow the box. In the fall of fifth grade, Miss Gentry gave me every edition printed from July 1959 to August 1960. Then I got a new one every month after—once she had the chance to read them through at least once. With some of the older ones that I had read a few times, I cut out my favorite articles, pasted them on poster boards, and hung them all over the walls of my room with pushpins. Five full-color maps from special editions hung on the walls, too.

The book showed some wear on the corner and on the burgundy spine. The gold lettering that read *Bible Stories for Children* across the front had faded from years of being held every day. The book was thick, and the first letter of each story was in different type than the rest of the words. They were the kind of letters that made me think of kings and queens. The pictures in my book looked like paintings that should be hanging in an art gallery somewhere, and I often wondered how closely they matched the real scene, the way it happened in history.

Samson and I sat back down on the couch, and he laid his head in my lap again while I read about Delilah tricking the biblical Samson and cutting off his hair. His ears seemed to perk up when I read the part about God giving Samson the strength to push down the pillars and destroy the temple.

"I'm glad you're here, Samson," I whispered to him as I closed the book when the story was over.

I grabbed a fuzzy blanket from the other end of the couch and pulled it over me and him both as I lay down to go to sleep. Samson curled up beside me there, and I settled my head on the arm of the couch and wrapped my arm around his chest as if he was a teddy bear.

I had spent lots of nights at home alone, and I didn't really get scared, at least not too often. But sometimes, I just felt better sleeping on the couch instead of in my room at the back of the house. That night, it was only because we were both too comfortable to get up. Feeling Samson's warmth there beside me, I knew I would get a good night's sleep.

Just before I slipped into slumber, a troubling thought roused me. *What if Bert comes home and catches me with a dog in the house? What will he do?*

At the very least, I knew he would kick Samson out. So, I closed my eyes, hugged my dog tighter, and prayed hard that Bert wasn't coming back.

Chapter Five

JOB HUNTING

THE DAY AFTER SAMSON ARRIVED, and two days after Bert left, was a Saturday. I was glad I didn't have to rush out the door to go to school that morning, so I could spend more time with my new friend. He had stayed with me on the couch all night until daybreak, when I woke to him scratching at the back door to go out, just as a rooster from the farm across the way sounded his morning song. It hadn't really occurred to me that Samson might use the bathroom in the house, so I was thankful that he proved he wouldn't.

After our shared breakfast of pork and beans, I got ready to head to town. It was time for me to be a man and find a job, seeing as how I had somebody to take care of other than myself. I needed money for dog food; plus, the bread and milk would run out soon, too, and I didn't want to have to eat just the canned food Bert had stocked in the pantry, even though I was glad to have it.

"Goodbye, boy," I said as I held on to either side of Samson's head and his floppy ears hung down over the backs of my hands. "I'll be back. I promise. I won't leave you for long. I promise. You can count on me." I trusted Samson to not make a mess in the house, but it was hard to leave him so soon.

Luckily for me, I stepped outside on that overcast morning right as Mr. Nelson's truck rolled to the end of his driveway with fresh heads of tightly bunched green leaves rounded up high in the bed. He was headed into town to sell his first harvest of lettuce.

The Nelsons were my closest neighbors. I could just make out the end of their driveway from my house, across the road and as far west as I could see. Most of the Nelsons' business was in their herd of dairy cows and apple orchard, but they had a small cash crop for every season.

Directly across the road from my house was their fields, and to the left of my house was their fields, too. Some of them lay fallow, and some still had lettuce. Mr. Nelson and his workers had recently planted potatoes in much of the well-tilled earth, which meant he would have a big harvest by Independence Day.

The land to the right of me and behind me was all woods, and I didn't know who it belonged to. Between the field and the forest, I had the little house with two tiny bedrooms, an insignificant front yard with one short dogwood tree, a small backyard full of dirt patches, a shed big enough only for a push mower and a few hand tools, and a short, gravel driveway. Everything about my domain was little, making it comically suited to me.

Mr. Nelson seemed glad for the company when I flagged him down for a ride. He leaned across the bench seat and pushed open the door for me to climb in. "Off to town this morning, Nate?" he asked.

"Yes, sir. Will it be any trouble?"

"Not at all, young man. That's the only place I'm heading today. Town and back again."

The Nelsons had always been nice neighbors, and I could count on one of them to drive me to town most any time I needed, if they weren't too busy working on the farm. Usually it was Mr. Nelson in his farm truck; but on a few occasions in recent months, I had ridden with Mrs. Nelson when she took the newer, shinier pickup out on a pie delivery. Mrs. Nelson was no doubt the best baker in the county. She made pies for people who were sick, or who just had a baby or a death in the family, or sometimes just to help neighbors celebrate a good harvest.

Every year at Christmas, the Nelsons brought us two pies and a bag of peppermint stick candy. The sweets were my favorite part of Christmas. There was usually a chocolate pie with fluffy meringue topping and an apple one with the fancy crisscrosses on top.

The year before, though, when they came, Bert was at home. I knew better than to answer the door instead of him, so I sat on the couch with my magazine and didn't move. He let them stand outside and knock three different times before he went to answer it, even though he wasn't even busy, only looking at some mail. When he finally opened the door, he didn't say a word of greeting to them. He just stood there until they handed him the gifts. He did say thank you, but he didn't say Merry Christmas back when they said it; and he closed the door before they'd even finished saying goodbye. I worried those were the last Christmas pies and candy we would ever get from Dell and Opal Nelson.

I looked out the window as the truck hummed along through a familiar pattern of curves and straightaways. *Nowhere else like it,* I thought, as we came to the most picturesque spot on the drive. It was a place where I could see mountains in three different directions. The trees opened up on that stretch because the earth sloped down into a gorge on one side of the road, revealing a panoramic view of rounded mountain tops covered in a fuzzy green blanket of forest foliage.

Sometimes, I imagined myself living in the middle of the rice terraces of China, or in a treehouse on the bank of the Amazon in Brazil, or any number of other places from my magazines. But I already knew that no place could match the beauty of those mountains that tied North Carolina and Tennessee together.

Little communities dotted my part of the high country, houses clumped together like islands wherever the land was flat enough, in the middle of all those fields and forests. Town was like an island, too, in the center of all the smaller islands of houses, and all the islands felt higher than the rest of the world, although the mountains continued to rise higher still for a long way beyond Copper Creek.

Town was close enough to be convenient if you had a car, but far enough away to make it impossible for me to walk all the way there. I was glad for lots of friendly people around, like Mr. Nelson, willing to give me, and plenty of other kids, rides back and forth.

Mr. Nelson drove with one hand on the wheel, and his other arm hung out the open window. He hummed along to the radio to a song by The Everly Brothers.

"Mr. Nelson," I said, pausing to make sure I had his attention. He turned down the radio. "I'm going in to town to see about any odd jobs I can do to make a little money."

"Oh, that's good, son," he said, nodding his head.

Mr. Nelson was a short man, and his round head had hair only around the back and sides. The lonely strip of light gray hair was so short, it almost wasn't there. He wore dark-colored overalls, the kind I'd seen other men wear, with a square tag in the middle of the chest with a picture of a hunting dog on point. They were crisp and clean and looked new; but by lunchtime, goodness-knows-what from his hard work on the farm would cover them.

I had never seen him with a big smile on his weathered face. But the corners of his mouth always turned up ever so slightly, like he remembered something happy or had a fun secret to share. He also never wore a mean look, or a worried look, or a tired look. If I had a camera and could take a picture of him there in the truck, I would have an image of what Mr. Nelson looked like in just about every situation.

"Mr. Nelson, do you have any work around your place I can do? I can help plant, or trim branches, or sweep porches. I bet I'd be pretty handy with a paint brush, too. Whatever you have that needs doing." *Please don't ask me why I need money,* I thought.

"Well, there's always plenty of work to be done around the farm, Nate. But I already pay a couple of good guys to help me out. I'm afraid I can't afford to pay another hand right now."

"Okay. I understand." I thought for a moment. "You know, if you have so much work to do, maybe I could come by and help out anyway. For all the rides into town you give me."

"That's mighty nice of ya, Nate. I just might take you up on that offer sometime."

We came to the stoplight at the main intersection of town, and Mr. Nelson parked to let me out in front of a row of shops.

"Check the bulletin board near the door at the Five and Dime, Nate," he said. "That's where people post for help."

"Okay! And thanks for the ride," I said as I hopped down from the truck.

"Good luck to you, Nate!"

"Oh, I'll find something. Surely, I will!"

The Five and Dime was as busy as I'd ever seen it. People from all the different islands of neighborhoods seemed to be there, carrying shopping baskets with everything from ladies' nylons to motor oil.

Farmer Nelson was right about the bulletin board. It hung on the wall right near the front door, covered in postings for odd jobs, mostly farm help. There were flyers for yard sales and lost pets, too, and a whole row of church cards. One advertisement on colored paper, with big, bold type, caught my attention. "This one looks good," I said out loud excitedly to no one. The headline on the flyer read, *Copper Creek Fair, April 22, Chester's Field.*

Chester's Field was literally a big, empty field owned by a man named Chester. It was home to the fair, two bluegrass concerts, and three Baptist tent revivals every year.

The flyer listed all the fair jobs available; and right off the bat, I saw one I could do. *Clean-up crew. That would be easy,* I thought.

The advertisement also listed opportunities for food vendors, craftsmen, and sideshow acts. I chuckled. Lots of people had commented on my height in my life, but I was pretty sure my small size wasn't freak-show worthy.

The fair is a week from today, I thought. *I shouldn't need money for anything before then, except some dog food. But it will work out. If God can send those ravens with food for Elijah, I guess He can feed me and my dog, too.*

"Hey, Nate," a lady's voice called from behind me. I hadn't expected anyone in the crowd to notice me, but I knew who called my name before I even turned around. The sweetest voice on earth belonged to my teacher.

"Hey, Miss Gentry," I said, spinning around. I shoved my hands in my jean pockets and rocked back and forth on my heels and toes, without looking away from her face.

"Have you read about any neat places lately?" she asked, winking at me. "I didn't have a chance to talk to you about it at school much this week."

She looked just like she always did at school, wearing a knee-length jumper dress with a round-neck top underneath and flat shoes with pointy toes. Her shoulder-length brown hair curled out on the ends, and her bangs swooped to the side.

I didn't take my eyes off her face, partly because I didn't want to look at the shopping basket on her arm in case it held lady things and other unmentionables and partly because she was so pretty.

"There's an article on the Northern Lights in the last volume you gave me. The photographs are just about the best ones I've seen!"

"Aurora Borealis is truly a wonder."

My teacher spoke with a deliberateness I had never heard in anyone else. She didn't speak just to make a noise.

"Yes, ma'am," I agreed.

"I'm glad you are still enjoying the magazines, Nate. I can't think of anyone else who I would rather have them. See you on Monday."

"Bye, Miss Gentry!"

I waved to her as she walked to the counter to pay for her things. I was so happy to have run into her, I almost forgot about the job search. Turning back to the bulletin board, I looked at the flyer again and made up my mind. *Next Saturday, I'm going to get my first paying job.*

Lots of cars and trucks cruised through town, and it didn't take long to find someone headed out to the highway going in the direction of my house. Instead of going home, though, I had the friendly stranger drop me off at Patrick's house. It was time he knew about my situation.

Chapter Six

BEING A KID

WE SPED DOWN THE ROAD like we had done countless times before. Patrick pedaled as fast as he could, while I balanced on the handlebars of his Colson Flyer and held on for dear life, enjoying the coolness of the wind in my face. His mama bought the bicycle at a flea market, somewhere down the mountain, and it was at least as old as we were. It was in decent shape, though, and he took special care of it, never leaving it out in the rain and making sure to grease the chain every few rides.

Imperceptible by just looking at it, the road declined between his house and mine, so gravity helped out when it came to him pedaling us both.

"So, what's this surprise of yours?" Patrick said, panting in between words.

"I told you. You'll find out when we get to my house," I yelled into the wind. I rehearsed the big announcements in my mind, playing it out like a great detective announcing how he'd solved the case. Having a secret to share felt special. I owned something no one else had, but I was willing to share my treasure only with Patrick.

We turned onto the driveway at my house, and I catapulted off the front of the bike to get a head start. Patrick dismounted and laid the bike down gently on its side in the yard. It was our tradition to race to the porch, though it was only a matter of a few yards. Patrick, with legs twice as long as mine, always won, but that never kept me from trying. I didn't mind losing to him because he didn't give me a hard time about it. It was just for fun.

As soon as we opened the door and stepped inside the house, Samson was there to greet us, tongue out and tail wagging.

"You got a dog!" Patrick exclaimed. "Oh, wow!" The look of surprise on his face was every bit as rewarding as I had expected.

Patrick plopped to the floor just inside the house and began rubbing Samson's head and back vigorously. Samson ate up the attention, and they were instant friends. I joined them in the floor in the patch of afternoon sun that came through the storm door. I relayed the story of how Samson had showed up in my backyard the day before; and I got back up, so I could exaggeratedly reenact my fall from the hammock.

"He's such a great dog," Patrick said. Samson had relaxed and lay in Patrick's lap. "And he sure is pretty. His fur is so soft, too."

"Yeah, he looks a lot better now than he did when he got here."

"But wait a minute. I thought Bert wouldn't let you have a dog. Did the old cheapskate change his mind?"

"Not exactly."

"Does he know yet? Has he seen him?" Patrick sounded worried. "You can't hide 'im, Nate. You'll be in a heap of trouble when Bert finds out. I know I would be if it were my stepdaddy."

"He doesn't know," I said. "That's the other thing I wanted to tell you about."

I got off the floor, walked to the chocolate-colored couch, and sat down. I scooted all the way back and let my legs dangle. I placed my hands in my lap with my fingers locked together.

Patrick and Samson followed. He seemed anxious to hear my news, so I waited a bit to speak, letting the suspense build. He ran his hand through his moppy, orange-tinted hair, the same way he did when he didn't know the answer to a question on a test.

"Bert's gone," I said matter-of-factly, looking Patrick in the eye as he sat down on the other end of the couch. Hearing myself say the words made it sink in for the first time.

"What do you mean, he's gone? He's gone all the time. But you know he'll be back soon," Patrick scoffed.

"I don't think so. When I came home from school the day before yesterday, all his clothes were gone, and his toothbrush and razor. And he stocked the pantry full, like he wanted me to have food for a good while." Patrick stared at me in disbelief, with his mouth hung open slightly. "I guess there's a chance he's coming back, but it beats me when it might be."

"So, you're just gonna stay here by yourself?"

"Yep. Can't be much different than normal, can it?"

"You okay doing that, Nate?"

I thought for just a second. "Yep, I'm okay."

"Well, why didn't you tell me at school yesterday?"

"I don't know. I just didn't."

I figured that if we had both been girls, the conversation would have been much different. We would probably have talked for hours about how I felt left alone, and if I was scared, and what effect I thought being an abandoned orphan would have on my hopes and dreams for the future. But Patrick left it alone, and so did I.

"Wanna go outside and play?" I asked.

"Let's go."

We turned my hammock into a tent and crawled under. Patrick took out the two matchbox cars that he always kept in his pockets. I was yellow, and he was blue. We drew lines in the dirt with sticks and made roads for our vehicles. Mine carried a family moving to a new city, but they kept breaking down and needed a mechanic. Patrick's car carried a grandma with a lead foot. When it was time for her to get a speeding ticket, my yellow car became a police cruiser.

Samson explored the backyard some, sniffing at ant hills and poking his nose under the back porch. The rest of the time, he stayed within an arm's reach of me and Patrick, showing no signs that he might wander off.

When we finished with our car games, I stood up, rubbed my hands together three times to loosen the dirt, then dusted the dirt off my pants three times, too. Patrick chuckled.

"Why do you do that, Nate?" he asked. "And the same way every time we play on the ground?"

"I don't know," I said. "I just don't like to stay dirty, I guess."

I brushed off the question just as I had the dirt and started dragging old cinder blocks out from underneath the porch. First, we put them in a straight line and took turns seeing who was best at using them for a balance beam. Next, we spaced a few of them out and tried to toss rocks in their hollow middles from different distances.

"Hey, I know what we should do! Let's play like we're marching around the wall of Jericho and make it fall down," I suggested.

"I don't want to play another story from your book, Nate. We act out those Bible stories all the time." Patrick sighed.

"Okay, then. How about one from my magazine?" I asked. "I'll be Captain Joseph Kittinger, Jr., and you can be a member of my flight crew."

"Who's Captain whatever-you-said?"

"*Who is he?* Kittinger is *only* the person who made the highest ever parachute jump from outer space!" I ran to the back-porch step and jumped off to illustrate my point. "Here, Patrick, help me into my pressurized suit to get ready."

The imaginary helmet was too small, and Patrick had to stand on the porch and push it onto my head while I stood on the ground.

"If there is an equipment failure," I said, making my voice quiver, "I'll be dead within two minutes—long before I hit the hard ground of the New Mexico desert."

"You learned all that from those magazines Miss Gentry gives you, Nate?"

"I'm not Nate."

"Sorry . . . Captain Kissenger."

"It's Kittinger." I stepped out of character to answer his question. "And, yes, the December nineteen sixty issue."

"Oh, got it. Okay, you're ready to go, Captain."

We took turns jumping eighteen-and-a-half miles above the earth from my four-feet tall porch.

"Hey, Nate. Why don't you read me some of that book you told me about?" Patrick asked when he was tired of playing. "Do you still have it? The one you were reading on the bus the other day?"

Patrick wasn't much for reading himself, but he enjoyed a good story and often would listen for as much as thirty minutes while I read.

"You mean *The Adventures of Tom Sawyer?*"

"Yeah, that's the one. That sounds pretty interesting."

I got the book—that I had borrowed from school and read three different times from start to finish—and Patrick and I went back to our place under the canopy between the trees.

He laid down on his belly with his chin in his hands. I sat cross-legged with the book on one leg and Samson's head on the other, and I read him the part where Tom and his friend Huckleberry Finn overhear plans to bury a stolen treasure.

For at least an hour, I didn't think about power bills, or stocked cupboards, or odd jobs. I just enjoyed being a kid and hanging out with my best friend and my dog, being anything we wanted to be.

"I better get home," Patrick said a little sadly. "I have to finish cutting the grass before my old man gets home. Otherwise, he'll be pretty mad, and I know I'll pay for it."

It reminded me of grown-up things again. I looked around at my own yard and realized that I would need to cut the grass soon, too. Bert had always done it himself. I wanted to learn how, but he liked it to look a certain way; and he said it took me too long to do.

I walked with Patrick to the front yard, where his bike was laying. "Hey, Patrick. Are you going to the fair next weekend?"

"I dunno. Are you?"

"Yeah, I'm hoping to get a job there, picking up trash and stuff."

"Job? Why do you need a job, Nate? You showed me all that food in there. You should be set for a good, long while."

"Sure, I have a lot of stuff, but I'll want a few other things for the refrigerator soon. Butter for my toast, and maybe some apples. It's my responsibility now. I gotta do for myself." I hooked my thumbs through the belt loops of my jeans and stood stiff-backed.

"But didn't you take care of yourself before, most of the time? Make your own food and stuff?"

"Yeah, I'm used to fixing it. But Bert always bought it for me. Anyway, what I need most is dog food for Samson here."

"Well, shoot, Nate. Why didn't you just ask me? I can give you some dog food."

It hadn't occurred to me to come out and ask somebody for what I needed.

Patrick righted his bike and stood gripping the handlebars. "Our dog, Rufus, could afford to lose a few pounds anyway," he continued. "Mama and Howard won't even notice if a little bit of kibble is missing. I'll put some in a paper sack and bring it to school on Monday. How's that?"

Samson came over and placed his head under Patrick's hand.

"That would be great, pal. I sure do appreciate it," I told him.

Like in the story, when Elijah got what he needed, it seemed that Patrick was my raven.

Chapter Seven

THE FAIR

PATRICK BROUGHT ENOUGH DOG FOOD to school on Monday to feed Samson for the rest of the week. At first, Samson acted like he missed the bread and pork and beans I had been giving him. He sniffed around at the new food and looked at me with a raised eyebrow, looking more like a person than a dog, just before he dove in and gobbled up the crunchy bits.

Other than having a four-legged friend at home with me, my week wasn't much different than before Bert left. I walked to the bus stop in the mornings, spent my days at school, and walked home from the bus stop in the afternoon, part of the way with Patrick. A couple of afternoons, when he didn't have chores to do, Patrick came over to my house to play with me and Samson. In the evenings, I did my homework, then warmed up dinner on the stove or made a sandwich. After dinner, I read my magazines or listened to a radio show, read my Bible storybook, and went to bed. The first week of being completely on my own passed without incident.

A few nights, I thought about Bert. I wondered where he might be or what he might be doing. I imagined he had simply decided to take off and see some of the places in my magazines, like I was thinking about doing, and the daydream made me jealous. A few times, I actually tried to think about what else, besides a desire to see the world, would cause a man to take off like Bert had, without even saying goodbye to his child. I didn't come up with any answers.

In the middle of the week, I paid a visit to Mr. Nelson to ask if he could give me a ride to the fair early on Saturday. I knew they would take the first group of decent workers that showed up. Every day, I thought about it and wondered how much money I could earn in a day of picking up trash, and I imagined the trip to the store where I would pick out what I wanted and pay for it myself.

I had been to the fair only one time before—by myself a couple years earlier. A nice stranger paid for me to ride a pony. I didn't know the man's name, but I never forgot his face. Even though I would be there to work instead of play, it made me excited to think about all the sights and sounds.

The fair wasn't nearly as large as the fairs in other towns, and it didn't have big rides. But there were lots of fun things to do and good things to eat. I hoped I might earn enough money to buy a candy apple before the day was over.

On Saturday, Mr. Nelson picked me up right at nine a.m. The bed of his truck held three goats he would enter in the livestock competition. Mrs. Nelson planned to meet him at the fair later, after she finished baking pies for the pie eating contest.

When we got there, I did as the flyer at the Five and Dime instructed. I made my way through rows of vendor tables, food trucks, and game booths to the information desk to ask for a Mr. Brindell.

"He'll be right back, dear," the lady volunteer at the desk told me. There were only two other guys milling around near me, who I assumed were there to ask about jobs, too. As I waited, I read through a program that listed all the times for competitions and shows. *It would be nice to see the magic show or play the knock-down-the-milk-bottle game,* I thought.

A big, burly man with a too-tight t-shirt walked over, munching on an ear of roasted corn, an odd sight for so early in the day.

"Yous guys here for a job?" he asked, pointing the ear of corn in the direction of me and the other two fellas.

"Yes, sir," I piped up before the other two. "I can help with clean-up."

"Us, too," the other guys chimed in.

"You're a little guy," the man said, coming closer and looking me up and down. "Can I really expect as much work out of you as these other guys can do?"

"Sure! I'm not fast, but I work hard."

"All right," he said. "Follow me."

The man led us to a maintenance station near the middle of the fairgrounds. He handed us each a long trash picker and several trash bags, and he gave out instructions.

"I want you all to split up. Keep trash off the ground. If you see trash, pick it up. There's trashcans all over the place. If you see one is full, empty it, replace the bag, and bring the full bags back here. Got it?"

We all nodded, but none of us moved, waiting for more details.

"Okay," he said. "Your shift is over at two p.m. I've got another crew coming in then. Meet me back here at that time, and I'll pay eacha yas six-fifty."

I took off, anxious to prove myself. There wasn't any trash to pick up yet because the fair was just starting; but with people coming from miles around, the field would be full soon.

Booths, stands, stages, tables, and tents stood in a line for almost as far as I could see. On one end of the fairgrounds was the livestock area with corrals, trailers, and pens set up to show off the animals. I was glad I didn't have to clean up what would be on the ground at that part of the fair.

I started near the food vendors, picking up a napkin here and there. As the crowd grew, so did the mess. But it was easy work.

Within an hour, a sea of people swallowed me. I ran into a few schoolmates and teachers. I avoided some and said hi to others, but I kept moving. The sounds around me were a blend heard only at fairs—guess-your-weight callers calling, live bluegrass playing, cows mooing, rock and roll blaring on loud speakers, roosters crowing, children laughing, and people cheering.

My first trash bag was almost full after a couple hours, and my legs and arms were still strong. *Two more hours to go,* I thought.

A new combination of sounds met my ears. A loud, steady drum beat alternated rhythm with the tinny clang of a high-hat, punctuated by intermittent honks of a bicycle horn. A kazoo rang out the melody, with additional rhythm provided from the strumming of a two-chord pattern on a ukulele.

As the one-man-band danced by me, I noticed that the shape of the man's head looked familiar. He played to the end of the row and turned around, headed back in my direction. The music wasn't good; but what the man lacked in talent, he made up for with enthusiasm. He walked with his knees bent as he made his way down the row, waddling and kicking and calling out to people as he passed them. When someone looked his way, he stopped strumming and held out his hat. Some people dropped coins into the man's hat, which he then scooped out and shoved into his pocket before returning the hat to his head and nodding his appreciation.

"Hey, I think I know you, kid!" the man with the instruments said. He had stopped right in front of me, and the music went silent, except for a soft drumbeat. "Aren't you one of my customers?"

The man from the power company! I thought. It was the man who had been so nice to me and had given me a hard candy to help my cough.

"I am! Hi, there, Mr. Smithson," I said. He was surprised I remembered his name.

"You came in just the other day to check on the bill." He stuck out his hand to shake mine. "You can call me Smithy. The name's Rodney Smithson, but everyone calls me Smithy." He was at an in-between age, twenty-four or twenty-five, where calling him mister didn't feel right, but calling him by his first name made me uncomfortable.

"I'm Nate," I said, "but, to tell you the truth, most people call me Weenie." I wasn't sure why I told him that.

I surveyed Smithy up and down. The instruments attached to his long, lanky body by a crudely welded metal frame mesmerized me. He wore the same smart suspenders I had seen on him at his office, and his coin-collecting receptacle of an outdated bowler hat cocked to one side of his head.

"Hmmm . . . " he said, looking at me squint-eyed. "I think Nate suits you much better."

"What are you doing here?" I couldn't help asking. I thought it odd that this person I had seen working at a desk in an office was busking for money at a fair.

He smiled and pointed to the trash picker and the bag in my hands. "Well . . . what are *you* doing?" he countered.

"I'm just trying to make a few bucks," I said. I was careful not to let my reasons slip.

"It looks like we're doing the same thing then. Just in different ways." He gave a playful triple clang of the high-hat by waving his left arm like a chicken's wing three times. He had one end of a rope tied around the bend of his left arm, and the other end was tied to the pedal of the high-hat.

"I like your band," I said. I was glad to stand and chat with him for a few minutes. It was the first time I had stood in one place for more than thirty seconds since I got to the fair.

"Here, want to honk the horn?" he asked, bending down so I could reach the bicycle horn mounted near his right shoulder. I squeezed the bulb of the horn, and the funny sound made me forget myself and flash a toothy smile at Smithy. I normally smiled with my lips together because I thought my two top front teeth were too big to match the rest of me.

"Hey, what time is your shift over?" Smithy asked.

"I finish up at two o'clock."

"Oh, good. That's when I get off, too."

I don't know how, but I could tell he was lying. I just didn't know why.

"Maybe we can walk around the fair after work," Smithy offered. "Play a few games or something."

I didn't see any harm, so I agreed to meet him at the maintenance station where I was supposed to get my money.

The last couple hours of my shift were the hardest. I was tired; plus, the amount of trash on the ground seemed to be growing exponentially. *I've sure learned one thing today*, I thought. *People are pigs.*

Finally, the time came to quit picking up trash. When I met up with the other guys at the station, I found I had collected as many bags as both of them combined, although they were much older than me. I almost lost my temper over it, but then I thought of the parable Jesus told about the vineyard workers, where some didn't do as much work as the others, but they still got the same amount of pay. I decided to calm down and just worry about myself and not the other guys.

The next shift of workers was there at the maintenance station, too. As we waited for Brindell to show up, I looked around for Smithy. I didn't see him, and I wondered if he had bailed on me.

At least I earned some cash today, I thought. *I might even buy Samson a rawhide with part of it.*

Brindell showed up ten minutes late with barbecue sauce stains down the front of his white shirt, gnawing at a turkey leg like he was afraid it could still run. I remembered then that I hadn't eaten since breakfast.

We had to wait for the boss man to give instructions to the new guys before we could get paid. The other guys on my shift stood with their hands out, palms up, impatiently.

Finally, our employer-for-the-day turned to us and reached for the money pouch tied around his waist. He leaned to one side to shift his belly out of the way, so he could retrieve the money.

I watched as he counted out a five-dollar bill, a one-dollar bill, and two quarters to each of the other two guys. They took off as soon as the money hit their palms. Sidling over to me, Brindell placed a single five-dollar bill in my open hand.

I looked at my hand, anticipating more. Instead, Brindell started to walk away.

"Excuse me, Mr. Brindell," I said, "this isn't six-fifty."

"I know," he replied coldly, without turning around.

I was afraid to go after him, but I needed that other dollar and a half, and I had earned it. My sense of justice urged me forward. I caught up with him and tapped him on the back. He spun around and looked down at me with disgust.

"Mr. Brindell, sir, why did you give me less than what we agreed on?" The directness of my question made me feel proud.

"Because I saws ya standing around talkin' to that joker with all the music stuff all over 'im. I's not payin' you to watch shows. I's payin' ya to pick up trash."

"But it was only for a minute, and I picked up more than those other two guys!"

"Look, kid. I paid ya what I thought you's worth, and I'm the boss. And I'm a lot bigger than you, too. Don't forget that."

My favorite picture in my book was of a boy and a giant. The boy had hardly anything on, save what looked like a towel wrapped around his waist and some kind of pouch hanging from it. The giant wore metal armor from head to toe and carried a giant-sized sword. I knew how the story ended in my book; but standing there in front of Mr. Brindell, I wasn't confident it would work out for me like it had for David.

He threw a cold sneer my way, then turned his back on me again, just as a voice called out from behind me. "Why don't you just give the kid his money? He worked hard for it."

I spun around. It was Smithy, and he was no longer wearing his instruments.

Mr. Brindell turned around for about half a second, then kept on walking, his pace getting quicker. He wasn't as ready for confrontation when it involved someone closer to his size. Smithy ran to catch up with him.

"Give the kid the dollar-fifty you owe him," Smithy said with authority.

He must have been watching for a while before he spoke up, I thought.

"Hey, why don't you mind your own business," Brindell snarled.

Smithy put his hand on Brindell's shoulder, which stopped him in his tracks. I fully expected the ogre of a man to slug Smithy in the jaw for daring to lay a hand on him. But Smithy looked him dead in the eyes with a look that said, *Go ahead and try it.*

"Why don't you just do the right thing?" Smithy said calmly.

Tired of being bothered, Brindell dug into the money pouch, pulled out the dollar-and-a-half—all in quarters—threw the coins on the ground, then stomped off mumbling curse words under his breath.

I ran to scoop up the rest of my money, perplexed by what had just happened. As I picked up the last quarter from the grass, tamped down by hours of foot traffic, I had a flashback of Susie's party and the look on Hershel's face when Susie's father had put him in his place.

"Thanks, Smithy," I said, as I got up off the ground. "That was nice of you."

"Aw, don't think anything of it. That guy's nothing but a smelly old monkey butt."

Smithy's assessment of Mr. Brindell made me giggle. I was glad to have my money, but since Smithy didn't know about the weeds in the pavement, he had no idea just how significant his coming to my rescue really was.

"So, you wanna check out the fair some more? Play some games?" he asked.

After all the excitement, I didn't really feel like hanging around any longer, and the muscles in my short legs felt like spaghetti noodles. I was ready to hitch a ride home.

Smithy seemed to understand.

"Can I ask you something, though?" I asked. He nodded *yes*. "Why did you want to hang out with me?"

"I dunno. You just seemed like you could use some company."

I left the fair that day with three reasons to be a happy boy. I had worked hard and earned a few dollars; I bought myself a candy apple on my way out; and someone had stood up for me.

Chapter Eight

THE SURPRISE GUEST

ON SUNDAY MORNING, I CLIMBED up onto the couch with Samson and my Bible book, turned on the radio, and me and my dog had church across the airwaves like I did every Sunday morning when Bert wasn't home. If he was home, I stayed in my room and read my book. Most folks around Copper Creek went to church on Sunday mornings, and I figured my mama would want me to go, too, if she were there. So, I did it the best way I could.

Most of the time, the preacher on the radio taught about things I couldn't find in my storybook. If I had a real Bible, I could've followed along better. But that Sunday, the commanding voice coming from the box in my lap told me to turn to the book of Daniel, and I was hopeful he would preach on a story I knew well. Then I recognized the subject of the sermon, from story number nine in my book—"Daniel in the Lions' Den."

Daniel was brave to keep on praying to God even when it meant being thrown into a pit full of hungry lions. I felt brave, too, staying there all by myself. But I wasn't nearly as good at the praying part. I had read that Bible storybook front to back no telling how many times, and I could tell every story in it almost word for word, but talking to God felt to me like a strange thing for a person to do, especially considering how busy He must always be. I did it from time to time, but I never felt sure if He heard me or not.

As the closing hymn of the church service rang out from the cone of the speaker on the little radio, there was a knock at the door, and I almost jumped out of my skin. Samson barked loudly and ran to the door to defend our house.

Maybe I should ignore it and wait for whoever it is to go away, I thought.

My curiosity got the better of me, and I wanted to quiet Samson's raucous barks. I switched off the radio and went to the door. I put my hand on his head, and my dog settled down.

The storm door was locked, so I opened the inside door, making sure to keep Samson between me and whoever was on the other side.

"Smithy?" I said in disbelief. "What are you doing here?"

"Um, well. I . . . I . . . wanted to check on you, you know, make sure you're doing okay. You seemed pretty shaken up yesterday after the run-in with that jerk at the fair, and I just wanted to see how you're feeling," he said through the screen.

"I'm fine," I said. His answer hadn't convinced me, and there was no hiding the confusion on my face. A few awkward seconds passed. I didn't want to invite him in, but neither was I inclined to send him away.

"That's good," he said. "I'm glad to hear it." Smithy tucked his thumbs under his suspenders, just below his shoulders, and looked away. He hadn't planned out what to say to me.

Samson stepped in place quickly, like a small child in need of a potty, anxious to greet our visitor. The pads of his paws made a tapping sound on the square of linoleum that distinguished the entryway from the carpeted living room.

"I like your dog," Smithy said.

"Thanks."

The awkwardness eventually outweighed my uneasiness, and I unlocked the door. "Come on in," I said.

Samson took to Smithy as much as he had taken to Patrick. I hoped what I had always heard about dogs being good judges of character was true. Samson's tail wagged, and his ears were relaxed, so I relaxed, too.

Smithy was the first person besides me, Bert, and Patrick, who had been inside my house since the Nelsons brought the Christmas present the December prior.

"So, I guess you think I looked pretty silly as a one-man-band, huh?" Smithy said. I wondered why Smithy cared what I thought.

"No, it was pretty neat," I said, sincerely. "I just wondered why you wanted to do that, since you already have a job working at the power company office."

"Well, that office job doesn't pay as much as you probably think. And I'm tryin' to earn money, so I can take a trip!" He hooked his thumbs underneath his suspenders again and pulled them out, letting them pop back against his chest. "I'm going to head out soon, take at least a week, get away from these mountains, and see the country. Now, don't that sound like fun?"

The talk of travel got my attention, and I realized I was being a bad host making him stand there.

"Why don't you have a seat at the table, Smithy? I'll get you a cup of water," I said. Miss Gentry always suggested a cup of water when someone in class was too hot, or was upset about something, or didn't feel well. It was the only thing I could think to offer, and I hoped it would solve uncomfortable situations.

Smithy followed me the few steps to the kitchen, and I motioned for him to sit down while I filled a cup with water from the faucet. *What are you really doing here?* I thought.

"Where do you want to go?" I asked.

"I'm not 'xactly sure; but wherever it is, it's gonna have a sandy beach and a big body of water. I'm thinkin' somewhere in Florida, or maybe down in New Orleans. Heck, I might just quit my job and head all the way to the Pacific. I can just picture it—me sittin' in a lounge chair in the sand with a big, cold drink. Won't that be the life?"

"Wait!" I interrupted. "How did you know where I live?"

I sat the water down on the table with a thud, splashing a little out, and gave him a look that let him know I expected answers.

He took a deep breath, ready to spill the beans.

"I know you're here by yourself, Nate. I just thought you might need lookin' in on."

"But how do *you* know? And how did you know where I live? Do you know Bert?"

"Kinda. Me and your pops have played pool together before. I don't know much about him. I just ran a couple bets agin him a while back. He schooled me both times." Smithy leaned the kitchen chair back on two legs and scratched the back of his head.

Maybe that's where he got all that money, I thought. *Gambling.* I stood there waiting for more explanation, hand on hip like I'd seen Miss Gentry do when she was interrogating a misbehaving student.

"He came into the office a couple weeks ago, and he wanted to pay the account in advance. The whole time he was in there, he just didn't seem right, y' know? Like, not right in the head. Was kinda mumblin' to himself. I heard him say somethin' about *the kid being alone* and about *gettin' out of town*. When you came to ask about the bill, I didn't put it all together right away. But later, it dawned on me whose kid you was and that you might be out here by yourself. I thought about comin' to check on you last week, since I had your address from your account. But when I saw you working at the fair, it kinda sealed it for me. How long has he been gone?"

"A little over a week."

I sat down at the table with him, relieved in some ways that some-one other than Patrick knew about my situation, but I also worried about what it meant for the future.

"Did Bert say anything else? About where he was going or if he was coming back?" I was more curious than hopeful.

"No. And I didn't ask any questions. Like I said, he didn't seem right."

"Are you going to turn me over to social services?"

"I don't know. What do you want to do? Do you have any other family around that could look after you? Is there somewhere I can take you?"

"I don't know of any family. I want to be left alone. I'm fine." My words were direct and my voice firm. "I don't want them to make me go to a new place where I don't know anybody. I can take care of myself just fine."

"But you're a kid! How are you gonna eat? How old are you, like six?"

"I'm ten! Almost eleven!" I shot back. I jumped up from the table and ran to reveal the cupboards, then the refrigerator. "I have plenty of canned food, and I went to the store on the way home yesterday. I bought bread and bologna and milk and cereal. That'll last me a good two weeks! And I got food for my dog, too." My indignation waned, and I remembered Smithy's kindness at the fair. "That was the main reason I earned the money—to get food for Samson here."

He looked impressed as he surveyed my little house, which he could see most of from where he sat. I was glad I had cleaned up so well. There were no dirty dishes in the sink, and I had swept the dirt up off the floor and dusted in the living room.

"All right, kid. I won't say anything to anybody, if that's how you want it." He waved a hand up by his ear and down again. "But you can't live forever by yourself. Do you have some sort of plan?"

"I'm going to stay until the power runs out. Then I'll figure something else out. But the plan for now is to stay put."

We sat there in awkward silence for a moment. Smithy, whom I had seen only three times in my life, had already shown more interest in me than my father had in months. It made me want to trust him, to believe that he was a good guy with good intentions.

"So, you want to travel, huh?" I broke the silence. "To tell you the truth, I'm thinking about taking a trip, too."

"Oh, yeah? Where to?"

I jumped up from the table again, ran to my room, and came back with a stack of my magazines in answer to his question.

"I don't know how I'd get there, but I'd love to see some place like this," I said as I opened one of the books to a story on Amalfi, Italy. "See how this mountain range sits between these two bodies of water? This one is called the Gulf of Naples, and this one is called the Gulf of Salerno." I pointed out the places. "Just look at these pictures! Wouldn't you want to go there?"

"Ohhhh, no," he said without hesitation. "Any place you can get to only by boat or by airplane, I don't 'spect I'll be goin' to anytime soon."

"Why not?"

"Well, for one thing, it costs too much. Plus, I am not too keen on heights, or water. And I especially don't want to be so high up in the air with the water underneath me. But I've got a car, and there's a lot of sights to be seen right here in these United States." He over-emphasized the first syllable of *United*. "These are neat books, though, kid."

"I want to see our country, too!" I said. "Hey, look, there's a great article in one of these books about California." I found the one I wanted to show him. "Look at all those sailboats in the cove and the people on the beach." He studied the pictures in the magazine I handed him, while I stood over his shoulder flipping through a different book, trying to find another article that might interest him.

"You can borrow one if you want," I said.

"Okay, kid. I think I will. Thanks!" It made me proud that he accepted my offer. "Look, I need to be hittin' the road soon," he said. "Is there anything you need before I go?"

I shoved my hands in my jeans pockets and looked down at my sneakers, shuffling my feet. It had dawned on me that morning about something I needed, but I was embarrassed to ask.

"Come on, kid. What is it?"

"Well, my hair is getting longer than I like it, and I'd rather not spend my money on a barber. We've got clippers. But if you don't have time, it's okay."

"Well, go grab 'em. I think I can manage that."

I fetched the clippers from underneath the bathroom counter and met Smithy on the porch. He had already taken a kitchen chair to the side porch off the kitchen for me.

As the clippers drove slowly across my scalp, I remembered the times Bert cut my hair. It wasn't very often. He usually gave me a dollar about once a month to get it cut in town.

The metal guard felt soothing on my head, like a massage, and the gentle hum calmed me. Tiny pieces of caramel-colored hair fell from my head like a light rain.

"Do you live close by?" I asked Smithy, chatting just like I did with the barber in town.

"Not too far," he said. "Just down Cider Hill Road a piece. I live with my sister. She's a few years older than me. Not married yet. It works out okay."

"Is she going on vacation with you? Where does she want to go?"

"Naw, I haven't talked to her about it much. I'm dead set on goin' in just a few weeks, and I don't think she's gonna like it too good."

"Why not?"

"Well, she's a bit of a homebody. And she worries over me like I'm a little baby. She's afraid I'm gonna take off one day and not come back. And don't think I haven't thought about it!" He came around to work on the top of my head. "She's gotten used to having me around the house to help her out with stuff and to help pay bills. I probably oughta stay gone, just so she'll want to look a little harder for a husband. She's almost an old maid as it is. And I don't want me and her to end up being the ones to grow old together." He stopped cutting to inspect his work. "You know, it's kinda funny that you ask. Most kids don't think about stuff like how some grown-up feels."

Smithy spoke with the same mountain accent we all shared in those parts, but he spoke a lot faster than most. His speech matched the upbeat cadence of the songs he played in his one-man band.

"All right, kid," Smithy said. "You're all done, and I gotta be hittin' the road. Meetin' some buddies in town in a little while."

"Okay," I said, getting up from the chair. Samson stood up, too, nervous that I was leaving. "Thanks for the haircut." I stood, rubbing the top of Samson's head with one hand and across the top of my own with the other. It felt good to have short hair again.

I followed Smithy around to the front of the house, where I noticed the jalopy that he drove sitting in the driveway.

"So, you're not going to tell anybody I'm by myself, right?" I asked, for reassurance.

"I won't say nothin'. But I'll be back to check on you. How about I drop in on Saturdays, just to make sure you're doin' alright."

I liked the idea. It seemed unnecessary, but I thought it would be nice to see him again.

"Works for me," I said.

"Okay, kid. You take care of yourself, and I'll see you in a week."

Samson and I stood there, one of us waving, and watched our unexpected new friend as he backed out of the dusty driveway. I already looked forward to Saturday.

Chapter Nine

ALONENESS

I SPENT PART OF THE rest of Sunday afternoon reading my yellow-covered magazines, paying special attention to articles about places in the United States. The Painted Desert, the lower Mississippi, Yosemite—I had pretty photographs of all those places, and reading about them made me feel like I was there. In my imagination, I visited the different sites in the past and in the present—one minute a cowboy out on the range, and the next a tourist with a fancy new camera snapping pictures at the Grand Canyon. Majestic images and grandiose daydreams transported me outside the walls of my quiet, little house for hours. I was always a head and shoulders taller than everyone around me in my fantasies, including Smithy, when I imagined me and him traveling across the country.

I read a description of *National Geographic* somewhere that called it a "publication about the world and its peoples." As much as I liked learning about the places, it was the *people* in the magazine that caught my attention the most. In all the pictures, no matter where they were taken, the people all looked the same. The skin was different, for sure, and the clothes were different; but all the ears were stuck on the same way, and they all had the same number of fingers and toes, and all the older people had the same kinds of lines around their eyes. In every image of a person's face shown up close, there was the same hungry look, even when the hunger was for different things.

Just before dusk, I stopped studying pages and took Samson outside for some exercise. The evening, mountain air was the perfect temperature for our playtime. If a dog could smile, he surely did, romping around after me, zigzagging across our patch of yard that seemed to be getting taller by the minute. He pounced on me, which I allowed during playtime. I fell to the ground, laughing. He licked my face, and I had the strangest thought that Samson resembled a picture of an angel in my Bible book. "Are you hiding wings underneath that white, fluffy fur?" I asked, looking up into his brown eyes.

I went back into the house and washed up for dinner; then I made myself a sandwich and flipped the switch on the radio before I sat down to eat. Samson sat at my feet, patiently waiting for me to toss the outside edge of the bologna from my sandwich to him. I let my feet swing back and forth to the rhythm of the country western song on the radio.

After the last bite of my sandwich, I pushed the aluminum-legged chair across the gold-and-green-patterned linoleum floor to the cupboard. I climbed up to get myself a glass, then poured some cold milk, which I gulped down. It was refreshing after how hard Samson and I had played, and I remembered he needed water in his bowl.

The singer's voice on the radio was hauntingly beautiful, but depressing, made even more so by the way the sound bounced off the walls of my empty house. I turned the radio off, but I could still hear her in my head, singing about falling to pieces when she saw the man who had left her lonely.

"At least I've got you, boy," I said to my dog.

We headed toward my little room at the back of the house. Before I went in, I peeked in Bert's old room across the hall for the first time since the day I found out he had left. For some reason, I still didn't want to go in there. He had never liked for me to be in his room.

I looked at the bed, neatly made, and at the tops of his nightstand and dresser, completely bare, like in a model house. No one had stepped on the shaggy carpet in days. The only evidence that someone had ever occupied the room was a large, framed portrait of my parents on the wall.

Boy, my mama sure was a pretty lady, I thought. I studied the straight, dark hair and thoughtful expression. She smiled like she had a secret. *I got my blue eyes from you, didn't I, Mama?*

And just like every time I had ever looked at the picture, I thought how odd it was to see Bert smiling.

He was wearing a suit that I was pretty sure he no longer owned and a long, skinny necktie. Mama wore a white dress with ruffles on the neck. The photograph in my book must have been made at the same time as the one on the wall because she had on the same dress in both pictures. I assumed it was sometime after they got married and before I came along. They were posed with Mama seated just slightly behind Bert, and her delicate hand rested on his shoulder. The smiling man wasn't bad-looking, but the years between the portrait and then had aged Bert faster than they should have.

I blew Mama a kiss before turning to my room.

Samson was on my bed before I even stepped foot in there. He was tired, and he was ready for me to lay down. But first, I had to lay out my clothes for the next day and set the alarm clock. It was a habit I had known for as long as I could remember.

I owned exactly fifteen pieces of clothing, not counting socks and underwear and my winter coat in the hall closet. I had two pairs of jeans, two pairs of denim overalls, one long-sleeved button-up shirt, five short-sleeved t-shirts, two sweatshirts, a pair of pajama pants, and two night shirts—one short-sleeved and the other long-sleeved. Most nights, when it was warm, I just took off my pants and slept in whatever shirt I had worn that day. On Saturday mornings, I washed all my clothes from the week out in the bathtub and hung them up to dry. I couldn't remember anybody ever teaching me to do it that way. It just seemed like I had always done it.

I took my blue jeans off and laid them across the foot of the bed to wear to school on Monday, and I picked out a red t-shirt from my drawer.

Soon, I was curled up with Samson, under the soft blue sheets of my comfortable bed. The only sound was my dog's subtle snoring. Like always, I had left the hall light on. I knew it would make the money on my account with the electric company run out sooner; but as brave as I felt, I couldn't let it be pitch black in the house.

As I drifted off to sleep, there was an uncomfortable rumble in my stomach. *I must've drank my milk too fast*, I thought. I assumed the discomfort would soon pass, but I was wrong. Soon after I went to sleep, I woke with an indescribable sick feeling that radiated from my stomach outward to my limbs, making my whole body feel hot and helpless. I ran on wobbly legs to the bathroom and dropped to my knees just in time in front of the toilet. My stomach involuntarily emptied its contents into the bowl. It was sudden, and it was violent; and I felt like I might pass out from the force of it.

For over an hour I stayed there, going back and forth from the toilet to the floor. Samson whined beside me. In between the bouts of vomiting, I pressed my face to the cool of the tile floor for a bit of relief. I didn't know what was wrong with me, but I knew it was something awful. As soon as I was able, I made my way to the kitchen for some water, taking only a tiny sip to wash the horrible taste from my mouth.

Back in bed, the nausea went away, but I was no better. I had a fever, and it seemed to be slowly cooking my strength away. *What is this?* I thought. *Where did this come from?* I had been sick before, but never in my short life could I remember having anything as bad. If I could have just gone to sleep, it would have been fine. But there was no rest.

The sweat dripped from my forehead. I could feel my heart pounding in my ears. I felt Samson nudge my hand with his nose, and I could hear him whimpering; but my body was so weak that I couldn't even lift my hand to reassure him that I was okay. I was not okay.

All through the night, I was trapped somewhere between asleep and awake. When the fever spiked, I had a dream, or maybe a hallucination. I was trapped in a crack in the road, my feet buried underneath the asphalt. I wriggled from side to side, struggling to break free, as a big-rig barreled down the highway toward me.

I looked at the clock. It was 4:15 a.m. The fever seemed to have finally broken, and my sheets were wet from sweat. I thought of the Bible storybook underneath my bed and the story of Jesus praying in the garden. The muscles in my neck fought for the strength to turn my head just enough to look at the pillow. I wanted to see if I had sweat drops of blood like Him.

Finally, I slept. And I didn't wake again for a very long time.

When my eyes opened, I forced myself to sit up, then to slowly stand, but only because I knew Samson needed to go outside. It took all my strength to get to the door to let him out and to fill his food and water bowl. After I took care of my dog, I made it as far as the couch before I couldn't go any further.

I wanted a sip of water badly, but I didn't have the strength to get it. I opened my mouth slightly to keep my furry-feeling tongue from sticking to the roof. *Jesus was thirsty like this once,* I thought. *Probably worse.*

Samson ate and drank, then came to rest on my feet on the couch.

Right before I fell back asleep again, a memory appeared from at least two years earlier. It was of another time when I was sick with some kind of stomach bug. I remembered Bert sitting on the edge of the bathtub and handing me a cold washcloth for my face while he rubbed my back. I struggled to understand if it was really a memory or just my fevered brain playing tricks on me. *No, it really happened,* I decided. *There were times he had really acted like a father.*

But why did he leave? I thought.

Lying there, feeling so helpless, I longed for a father. I longed for Bert. It felt like the aloneness would swallow me whole. And then I understood. He was sick, too. That's why he had left me alone. He had a kind of sickness. It wasn't nausea or fever, but something that kept him from being able to be my daddy. *That's what it is,* I thought. *Bert is sick.*

As exhaustion took over, I whispered something I had memorized from my book: "Our Father, Who art in Heaven . . . "

When I awoke again, it was dark; Samson was whining to go out; and I found that I had strength enough to let him out and finally get myself some water from the kitchen faucet for my dry throat. My lips felt like fall leaves on the ground against the smoothness of the glass. After letting Samson back in, I filled my glass again, so I would have it beside me when I laid back down on the couch.

Even after the revelation about Bert being sick, I felt mad at him for the first time. *It's not fair,* I thought. *It's not fair that there's nobody here to take care of me when I'm this sick.* I felt sorry for myself and mad at Bert. I needed to be at a hospital, not on a couch all alone, except for my dog. *Why couldn't he even get us a telephone?*

It was much of the same for a little while longer. Forcing myself to get up to take care of Samson, getting water, then crashing again, until eventually I was able to get the cereal down from the cupboard and eat it from the box. I moved on to peaches when I was able, as I slowly recovered from whatever evil ailment had attacked me.

I had been so sick, I hadn't even thought about school or what was going on there. Sometimes, I couldn't tell if it was night or day. It felt like the world around me had stopped.

At some point, I realized why no one had been by to check on me. Patrick and his family were visiting relatives in Ohio for the week. Without him missing me at school, there was no hope of anyone coming to my rescue until Smithy's scheduled visit on Saturday. That's what I thought—until my doorbell rang.

My furry sentry bolted to the door, waiting to defend me if necessary. But he didn't bark this time. It took a while for me to come to myself and realize I needed to see who was at the door. Then I realized I wasn't wearing any pants.

It took so long to get to the door after retrieving my blue jeans from my room and putting them on, I was sure whoever it was had given up and left. But she was still there. Susie Pennywell stood on my front porch.

"Nate, you look awful!" the normally polite Susie said when I opened the door. "What's wrong with you?"

Seeing her seemed to stun some strength back into my body. I opened the door, allowing her to come inside.

"I've had some kind of really bad bug," I said, confused by the presence of a second new guest in less than a week. "I hope I'm not still contagious. I'd hate for you to catch it. What are you doing here?"

"I came to bring you your schoolwork, so you wouldn't be too far behind. My mom is waiting in the car outside." She stared at me like I had two heads, but she managed a sweet smile. "I remembered that you said you live across from the Nelsons' farm. We buy eggs from them sometimes."

"Oh. That's really nice of you. Thank you." I took the stack of books and papers from her hands and sat them on the end table beside the couch. I had to sit. I didn't want to be rude, but I still wasn't strong enough to stand there and carry on a conversation.

Susie didn't ask me about my father, so I didn't have to worry about her finding out he was gone. She just kept asking me over and over if I was really okay.

"Did the doctor give you some medicine?" she asked, standing across the room from me.

Medicine, I thought. *I bet there's something in the house that would help me, if I can find it.* It hadn't even crossed my mind, and although the fever was gone, my whole body was achy and weak.

"No," I answered, not elaborating so I wouldn't have to lie.

"Well, do you want me to tell Miss Gentry you won't be there to-morrow?" she asked.

"Yes, please," I said. "I don't think I'll be able to go tomorrow either. Wait . . . uh . . . what . . . what day is it?"

She looked surprised by the question. "It's Thursday."

The days and nights had mixed together in my sick, sleepy, dazed delirium.

I wanted so badly to tell Susie what was going on, to have someone else know my secret, other than Smithy and Patrick. I wanted to ask for help. Right outside, in the driveway, there was a mother—Susie's mother—who could nurse me back to health and would be happy to do it. But it was too risky.

"I'm sure I'll see you next week, Susie," I said, hinting that I needed to lie down. "Thank you for bringing my work."

"Okay, Nate." She acted like she didn't want to leave. "Feel better!" she called, and I waved to her as she went out the door and closed it behind her.

As my head hit the arm of the couch, I said out loud, "Susie Pennywell came to my house." I thought it might have been another hallucination.

Why didn't I just tell her? I thought. I was afraid of going to foster care and losing my dog and having to leave my house where I felt like king of the castle, but there was another reason. Deep down, I hoped to see Bert again, and I didn't want him to get in trouble for leaving me.

After a rest, I made my way to the bathroom. I stood on my tiptoes and rummaged in the cabinet behind the mirror, looking for any kind of medicine that might make me feel normal again, but there was nothing there except for antacid and hemorrhoid cream.

I had to look in Bert's room, although I was still reluctant to be there. My energy was spent from talking to Susie, so I had to crawl. The shaggy carpet was soft on my hands. *Like a clown wig*, I thought.

After finding a couple of empty drawers, where Bert's clothes had been, I found the bottom middle drawer in Bert's dresser to be full of stuff. There were medicine bottles, many prescriptions with Bert's name on them. And I found what I was looking for—some aspirin to bring a little relief.

Then something else caught my eye. In the back of the drawer was a lidless shoebox full of papers. Pulling it out and sitting down with my back leaning against the dresser, my trembling fingers sorted through cards, envelopes, and pictures I had never seen before. It felt like I had uncovered a secret treasure, and my eyes were wide searching the box's contents.

But I was still too weak to understand the discovery. Uncovering the box's secrets would have to wait until the medicine, and another night's rest, had helped me recover enough to handle what I had found.

Chapter Ten

THE BOX

WHEN I WAS FEELING BETTER, the reality of how bad my ordeal had been slowly faded from my memory. I rested all day Friday; and by Saturday, I was able to wash my clothes and clean myself. The shower was long overdue, and I even cleaned up around the house—not as much as I wanted, but some.

The school work that Susie brought still sat on the end table, along with the box I found in Bert's dresser drawer. I had stared at them since Thursday but hadn't touched them. After my chores, I decided it was time.

I started with the stack of schoolwork, and I was happy to find a new copy of *National Geographic* among the math worksheets and the reading book with marked pages for me to work on. As much as I wanted to flip through the glossy magazine and discover something new about the world, I laid it aside and picked up the shoe box. It appeared to be full of only papers, but it felt heavy in my hands, weighted with importance. I thought it might hold new information about the world, too.

My heart raced as I picked up an envelope, the first one on top of the stack. As I turned it over to read the front, I was filled with fear that Bert would walk through the door any minute and catch me with his things. The envelope had Bert's name and our address, and it was postmarked only a month before. There was no return address.

Before I could open it, a photograph in the box caught my eye. It was a picture of Bert and Mama, and me and Colleen, right after the girl was born. Pictures of my mama were worth more than gold to me; but to have one of my whole family, the way we were supposed to be—it was hard to believe. *Why have I never seen this?* I thought. *This is my family.* I stared at it, letting myself think about what life would have been like if Mama hadn't gotten sick.

I lay the picture in my lap and carefully opened the envelope. Before I drew out the paper, there was a knock on the door. *It's Smithy,* I thought. The box of treasure would have to wait.

"Heya, kid! I got somethin' for ya," he said rather proudly as he entered. "Well, I guess it's really for your dog." He laughed. Smithy's arms were wrapped around a giant bag of dog food.

"But . . . why? What's this for?" I said, amazed.

"What is all dog food for, silly? For your dog to eat." He shook his head, pretending I was stupid for asking.

"I mean . . . why'd you buy this for me?"

"You ever heard the sayin', 'Don't look a gift horse in the mouth'? I know you got plenty of food for yourself for a while, but I figured Samson would be runnin' out soon, so I wanted to help you out. Can't a guy just do somethin' nice?"

I wanted to run to him and hug him, but that seemed like a weird thing for me to do.

"Thank you. Right nice of ya," I said. I left it at that.

He sat the bag down in a kitchen chair. I wasn't sure if I would be able to lift it, even when I was completely well.

Smithy opened the cupboards, assessing my provisions. He looked in the refrigerator to see if there was still milk, and his brow furrowed at the sight of the gallon jug almost empty. I didn't mind the way he made himself at home. I knew why he did it, and I appreciated it.

He looked around the house and noticed the results of my morning's labor. "Boy, it looks good in here! You sure you haven't hired a maid?" he said with a laugh. Before I could respond, Smithy got a good look at me, and his expression changed quickly. "Nate, what's wrong with you? You've wasted away to nothin'! And you're white as a sheet!"

I had debated whether to tell him about my sickness or not, but my sunken cheeks and hollow eyes gave me away.

"I'm better now. Really."

"Have you been sick?"

I continued to sugarcoat things, saying I had some kind of virus, I guessed, and that it had been pretty rough. But eventually, I broke down. It all came back to me, and I sat down on the couch and poured my heart out to him. I even told him about the times during my sickness when I wished I could just die and go be with my mama. But, somehow, I managed to not cry.

"You shouldn't be here in this house by yourself, no phone and no way to get help," he said, sitting beside me on the couch. "And it ain't right me lettin' you do it. If you woulda died and somebody found out that I knew you was here by yourself, they mighta thrown me in jail."

"But I'm okay," I replied, wondering if Smithy was right and he really could get in trouble for leaving me there alone. I didn't want to get him in trouble, just like I didn't want Bert to get in trouble for leaving me.

"What can I do for ya now? Do you need any medicine? Do you think you still need to go see a doctor? Doctor Edwards in town ain't open on Saturdays, so I'll take you over to the county hospital in Clyde. My sister had to go there once when she stepped on a rusty rake barefooted. They fixed her up good."

"No, I'm okay."

"Maybe I can let you come home with me, look after you for a while. Regina won't mind, I don't reckon." He scratched his head like he was figuring things out. I guessed Regina was his sister.

"No. I want to stay here. I don't want anybody else finding out Bert is gone."

"But . . . I don't know, Nate . . . " He sunk back against the couch. "Maybe you'd be better off if they did know you're here alone. Maybe you could find some real nice parents. Maybe even a family with a brother or sister to play with."

"I just need one thing right now," I said firmly. "Can you write me an excuse note for school? I missed a whole week, and my teacher is going to expect a note from Bert."

Smithy dropped the argument. He had no problem writing the note, and he signed Bert Dooley at the bottom just like I asked him to. I couldn't lie, but I told myself it wasn't wrong to let somebody else do it for me.

"I still don't know about leaving ya here," he said. "I feel awful for what you went through." From the look on his face, he meant it.

"It's not your fault. I can still do this. And next weekend, I'll go find some porches to sweep or something to make a little money, so I can buy a few things. I don't need much. I'm doing okay!"

Smithy went back to rifling through the cupboards, eventually pulling out a can of condensed soup I didn't even know was up there.

He set about heating the soup, and I watched as he made lunch for me in my own kitchen, without me asking him.

"I'm coming back in the middle of the week sometime, too," he said.

"If you wanna," I said. It made little difference what I thought of Smithy's plan. If I wanted to stay in my home, I was going to have to abide by some of his rules.

"Did you read the magazine I gave you?" I asked to lighten up the conversation.

"Yeah, I sure did. I'll bring it back to you next time I stop in. Interesting stuff in there. I didn't know that the country's tallest totem pole was in Washington state."

"Have you decided which way you're headed yet this summer?"

"Naw, I'm still plannin', and I'm not in a hurry to make up my mind. Part of the fun is dreamin' up where it might be." He flashed a Cheshire cat grin at me, as he put two pieces of bread in the toaster.

Smithy poured the soup into bowls and set them on the kitchen table; then he pulled a watch on a chain from one of the two pockets on the front of his pointy-collared shirt and checked the time.

"That's a nice watch," I said, admiring it from my seat on the couch. "I've got a watch, too. I found it on the sidewalk in town last month. It's one that fastens on your wrist, but I don't wear it. My wrists are so little that it slips and slides around. But you don't have that problem with a pocket watch, do you?"

"Nah, I guess not." Smithy looked amused.

"I don't really need to know the time that often, anyway; but sometimes, it'd be nice to have a watch. Hey, yours is shined up really pretty. Is it new? I bet it is," I said.

I was overly chatty, but other than my five-minute interaction with Susie a couple days before, I hadn't talked to another human soul in almost a week.

"Actually, it's been around for a good while." He paused the subject. "Come on over here and eat something, kid." I did as Smithy instructed.

"Where'd ya get it, Smithy, if you don't mind me asking?"

"Well . . . it belonged to my daddy." Smithy looked proud. "He was a railroad man, and he earned this here watch for his years of *exemplary* service to the rail line. He's been gone a while, though."

I sat down at the table to eat my soup, wondering if he meant *gone* like Bert was gone, *gone* as in *retired from the railroad*, or *gone* like *dead*, but I didn't ask.

"I've always wanted to ride a train," I said. Smithy looked relieved that I'd found something new to talk about. "When I decide to leave here, I reckon that's how I'll head out."

Smithy looked at me hard, like he was worried.

"Well, nobody travels by train no more, Nate," he said. He leaned on the back of a chair and motioned for me to start eating.

"But I hear the train whistle all the time," I insisted. I tried to eat, but my first spoonful was too hot. "There's a station not far from here."

"Trains are still running, Nate, but they carry more lumber than people now," he explained.

"Yeah, but that won't matter if I'm not buying a ticket. It can still get me somewhere. I think some of the trains go over the mountains into Tennessee, and some of them go south to Florida."

"Now, don't ya think about hoppin' a train, Nate. You'll get yourself in a heap of trouble, for sure. If you need to go anywhere, how about you ask me first?"

"Okay, Smithy," I said. The soup was a tolerable temperature, and I slurped it fast, grateful for the warmth and flavor of the broth.

"Besides, I think you'd be pretty easy to spot with this mutt taggin' along," he said, and he reached down and stroked the top of Samson's head. I hadn't considered it—how Samson might make traveling more difficult. But I planned to take him wherever I decided to go.

"Alrighty, now. I'm gonna be outside for a while," Smithy said. "You just rest yourself in here."

Before I could ask what he was going to do, Smithy was out the door; and in a few minutes, the steady rumble of a lawnmower came from right outside the window. He started in the front; and from my seat at the table, I watched him for a while. His long legs made quick work of the task; and soon, the jungle was tamed, and my yard looked like a yard again.

I set my soup bowl in the sink, then laid down on the couch. The mower roared, and it felt good to know Smithy was in the backyard, close by. Then I remembered the letter.

My fingers trembled as I pulled out a piece of fancy, linen-colored stationery. It was monogrammed at the top with the initials M.K.D., and the swirly handwriting was perfect.

Dearest Brother,

We've had an early spring here at home. I'm glad for it after the miserable winter. I hope the weather is pleasant where you are, too. There isn't much for me to say. I know most of my letters all say the same thing. But I will keep writing, so you never forget that you are loved and missed, and you have family that cares. As always, please give my love to my nephew, whom I long to see, as well as you.

Miriam

My heart raced. I folded the paper back the way I had found it and slowly and carefully slid it back into the envelope.

Miriam. The name felt like sunshine and roses hidden under a pile of manure. *Miriam.* My brain could say the name, but it wouldn't let me piece together the rest of the information I had uncovered. I lay there with the letter in my hands until I no longer heard the mower. Then I dropped it back into the box.

"Alrighty!" Smithy said loudly as he swung open the screen door and came into the house. "It looks a might better out there, I tell ya."

I wanted to dig through the box, to devour all its secrets at once. But that would have to wait.

"Thank you. You didn't have to do it, but I'm glad you did."

"Ain't nothing."

I admired his modesty.

"Say, Nate," Smithy said, concerned, "you sure you're not still sick? You really don't look good, kid."

It wasn't the effects of the illness that he read on my face. He saw the revelations of the box in my expression.

"I'm feeling fine. Really."

To my surprise, Smithy hung around for a while. He asked me to bring out my magazines. I thought about getting the Bible storybook to show him, too, but I decided against it.

We sat on the couch together, thumbing through volumes of *National Geographic* magazine, reading sections of articles out loud and pointing out pictures to one another. Samson sat on the other side of me on the couch, and I was a long way away from the place where I had prayed to die days before.

"Okay. Wednesdays and Saturdays now, right?" he said when he was ready to leave.

"Wednesday and Saturdays," I agreed.

"See ya in a few days, Nate."

"See ya, Smithy."

I followed him out and stood on the porch waving as the clunker of a car backed out of my driveway and into the road, leaving a cloud of dust behind it.

I went out into the backyard. The mountain air made my sickly skin wake up again.

I laid in the hammock, and Samson laid under it, until it was dark.

Bert has a sister. I have an aunt. She wants to see me. Smithy came and mowed my yard. And he brought food for my dog.

I said my new relative's first name over and over in my head, then tried it out with her title.

Aunt Miriam.

Moses had a sister named Miriam.

Back inside the house, I read the letter again, this time out loud to Samson. It felt like Miriam was actually in the house with me—this person that I didn't know, but who wanted to know me. I dug through the box, finding letter after letter. They were all addressed in the same swirly handwriting. I decided not to read any more until later. I wanted to space them out, so I could have that same feeling of not being alone every night.

Laying in my bed with Samson at my feet, I flipped through the Bible storybook. For the first time I could remember, I wasn't able to read. So, I prayed.

God, show me where I belong.

Chapter Eleven

A NEW DAY

MY SUNDAY MORNING STARTED OUT like most Sunday mornings. I sat on the couch with the radio in my lap and Samson beside me. The preacher was loud, and his voice sounded angry, but I didn't understand why. I tried to follow what he was talking about.

Halfway through the sermon, someone rapped on my front door. *Why are all these people showing up at my house?* I thought as I got up to answer it.

"Mrs. Nelson!"

My feet froze in place. I couldn't move to open the screen door.

"Good morning, Nate. I hope you're doing well on this last day of April."

Mrs. Nelson was a sturdy woman who, unlike her husband, wore her feelings on her face. She must have been feeling cheerful standing on my porch because her smile was easily the width of two slices of orange. She wore a suit dress in a pretty, powdery blue color and a matching hat with some kind of feathery stuff on it. The hat hid all of her white hair, except the part that hung down over her ears.

"I was wondering if you would like to go to church with me and Mr. Nelson this morning, Nate. I noticed your father's car isn't out front. Is he away? Do you think he'll mind if you come with us? We'd love to have you." Her words came at me quickly through the screen.

"Um, well, no, ma'am. He won't mind."

She looked past me into the house. I felt rude not inviting her in, but I couldn't risk her somehow finding out about my situation.

"Do I look okay to go to church?" I asked. I didn't stop to think about whether I actually wanted to go or not, but I was instinctively agreeable.

"Oh, you look just fine to me," she said.

Before I knew it, I had said goodbye to Samson and was in the pick-up truck, wedged between Mr. and Mrs. Nelson. Just after we pulled out of the driveway, I felt relieved that I wasn't still in my pajamas when she came.

"Something just told me I needed to stop by and invite you to church this morning, Nate," Mrs. Nelson said as we headed up the mountain. The trip was windy and steep, and I felt like a ping-pong ball between Mr. Nelson's right shoulder and Mrs. Nelson's left. The combination of windy roads and the overwhelming smell of Mrs. Nelson's perfume made me queasy. I wasn't one hundred percent back to normal from my sickness, either.

Turning off the main road, the truck bumped and bounced along a long gravel road lined with tall, white pines and bushy hemlocks; then we pulled in front of a white church with a sharply slanted roof. Three steps covered in green outdoor carpet led up to the double doors. Cars were parked in the dirt on both sides of the church; and in front, some pulled between trees. A mountain stream flowed swiftly just behind the church. Without the cars, the scene would have looked like a painting pretty enough to hang on a wall.

"I haven't been inside a real church building since I was little," I confessed as I slid across the bench seat and made the leap to the ground. I knew Mama had taken me some, but I couldn't remember it.

"Well, we're happy you're with us today," Mr. Nelson said. He put his hand on my shoulder and guided me inside. "This is a special place to us."

The way Mr. Nelson said *special* made the word feel holy.

There was no lobby; the doors of the church opened right into the sanctuary. The church was wide enough for only one section of wooden benches; but the room was long, and there were doors on either side of the podium up front. I wondered where they led.

From my seat on the couch at home to the middle of a hard bench in the back of a church with a Nelson on either side of me, it was a whirlwind of a morning.

As people continued to file in down both side aisles, greeting one another with handshakes and hugs, I surveyed the crowd. Two rows from the front sat a woman with a familiar-shaped head. I patted Mrs. Nelson's arm excitedly. "That's my teacher!" I said, pointing.

"Kate Gentry is your teacher? How nice! She's a sweet girl," Mrs. Nelson whispered back as the preacher walked up to the podium. I kept my eyes on Miss Gentry, copying her as she stood and opened her hymnal to sing. She appeared to be there with the lady who sat beside her. From her profile, I could tell that the lady was pretty—but not as pretty as Miss Gentry—and her ears stuck out a bit underneath her bobbed hair. She looked to be just a few years older than Miss Gentry.

There were no instruments, and the hymns went on for at least twenty minutes, with the preacher leading all of them. I knew the

songs from the church programs on the radio, so I followed along in
the hymnal and sang loudly. My favorite was "Victory in Jesus." Except
for the Christmas pageant at school in third grade, I had never heard
that many people singing in the same place in person before.

The preacher started talking, and I was happy that he didn't yell
like the preacher on the radio. He sounded joyful. His voice felt like
the candy apple I got at the fair, and I wondered how he still had a
voice to preach with after all that singing.

"Showing love the way God commands us to isn't always easy,
friends," the preacher said somewhere in the first half of his sermon.
"Especially when we've been wronged. But in Matthew, chapter five,
Jesus said, 'Ye have heard that it hath been said, Thou shalt love thy
neighbor, and hate thine enemy.'" He paused and scanned the room,
then continued reading Jesus' words. "'But I say unto you, Love your
enemies, bless them that curse you, do good to them that hate you,
and pray for them which despitefully use you, and persecute you.'"

I thought of all the kids at school who picked on me about being
little, the ones who made my nickname sound like a curse word.

The service ended sooner than I expected. The Nelsons and I filed
out like everyone else, but like them, we stood outside for a long time
talking. The sound of the stream, the bright sun on my face, and the
freshness of the springtime mountain air made the church parking
lot feel like a holy place, too.

I was standing next to Mr. Nelson as he complimented the preacher
on his sermon when Miss Gentry spotted me. I had been watching her,
hoping for the chance to speak.

"Nate Dooley, I've been so worried about you!" she said rushing
over. "It's nice to see you at church!"

I expected the handshake or pat on the back that she gave freely to her students; but instead, she wrapped her arm around my shoulder and pulled me in close to her, laying her head over on top of mine for a second.

"Hey," I said, unable to come up with anything else.

"Where were you this week? Without you and Patrick in class, the room just felt empty!" Her normal demure tone was gone. "I know you don't have a phone at home, or I would have called to check on you."

"That's okay. I was sick, but I'm better now. I'll be in class tomorrow, Miss Gentry."

"I'm glad you're better, Nate. I missed you."

My cheeks felt red hot.

"Most of my students go to church near town, I believe. Are you here with the Nelsons today?" she asked.

"Yes, ma'am. They're my neighbors," I explained.

"Oh, it looks like my friend Regina is ready to go." Her normal tone was back. "I hope you come back again. See you tomorrow, Nate."

"Bye."

Mrs. Nelson left a group of ladies and came over to me. "Would you like to join us for lunch at our house?" she asked.

"Yes, ma'am."

"Will your father miss you?"

"No, ma'am."

"Okay, then!"

My whirlwind of a day continued. Further back down the mountain and past my house, we turned into the Nelsons' driveway. The farmhouse was set far back from the road. A tire swing hung from a big oak in the front yard. On the left side of the house grew a small forest of tiny fir trees that, in a few more years, would be Christmas trees.

"Come on in and make yourself at home, Nate. The chicken pie is already cooked. I just need to warm it back up in the oven for a bit," Mrs. Nelson said. She unpinned her hat from her head and hung it on a rack near the front door.

Mrs. Nelson didn't speak like everyone else in Copper Creek. Her *t*'s were crisp, and her long *i* wasn't longer than it needed to be.

"Here, Nate, have a seat in the living room with me while we wait on lunch," Mr. Nelson said.

The house was open and inviting, quiet and calm. Mr. Nelson sat in a rocking chair, with an ankle rested on a knee. I sat on the couch in front of a double window with billowy, white curtains.

He picked up a newspaper and opened it, but he didn't read. Instead, he turned to me.

"It's a shame that we don't see more of one another, being neighbors and all. I guess you've never been in our house, have you?"

"No, sir. It's real nice." I had knocked on their door many times to ask for a ride but had never been inside.

"Well, tell me a bit about yourself, Nate. What do you like to do for fun?"

"I like to read and listen to the radio and play with my dog."

"I like reading, too," he said. "That's why I haven't bought that television set like Mrs. Nelson's been asking me to. Too much noise. I think a good book is much better."

I looked around the room and noticed the full bookshelves. I hadn't even noticed the absence of a television.

"I thought I was the only one around who doesn't have one," I said.

"Naw, you're not the only one. There's plenty of families around that can't afford one or just don't want one. I reckon' we'll end up with one eventually, but the telephone is enough distraction. Ever since we had it put in, it feels like somebody's always needin' something. Don't get me wrong, Nate—I don't mind helping folk. Sometimes, it just feels like we've forgotten how to think for ourselves, since somebody else that might have the answer is only a phone call away."

When lunch was ready, Mrs. Nelson called to us from the dining room.

"Is somebody else coming?" I asked when I walked in and saw the spread on the table.

"Oh no, dear, I just wanted to make sure our guest has plenty to eat. A strong, growing boy like you needs to eat!" There wasn't a hint of irony or sarcasm in her voice.

I almost laughed. It was funny to hear someone describe me as *strong* or *growing*.

Four chairs sat around the oval-shaped table. I hung back, trying to figure out which seat was for me. The Nelsons sat down across from one another, at the narrow ends, leaving an empty place for me between them, but I stood there until Mrs. Nelson motioned for me to sit.

After Mr. Nelson said the blessing, I dove into the plate of chicken pie, mashed potatoes, and green beans Mrs. Nelson had dipped for me. I started fast but slowed down to enjoy it.

"Is Nate the name you go by at school?" Mrs. Nelson asked me from above the rim of a glass of sweet tea.

It seemed like a weird question, but I didn't mind telling her the truth.

"No, ma'am. Most people call me Weenie."

"*Weenie? Well, why on earth . . . ?* I'm sorry, son. What I meant was, is Nate short for Nathan, or maybe Nathaniel?"

"Oh . . . " I was embarrassed. "It's Nathaniel. I'm Nathaniel James," I said.

"Well, how nice, to have two disciple names."

"Two?"

"Yes. Nathaniel and James were both disciples. The *King James* spells it differently than you, I bet; and in some places, Nathaniel is called Bartholomew instead."

"Bartholomew! That's what it says in my book," I said.

"What book is that?" Mr. Nelson chimed.

"The book of Bible stories that my mama gave me. I read it every day. There's a story in there about Jesus picking out his disciples, but I never knew one of them was Nathaniel."

"I think it is wonderful that you read your Bible book, dear," Mrs. Nelson said sweetly.

"Well, I think it would make my mama happy, if she were here."

"Yes, Nate, I'm certain it would."

"Do you have a real Bible in your house?" Mr. Nelson asked.

"No, sir. Not that I know of."

He got up from the table and left the room. *Did I say something wrong?* I wondered. But shortly, he returned with a brown book in his hand.

"Here, take this. Keep reading your book of stories from the Bible, but try to read this one, too."

I took the Bible from him, not sure what to say. I never quite understood if my mama could see me from where she was. But just in case she could, I planned to read it just like my storybook.

"Would you like to come to church with us again next week?" Mrs. Nelson asked when lunch was over.

"Yes, ma'am. Thank you."

"Should I come by and ask your father first this time? To make sure it's okay with him?"

"No!" I said, too quickly. My outburst made Mrs. Nelson jump. Catching myself, I added, "No, ma'am. He'll be okay with it."

"Do you want me to drive you over to your house now, Nate?" Mr. Nelson asked.

"No, thank you. I can walk. Thank you for lunch. It was wonderful."

As they walked with me out on the front porch, Mr. Nelson said, "You come back sometime this week, and I'll show you around the farm, son. Drop in any time."

"Yes, sir. I'd like that," I said, as Mrs. Nelson shoved a container of leftover chicken pie into my hands.

I turned from halfway up the driveway to see them both standing there waving at me.

Samson was happy to see me when I got home. He sniffed at my hands and my clothes, smelling the food and the new place on me.

"What an unexpected day," I said to him. I plopped on the couch, and he jumped on top of me to lay down.

Unexpected, I thought. The word reminded me of the box and Aunt Miriam's letters.

"Samson, it's time to see what else she has to say."

Chapter Twelve

HOW TO LOVE YOUR ENEMIES

DEAREST BROTHER,

I have no way to know if you will read this, but I hope so.

Unlike the first one I had read, this letter from Aunt Miriam had a date. In the top left corner, she had written *July 16, 1956.*

Almost five years ago, I thought.

I hadn't even noticed the postmark. I wondered if I should stop and sort them in order—newest to oldest or oldest to newest—but I decided to keep reading and think about that later.

You should know that Father died. It was peaceful. He didn't suffer. It was just his time and the natural way of things. Augusta and I are alone here now. I wish you were here, too.

Your sister,

Miriam

The letter introduced me to my grandfather and told me about his death at the same time. I felt sorry for Miriam.

He left her like he did me, I thought. *I wonder who Augusta is.*

That night, I slept on the couch with Samson and kept the letter on my chest.

The next morning, before I left to catch the school bus, I grabbed the excuse note Smithy had written. Patrick and I met up at our usual spot, and we walked to meet the bus together. He was full of excitement about his trip to Ohio, and he couldn't stop talking about it. I listened for a long time; but when the bus was almost to school, I jumped in to tell him about Smithy.

"Somebody else knows my secret," I said.

"What secret?" He looked at me funny, then exclaimed, "Gosh, Nate! I almost forgot about Bert leaving you. Who else knows?"

I put my finger over my lips and looked at him wide-eyed. Patrick's volume had nearly given me away.

"It sounds weird, but it's the man from the power company that I told you about." I told him about seeing Smithy at the fair and about him standing up for me. I explained how Smithy knew I was alone, and I told Patrick about him coming to my house twice. I decided to leave out the part about me being so sick for a week. There wasn't time, anyway, because the bus pulled up in front of our school.

When I got to my classroom and laid the note on Miss Gentry's desk at the back of the room, I had a twinge of guilt about Smithy's forgery, but not enough for me to tell her about Bert being gone. It was too risky.

At recess, I sat against the fence around the kickball field with Patrick, who was still talking about Ohio.

"For a few days, we stayed with my grandma, but then we stayed in a motel the next couple of nights. Have you ever stayed in a motel, Nate?"

"Now, when would I have done that?"

"I dunno, Nate. I's just asking."

"Listen," I interrupted him. "I found some stuff in Bert's room."

"What kind of stuff?"

"A bunch of letters, and they're from Bert's sister."

He sat back against the fence. "Man, a lot happened while I was gone, huh?"

"Can you believe it? I have an aunt, and she lives in Tennessee. At least, I guess so, 'cause that's where the letters are postmarked from."

Before Patrick had a chance to ask me what the letters said, there was a commotion. The kickball game came to a halt. A group of girls stopped hula hooping, and, in another part of the fenced play yard, the thrower held onto the Frisbee. Everyone stared toward the tetherball court.

Miss Gentry wasn't around. She had taken Cynthia Poindexter inside to get a band-aid after she skinned her knee playing hopscotch. That's when Peter Dotson saw his chance to prove he was the toughest kid in class by picking on the biggest kid in class, which was Hershel West.

Peter wailed on Hershel with the tetherball, holding the rope in his hand and knocking Hershel in the head with the ball. Nobody could believe it was happening.

At first, it felt good to see Hershel getting a taste of his own medicine; but as I watched him hunker down and cover his head, trying to dodge the blows, something happened to me. Without thinking, I ran over to them and yelled at Peter as loudly as I could yell, "Hey! Stop it!"

Peter turned around and stared down at me in surprise.

"Nate, what are you doing?" Patrick asked frantically from right behind me. I didn't answer him. The truth was, I didn't know.

"It's not nice to pick on people," I said.

He turned around and hit Hershel over the head again, then turned back around and gawked at me. I couldn't understand why Hershel just stood there, letting it happen.

"I said, it's not nice to pick on people!" I was standing closer to Peter, but I couldn't remember how I got there.

Peter finally spoke. "Oh, don't worry, Weenie. Hershel's not a *person*. He's a big, dumb sheep. It's okay to pick on them."

My clenched hands came out of my pockets at the same time, and the left one traveled swiftly upward toward Peter's right eye. It didn't knock him down, but the blow to the eye made him stumble backward a few steps. Before he had a chance to make an end of me, Miss Gentry was there between us, and Patrick was pulling me back.

I'm gonna be found out for sure now, I thought.

After the whole class filed inside and back to the room, Miss Gentry made me stay out in the hallway. *She's gonna find out Bert is gone and call social services, and they will take me away from my house and from Samson.*

Miss Gentry was inside the classroom checking on Peter's eye. She opened the door and called me in, while at the same time sending Peter down the hall to see the nurse.

My teacher led me to a corner in the back of the room. Everyone's eyes followed us there; but she snapped her fingers, and they went back to looking at the reading assignment.

Without saying anything, Miss Gentry handed me a folded piece of paper.

"What is this?"

"It's a note for your father. I can't call him at your house, and I don't have a work phone number for him on file. But I think he needs to come in and speak with me. I'm inviting him to have a conference on Friday."

"But I never get into trouble, Miss Gentry." There was genuine shame in my voice.

"Nate, you've been daydreaming in class for weeks; then you missed a week of school. Now, on the first day back, you've done something very out of character for you. You're one of my best students, Nate. Probably *the* best. And I need to figure out what's going on with you."

Her words didn't comfort me any. I had disappointed the person I most respected; and on top of that, she was going to find out about Bert being gone.

"Now, I already know you were standing up for Hershel. And to tell you the truth, I'm not mad at you. But your behavior is still unacceptable."

"But the preacher said to love your enemies. And Hershel has been my enemy for as long as I've been in school. So if I can show love to him by helping him out of a pickle, isn't that a good thing? You know, it's funny. Hershel doesn't seem so much like an enemy anymore."

"I understand, Nate. But did you show love for Peter when you socked him in the eye?"

She had a point, and I couldn't argue.

I thought about the predicament I was in for the rest of the day, and there was only one thing for me to do. I needed Smithy's help.

For all the trouble I was in, I didn't regret what happened, especially since when the bell rang at the end of the day, Susie came over to talk to me before I even stood up from my desk.

"I thought that was really brave what you did, Nate," she said.

"Thanks." I smiled. "But I think I'm going to be in a lot of trouble now."

"That makes you all the braver for doing it," she said. Then Susie Pennywell planted a kiss on the side of my face and ran out the door. No one saw it; but it happened, and I could hardly believe it.

After school, I went to the power company office. I skipped half-way there, thinking about Susie; then I thought about my problems again and slowed down to the pace of a funeral dirge.

I had to wait for a few customers to leave, but then Smithy was free for me to tell him about the fight, and the conference, and how I needed his help.

"If you come with me to the conference, you can be sort of a stand-in for Bert. Tell my teacher that he can't make it and that you'll tell him everything he needs to know."

"Kid, you've lost your mind."

"It's not like you'd have to lie. He *can't* make it! And if you ever see him again, then you can tell him everything that she said! Please, Smithy. I don't want to have to leave my house. The conference is on Friday. Can you get off work to talk to her at three o'clock?"

He looked at me with a clenched jaw, and I thought he might have already written me off.

"All right, kid. I'll do it. Now get out of here; there's a customer coming. I'll check on you at your place Wednesday night."

I rushed out before he could change his mind.

When I got home, Samson and I read another letter from Aunt Miriam, but it was just about the weather wherever she was. Still, I liked hearing the voice I had made up for her in my head when I read the letters.

For dinner, I had leftover chicken pie, pork and beans, green beans, and peaches while I listened to a Wild West shootout scene on the radio. Like Mrs. Nelson had said, I was a strong and growing boy.

Chapter Thirteen

WHERE THE SOIL IS ROCKY

THE KIDS AT SCHOOL LOOKED at me differently on the second day of May. A couple of them even called me by my real name for the first time. And Susie hung out with me and Patrick for all of recess.

The biggest change was Hershel. During lunch, he walked by my table and slipped a note under my tray. I waited until I went to the bathroom to read it, so no one would see.

Nate—What you did for me was real nise. I'm sorry for calling you all them names. Your a good friend. Sinseerly, Hershel

Hershel West had called me his friend.

After school, I went home and let Samson out. It was a pretty day, so he and I decided to pay a visit to Mr. and Mrs. Nelson together.

Mrs. Nelson answered the door wearing an apron. White powder covered her hands. Underneath the apron was a dusty blue dress with tiny yellow flowers, and I remembered seeing the same material for sale over at the Five and Dime.

"Well, Nate, it's good to see you! I was just making a pie, but you're welcome to come in."

I looked over at Samson, wondering if he was welcomed, too.

"Oh, I didn't notice your friend. I wish he could come in, Nate, but I just mopped my floors. I hope you understand. I know Mr. Nelson would love to see you. He's out around the farm somewhere. Why don't you go play on that old tire swing while I finish up. Then we'll go find him together."

"Yes, ma'am."

The rope of the tire swing showed lots of wear from time and weather, but it was still strong. The rope was tied to a limb so high up, I wondered how it was possible to get up there. *Maybe they climbed the tree just like Zacchaeus*, I thought.

I hopped in the tire and let it take me away. Samson ran back and forth under me, barking loudly, as I kicked my little legs to move higher. I couldn't tell if he thought it was a game or if he barked because he was afraid I would get hurt.

"I wonder why the Nelsons have this old swing in their yard, boy," I said to Samson. I imagined them taking turns riding in it, although they surely wouldn't fit inside the tire.

I didn't have to wait for Mrs. Nelson long. She came out of the door soon wiping her dusty hands on her apron.

"Okay, friend, let's go on a walk."

Samson and I followed as she led us across the property. The area behind their house was a beautiful mix of flat patches and hills, and they had figured out how to use them both for their purposes.

"He's in the barn milking right now. He'll be happy to see you."

The barn was in the distance, set down in a little valley next to the big pasture where the cows grazed.

The landscape all around made me think of the Garden of Eden, lush and green. It was peaceful there, but I knew Mr. Nelson worked hard to tame the earth, to keep the land managed and calm.

I stopped in my tracks, and Samson and Mrs. Nelson stopped to see why I wasn't moving.

"What is *that*?" I asked, with my mouth gaped open.

It was a sea of white, an entire hillside covered in bushes spaced about a foot apart, and the bushes were covered in tiny white buds that looked like snow.

"Oh, that's my special garden," she answered, smiling. "Mr. Nelson planted it for me a few years ago. It's grown up fast. It didn't bloom the first year; it had tiny buds the second year; and this year, well, you can see how it's turned out. But it's the strangest thing! They've bloomed much, much earlier this year than they are supposed to. We can't figure out why it happened."

"I've never seen anything like it."

It was rows and rows and rows of just *pretty*.

"It is beautiful, isn't it? We'd never been able to grow much on that hill, because the soil is too rocky. But my lavender does well there, and from that space, they look right at the sun most of the day."

"But I thought lavender was a purple flower?"

"Usually it is. Those are special white lavender." She looked proud as she told me about them. "Mr. Nelson had to order the seeds. He had them sent here all the way from Europe. He studied to get just the right thing to plant there, and he picked the white kind because he wanted something bright to lift my spirits." Her face glowed while she told me about Dell's special present to her. "It took him weeks to plant it all, with all his other work around the farm. But it was worth it. I can see that hill from my kitchen window. We're not going to harvest the stems, just leave them to enjoy until the blooms fall off and wait on them to come back next year."

"Lift your spirits?" As soon as I asked it, I regretted it. Mrs. Nelson was a new friend, and the question was prying.

"Let's sit and visit for a minute," she said, inviting me to a picnic table right behind the house.

I sat down with her and noticed her normally bright smile had faded to a dim straight mouth.

"Do you want me to tell you why Mr. Nelson planted that garden for me?" she asked. I nodded yes.

"It hasn't always been just me and Dell here by ourselves," she began. "We have one daughter, and she lived here with us until about four years ago."

I folded my arms on the table and rested my chin on them, looking up at Mrs. Nelson intently. She had chosen to share something important with me, and it deserved my full attention.

"What's her name?" I asked.

"Her name is Jenny. And she has the most beautiful green eyes you've ever seen. And the most contagious laughter."

Mrs. Nelson's smile returned, but for only a few seconds.

"But Jenny decided she wanted to move away from here, after she got grown. And I don't see her anymore. I don't even know where she is right now. And that makes this mama's heart very sad."

I didn't know what to say to her, and I didn't know why she was telling me about her daughter. Samson sensed her sadness, though, and he rested his head on the seat beside her, nuzzling in close. She stroked his head in return.

"But Dell has been very patient with me, and he has been a good helper. Even when I lost my faith in God, and he had to go to church alone for a very long time."

I sat up at the revelation.

"You didn't go to church? I can't imagine that. You're the most churchy person I know!"

She laughed. "Thank you, I think!"

"I mean, you seem so happy and excited about going."

"Oh, I am now. But it took me a while. You see, when somebody loses someone, it can change who they are. And I blamed God for letting my Jenny leave me, even though it was all her choice. I was mad at Him. And then I questioned whether or not He was really there. I spent a lot of time in this house, moping around, feeling sorry for myself and being mad at God. One day, I looked out the window and saw Dell on that hill that wasn't much good for growing anything, and I thought, *What is he doing?* Then I found out about his plans—how he had found those plants that are pretty, and they smell good, and they grow well even with all those rocks in the ground. And he went to all that trouble for no other reason but to make me happy."

When Mrs. Nelson cheered up, Samson came back around the table to be with me. Mrs. Nelson looked up at the sky and followed a cardinal across it; then she spoke again. "I thought maybe you would understand my story, since you've lost someone, too."

I froze—except for my eyes, which darted back and forth in confusion. *How does she know? How did she find out about Bert?* I thought.

"Although, it's been a long time since your mother passed, hasn't it?" she asked.

"Yes, ma'am. A very long time," I relied, holding in a sigh of relief.

"As simple as it sounds, the beauty of that hill over there reminded me Who created all beautiful things. The same God Who made the lavender, and me, and my Jenny—I knew He could make my life beautiful again if I would just let Him."

"I'm glad you're happy again, Mrs. Nelson. And I surely do like your lavender garden."

"Well, thank you for listening to me, Nate. And I hope you know if you ever need someone to talk to, you can come talk to me." She reached across the table and patted my hand. "And since we're getting to know each other so well, why don't you call me Opal?"

"Yes, ma'am."

"Oh, look. Here comes Mr. Nelson," she said. "Look who came to see us, Dell!" she called to him. He was halfway between the barn and the house, and he picked up his pace to greet me.

"How's it going, young sir?" Mr. Nelson asked with a wave of his hand. His eyes smiled, even if his mouth didn't.

"I'm good, Mr. Nelson. You told me to come by and you would show me the farm. I thought today might be a good day. And I brought my dog, Samson."

"It is indeed a good day," he said with a nod as he pulled off his work gloves. "And I've seen your dog before."

"You have? I've had him for only a couple weeks, but it feels like we've known each other forever."

"Yeah, he hung out here for a while. I gave him some scraps, but he would never come near me. He seems really friendly now, though. And a right smart cleaner, too."

"He wouldn't come near you? That's weird. He's the friendliest dog I've ever met. He showed up at my house one day acting like he was mine and won't leave my side. He's a good friend. Aren't you, boy?" I squatted down and scratched Samson behind the ears with both hands.

"Well, maybe he just knew he didn't belong here because he was supposed to find you."

As if he knew what we were saying, Samson trotted over to Mr. Nelson, let him pet him, then came back over to me.

"He's definitely your dog, Nate," remarked Mr. Nelson. "Now how's about I show you the cows? Come on with me."

"You boys have fun," Mrs. Nelson said. "I'm going to go check on my pie."

Not only did Mr. Nelson introduce me to his whole herd of dairy cows and his few chickens, but he also walked me over the entire property, except the potato fields and the fallow ones. The apple orchard impressed me the most. He had some great climbing trees, and he waited on me to try out a few of them before we headed back up to the house. All in all, it was a good way to spend an afternoon.

When I got back to my house, I remembered to check the mail for the first time in days. The mailbox was usually empty, but ever since I had found the letters from Miriam, I wondered when she might send another. There was no letter, but there was an account statement from the power company. Like I expected, the paper said I didn't owe anything. But I was that much closer to either having to pay, living in the dark, or leaving Copper Creek.

I had ideas about where I might go, but nothing set. *East or West? North or South?* If Bert didn't come back, or maybe even if he did, I had to make up my mind which direction I would head.

After dinner and homework, and before I opened another letter from Aunt Miriam, I picked up the Bible Mr. Nelson had given me. I hadn't kept the promise to myself to read it yet, and I didn't know where to start. But when I opened it, it fell to the book of Ecclesiastes.

In the third chapter, I read something that made me think of Opal, and about losing my mama, and about Bert leaving. It brought to mind the way I had found Samson, or rather, how he had found me. I thought about meeting Smithy and getting to know the Nelsons, and I couldn't help but wonder what else might be in store.

He hath made every thing beautiful in his time: also he hath set the world in their heart, so that no man can find out the work that God maketh from the beginning to the end.[1]

---

1 Ecclesiastes 3:11

Chapter Fourteen
THE POOL LESSON

SMITHY CAME OVER ON WEDNESDAY evening, and again, he brought gifts—bread, milk, apple juice, and bologna. As an extra treat, he even came with three doughnuts, wrapped in special paper, from the bakery inside the grocery store in town.

I wanted those doughnuts something terrible, but the gifts felt strange.

"Smithy, I appreciate this, but I don't feel right taking all your charity."

He seemed hurt by my resistance.

"You talk too much like a grown-up. Talkin' 'bout *charity*." He shot me a look of disapproval. "You need to lighten up and just accept that somebody wants to help you."

"It's just that . . . the day Bert left, almost three weeks ago, I decided to work for what I need. Earn my keep."

Smithy set about putting the groceries away, all the while shaking his head.

"Okay, then," he said, closing the refrigerator. "You can pay me back by comin' out to play pool with me and some of my buddies tonight. All you do is go to school and stay cooped up in this house by yourself."

"That's not true," I replied.

"Ain't it?" His face mocked me. "No matter. You still need to get out more."

"Well, I don't know. It's a school night, and it's already getting a little late."

"There you go agin, talkin' like a grown-up."

Smithy had been good to me, and I wanted to make him happy. Eventually, I gave in; and just like Sunday morning, I found myself taking an unexpected trip.

We drove for what seemed like forever. I fiddled with the knob on the window crank, looking out at dark scenes I didn't recognize.

"Where is this place we're going to, Smithy?" I asked.

"Not much farther. There's nowhere to play pool in Copper Creek. This place is just over the county line. A little hole-in-the-wall joint where I meet up with the guys. It's where I ran into your daddy a few times."

My stomach turned. I recognized Bert as my father and had probably referred to him as *Dad* in my brain a few times. But he had never been *Daddy*.

We pulled up in front of the place Smithy had described—a long, squatty building with tiny windows high up close to the broad overhang of the roof. Smoke wafted out of the entrance, a screened door with duct tape patched over the rips in the mesh.

"Come on, Nate. I'm gonna show you how to play pool. If we're lucky, we can get a table to ourselves."

The inside was one long room with a concrete floor, except for two doors—one was labeled *Bathroom* and the other was an open closet. A man sat on a barstool behind a counter near the front door. A box full of Nabs with a five-cent price tag sat on the counter. A drink cooler filled with Pepsi and beer stood against the wall at the other end of the room. Four pool tables were the main attraction, and all of them were taken.

"Smithy! Ya old son of a gun. Hadn't seen you 'round in a spell," called out a large, middle-aged fella holding a pool stick.

"How's it goin', Big Lou?" Smithy answered. I stayed close behind Smithy, trying not to cough from the cloud of smoke that hung in the air.

"We were just getting ready to rack 'em for a new game. Why don't you join us?" Big Lou motioned toward the table. "Hey, who's the little guy?"

"This is my friend, Nate," Smithy said. "I want to teach him how to play some eight-ball."

"He can be on my team," Big Lou said. "Smithy, you can team up with Kenneth here."

Kenneth was short like me, but had a beard so long it covered his neck. He wore overalls like me, too, but he didn't wear a shirt underneath, and both arms were tattooed so that no undecorated skin showed above the wrists.

The whole thing felt like a strange dream. Just two days earlier, I had stood up to Peter Dotson on the playground at school, but I was in way over my head hanging out with strangers in a smoky pool hall. Smithy nodded at me, trying to reassure me, but it didn't help very much.

It turned out, my first ever game of pool wasn't too bad, despite my inhibitions. It went quickly; and Big Lou and I won, although I got only one ball in a pocket.

"You're a little rusty, aren't ya, Smithson?" Big Lou taunted at the start of the second game.

"Just gettin' warmed up," Smithy said. "How about we put a fiver on this one?"

"You got it. Except this time, we switch partners."

"Fine with me," Smithy replied. "C'mere, Nate."

I didn't understand what was going on, but I did as Smithy asked and joined him on the other side of the table.

The game was different this time. Smithy was on fire, and he made jabs at Big Lou on every turn.

"Hey, Lou. Who's rusty now, huh?"

"I think that big gut of yours is throwin' off your shot."

"What happened to your game, Big Lou?"

"Maybe I'll let you keep your money, so you can buy some glasses."

The way he talked made me nervous.

Smithy helped me line up a shot, told me exactly how and where to hit the cue ball to bank it off the wall of the table to hit the green number six ball. He high-fived me when I sunk the shot, my second of the game, and the pride I felt helped erase the nervousness for just a little while.

"Lou, I think this kid was hustling you the first time." Smithy laughed.

Kenneth took his turn and missed the shot. Big Lou knew he was close to losing five dollars, and he looked agitated. He was tired of listening to Smithy's smart aleck mouth. "Hey, Smithy," he said, "That five you're bettin', did that come out of your paycheck this time or somebody else's pocket?"

Smithy had an easy shot lined up, but Lou's question shook him, and he missed. Smithy ignored him.

"Why so quiet? I just wanna know whose money I'm gittin' ready to win." Big Lou landed a ball with a red stripe in a side pocket.

"Hey, not in front of the kid, all right?" Smithy warned.

It was my turn, but I just stood there with my cue resting on the floor, trying to figure out what they were talking about.

"Oh, I'm sorry," Big Lou mocked. "You don't want him to find out what your little musical gig is all about?"

"Shut up, Lou," Smithy shot from between his gritted teeth.

"What's he talkin' about, Smithy?" I asked. I didn't want to believe what Big Lou seemed to be saying.

"You don't know your buddy here is a crook? That one-man band is a big one-man scam." He threw his head back and laughed a nerve-grating laugh. He turned to Smithy. "How many wallets did you score while you were wearing that stupid get-up the last time? I still don't know how you do it—sneak up and pick people's pockets covered in all those noisy instruments. You must have a real talent. It sure as heck ain't for playing music, though." He rubbed elbows with Kenneth, who was laughing along with him.

"Nate, it's your turn," Smithy said dryly.

I made myself shoot, even though I wanted to run out the door.

When our team won, Smithy took Big Lou's money and his own off the table. Before we could make our exit, though, Big Lou shoved Smithy hard against the cinderblock wall.

"Hey, man, look, you can have your five dollars back. I don't care," Smithy said.

"No! I don't want that. You won that fair and square." His voice was greasy and mocking. "But you do need to pay for your big mouth, and I'm gonna take payment out of your hide."

Smithy could have taken him down without breaking a sweat, but it wasn't hard to see that he didn't want to do it in front of me, especially after what I had just learned about him.

"Take it easy, Lou. It was just a game."

The man behind the counter didn't get off his stool, but watched Smithy and Lou intensely, waiting to see what developed. I suspected he was used to people being shoved against walls in his establishment.

Lou stood blocking Smithy's way, in between the two of us. Kenneth came and stood uncomfortably close behind me.

"Here, Lou. How about you take this, and we'll call a truce, huh?" He took the shiny timepiece from his shirt pocket and handed it over.

"But your father gave you that watch he got for working the railroad!" I cried.

Lou laughed his obnoxious laugh again; then Kenneth joined in the talking for the first time.

"Railroad? Ha! Smithy's daddy weren't no railroad man." Kenneth chuckled. "He was a thief and a crook just like his boy here."

I didn't care if Smithy got roughed up or not. I had to get out of there.

I ducked by Kenneth and ran as fast as I could out the door, letting the screen slam behind me. By the time I reached the car, Smithy had managed to get out, too, and had already caught up with me. I jumped in the car and slammed the door. Neither of us spoke for at least three miles.

"Nate, listen," Smithy finally began.

"Why'd you take me there?" I interrupted, fighting to keep calm.

"I really did just want to show you a good time. There's usually some nice guys in there. I didn't know those clowns were gonna try to start something."

"And was what they said about you true? Are you a thief? That day at the fair, were you stealing from people?"

Smithy took a deep breath.

"Look, I won't lie to you. I used to try to get things the easy way. I stole from people. But that's been a while back. I decided I don't want to be like my daddy. I got a job now, and I work for my money. And when you saw me at the fair, I really was working just for the tips. I swear it."

I didn't know what to think of his story, but I felt like I had been punched in the gut. I didn't speak again until he dropped me off at my house.

"Thanks again for the groceries," I muttered as I got out of the car.

"Hey, I'll see you Friday, at your school."

I didn't respond. I made my way into the house, with my head hung down, heavy with hurt.

"At least I can trust you, right, Samson?" I whispered to my dog who was waiting for me behind the front door.

It was close to eleven o'clock, but I read my Bible storybook anyway. My brain needed something that didn't feel dirty or wrong. I read the story of Joseph, who was betrayed by his brothers. Part one of the story ended with Joseph becoming a successful leader in Egypt. I read on to part two because I knew what it was about, and I needed to read it. I needed how it felt. In part two, Joseph forgave his brothers and helped them, even though they had done very bad things.

I randomly grabbed a letter from Miriam out of the shoebox that was hiding under my bed next to the box where I kept the Bible story-book. The letter was postmarked the day after Christmas, 1960.

Dearest Bert,

I like to imagine that you write to me often. I pretend that the postman keeps losing your letters, or you have managed to forget the correct number.

Maybe another Miriam Dooley has been getting my mail. Just in case you need it, the envelope has the return address.

Christmas was lonely without Augusta here, but the boy who delivers my groceries to me brought a box of peppermint sticks as a gift from the grocer. I gave him an extra dollar tip, and he hugged me for it.

I wonder if our Nathaniel might look like the delivery boy. That's how I picture him, since I have no way to know.

Brother, I know things aren't easy for you now. But we could be a family together. Please write to me.

Your sister,

Miriam

My heart ached for Miriam; and I knew that somehow, I had to set things right.

Chapter Fifteen

THE CONFERENCE

MY STOMACH FELT LIKE A whole kaleidoscope of monarchs had taken up residence inside. School was over for the day, and I waited for Smithy outside. Miss Gentry waited to talk to us both, although she thought she was waiting to talk to Bert.

For a spell the night before, it seemed like Bert and Smithy were two peas in a pod—I didn't really know either of them, and I couldn't trust them any further than I could throw them. But I had studied on it all day at school—the red hard candy at the power company office, Smithy sticking up for me with Mr. Brindell, the haircut on the front porch, and all the groceries he didn't have to buy but did. *Smithy's no saint, but he's not a bad guy, either,* I thought. I wanted to tell him so as soon as I saw him.

The baby blue and rust-colored car with the low hanging rear bumper came rumbling into the school parking lot at two minutes 'til three. Smithy parked and rushed up to me faster than I'd seen him move before.

"Am I late?" he asked, out of breath.

"No, you're just fine," I assured him. "Smithy, before we go in, I need to say something. I want to say thank you for doing this. And, I, um . . . I . . . I know what a good heart you have."

He tried to mask the relief on his face, but he couldn't.

"Come on, kid," he said, gripping my shoulder, "let's get this over with."

Past the front office of the school was a long hall with rows of doors on either side, each directly across from one another and in grade order. There were two classes of each grade. To the left and right were two first grade classrooms, then two second-grade classes opposite one another, then the third-grade classes faced off, and so on. We came to the fifth-grade rooms at the end of the hall. Mine was on the right and had a big poster with all our names on the door.

Any hope I had of a successful ruse was squashed as soon as Smithy and I stepped into the classroom.

Miss Gentry looked up from her desk and shouted, "What are you doing here?" Her tone was very uncharacteristic.

"No way!" Smithy said to me. "Why didn't you tell me she was your teacher?"

"You didn't ask!" I said, with my head in my hands. I didn't quite know what was going on, but it didn't seem good.

Smithy took his hat off and made an attempt to salvage the beginning of the meeting. "Kate, I'm here to talk to you about my friend, Nate, here."

I had never realized mine and my teacher's names rhymed until I heard Smithy say them, and it made me want to giggle; but it wasn't the time.

"The conference was supposed to be with Nate's father, Bert Dooley. I know you! And I know you're not Bert Dooley. You're Rodney Smithson, Regina's brother, and the most unbearable human being I've ever met."

The friend I saw with her at church is Smithy's sister! I realized.

"I know I'm not the boy's father," Smithy said. "But I'm a friend, and his father couldn't make it, so why don't we just sit down and talk about what's been going on with him?"

Smithy casually strolled to the seat Miss Gentry had positioned in front of her desk and sat down. He was masterful, the way he took charge and acted so calm. She wasn't falling for it, though.

"Smithy, I can't talk to you about Nate. I need to talk to his father."

"Well, like I told you, he's not available, but I can speak for him."

"How do you even know them?"

"I'm a friend, I told you. A friend of the family. And Nate here just goes on and on about how wonderful his teacher is. He even let me borrow some of those magazines you gave him. I think he learns a heap from those. You know, I really appreciate you bein' so generous to him."

I stood back watching their interaction, him trying to flatter her and make himself sound like he had every right to be there. She had her head cocked to one side and her mouth half open like she didn't know what to make of it.

This isn't going to work, I thought. *This isn't going to work!*

After several awkward seconds, she motioned for me to come closer. I came to stand beside her desk, but she waved for me to come even closer. I did, and she gently took hold of both my arms at the elbows.

"Nate," she said, her gentle and deliberate tone returning, "what's going on? Where's your dad, Nate?"

I turned to Smithy, and we shared a look that meant the jig was up. Moses and that stone tablet were right there in the room with me, and I couldn't lie to my teacher.

"I don't know where Bert is," I said. "He's been gone for three weeks."

Has it really been only three weeks? I thought. It felt like he had been gone much longer.

Miss Gentry dropped her head down, then, toward Smithy as if he were to blame.

"Do you know where Nate's father is?"

"Kate, I don't even know how I got involved in this mess. Trust me, I don't know where the boy's daddy is."

He had used that word again, the one that made me queasy.

"Wait a minute!" she said. "He's been gone three weeks? But you brought me a note from him. When you came back from being sick, you brought an excuse note signed by your father."

"Well, it was signed Bert Dooley, but Bert didn't sign it," I confessed. She shot Smithy a knowing look, and he hid the side of his face with his cupped hand as if he was the student instead of me.

"Sit down, Nate. I want you to tell me whatever you can. I want to help you."

She turned to Smithy. "And I think you can go now. I'll take Nate home when we're finished."

"Let him stay," I insisted. "He is my friend. He's been checking in on me. He even bought me groceries. Even though I coulda worked for 'em." I shuffled my feet, still balking at the idea of charity.

"He has?" she asked me, her voice filled with disbelief.

"You've been worrying about somebody besides yourself for a change?" she asked Smithy sarcastically.

I had never heard my teacher be so loose with her words. I didn't like it. I liked it when she sounded in control and collected.

"Go on, Nate. Let's hear it."

I spilled my story—about Bert disappearing, and the power bill, and seeing Smithy at the fair. Then, as I feared, I sat there while grown-ups discussed my fate as if I had no say and as if I didn't already have my own plans to head out on an adventure when the summer came.

"He has no emergency contact in his file," Miss Gentry said.

"And I really don't know nothing about his daddy," Smithy said.

Why does he keep calling him that? I thought.

"He does real good by himself," Smithy vouched. "He's a smart kid. And staying at home is how he wanted it."

"I know how smart Nate is," Miss Gentry said. "He's an exceptional boy, and he deserves better than what he's got." Her words made my heart swell up. "He can't stay by himself anymore. I think I need to tell Administration. And they will probably have to call the County."

"Miss Gentry, please! Please don't do that. I don't want to go to an orphanage. I'll have to leave my dog and my house. And what if Bert comes back? He'll get in trouble because of me. Please! If I can't stay alone, maybe you can take me."

She let my words soak in, then continued, "Nate, if your father gets into trouble, it won't be your fault. You are not responsible for him. And as far as letting you live with me, I don't know if I'm allowed to do that." She reached up and put her soft hand against my cheek. "I would, but, I'm your teacher, and . . . well, anyway, my apartment doesn't allow dogs."

"Maybe I should just take him home with me," Smithy chimed in.

"No, he doesn't need to be with you," she countered sharply. "Maybe with Regina, but not with you."

They made me feel like a lost puppy, but I was glad the enemies had found common ground.

"If we can't find a family member to care for him, the County will need to get involved. They need to have record of his . . . situation," Miss Gentry said slowly. "We can't just make decisions about him because we're not his family."

"I have an aunt!" I shouted out before my brain knew what my mouth had done. "I found letters from her, and I know she wants to meet me."

Smithy and Miss Gentry both stared at me, not sure how to respond.

"I don't know if she has a telephone, but I found an address in one of her letters. She lives in Tennessee, in a town called Topknot. I looked it up in the atlas. It's just over the mountain a ways. I plan to write to her. I don't want to leave Copper Creek forever; but maybe I could go visit her, and she could help me decide what to do."

"But what will we do in the meantime, until you make arrangements to visit? There's three more weeks of school left, and I think it would be best for you to stay until summer break."

"I'll ask the Nelsons for help. Between them and you and Smithy, y'all can make sure I'm okay until I can get to my aunt."

"But how will you get to Tennessee, Nate?" Miss Gentry asked.

"That's easy," Smithy said. "I'll take him to meet his aunt. And I won't leave him unless it's a good place for him to be. I'll stay long enough to make sure of it. I was plannin' on takin' some time away from work, anyway, to do a little traveling."

"But, Smithy, you don't want to waste your vacation on me. What about seeing the country? Making it to the Pacific?'

"Don't worry about it, kid."

Miss Gentry's face had started out looking troubled, but while she listened to Smithy's plan, it gradually softened into an expression that resembled admiration.

"I think the Nelsons are a good option, Nate. Will you be going to church with them again this Sunday?" Miss Gentry asked me. Smithy shot me a strange look.

"Yes, ma'am."

"Why don't we wait and talk to them together then on Sunday morning? Will you be okay until then?"

"That sounds good, Miss Gentry. I really am fine on my own."

"Everybody needs *somebody*, sweetie." She smiled. "I am proud of how you've managed, though. Do you need anything between now and when we talk to the Nelsons?"

"No, ma'am. Smithy already made sure of that."

He tried to hide the look of pride on his face. "Kate, I'll take him home now," Smithy said. She hugged me before I left the classroom, and I took the smell of her perfume with me.

Since Miss Gentry knew about my secret, too, it felt like a weight had been lifted off my shoulders. I wasn't sure about leaving Copper Creek for a destination I hadn't planned, but I was hopeful things were going to work out okay.

When we got in the car, I explained to Smithy about my neighbors, the Nelsons, and thanked him for trying to make the conference work. Then I hung my head in silence.

He let me sulk for about half the drive then said, "What's the matter, Nate? Are you worried about going to see your aunt and maybe having to stay there?"

"Well, yeah, that's part of it," I said.

"Are you nervous about asking these Nelson people if you can stay there for a while?"

"Not really."

"Well, what is it?" Smithy asked. "What's bothering you the most?"

"I don't want you to have to give up your dream vacation for me!" My eyes brimmed with tears for the first time in front of Smithy. "It's not right for me to do that to you!"

"Oh, hey now! Did I forget to tell you?" His voice was upbeat and cheerful. "I finally decided where I wanted to go on my trip. You see," he leaned over toward my side of the car, "I decided I don't really want to go to the ocean after all. I don't look very good in shorts, plus the sand just sticks to you when you sweat, I hear. And I don't think I'd like that at all."

My tears stopped, and I looked at him, wanting to believe what he was saying.

"Yeah," Smithy continued, "the other day I pulled out a map and decided I would start out small, just on the other side of the Smokies. I've been all around them, but I've not got to the other side yet. So, this works out just perfect for me, since I was planning on heading that way anyhow."

I smiled. I realized he was lying, but it seemed like a good kind of lie—if there was such a thing. For sure, it didn't feel like he was breaking any rules on Moses' stone tablet in my book.

"I'll swing by tomorrow evening for a bit. Okay, kid?" he asked, as I got out of the car in my driveway.

"Okay."

I bounded up the steps and was surprised to find a note taped to my front door. It read:

I'm going fishing in the morning. If you'd like to come, meet me at my house at 9:00 a.m. Bring along a friend if you want.

Dell

Chapter Sixteen

REVELATIONS ON THE RIVERBANK

I WOKE UP AT EIGHT o'clock and threw on my clothes. Before he and I left home, I bent down and whispered in Samson's ear, "Okay, boy. We have to be extra nice today. The Nelsons don't know yet that we need their help. Let's show them how good we can be." I didn't have to worry about Samson, though. He was the most well-behaved dog I'd ever seen, never chasing or barking too much and jumping up only when it was playtime.

Samson and I bolted out the door and started running as fast as I could go to Patrick's house. Samson could have gone faster, but he kept pace with me. All the way, I hoped I wasn't running for nothing and that Patrick would be able to come back with me—partly because I really wanted him to go fishing and partly because I wanted to ride back on the handlebars of his bicycle instead of having to run.

"Wooohoooo!" I exclaimed, when Patrick's stepdad agreed to let him go, only I waited until he closed the door of the house and we were already on the bicycle. I held onto Patrick's fishing rod as he pedaled. I didn't have a fishing rod of my own, but Mr. Nelson wouldn't have invited me if he didn't have one to share.

"You'll like Mr. Nelson," I said to Patrick.

"I know, Nate. You told me all about him at school. I'm just excited for the chance to go fishing. I haven't even been yet this spring!" Patrick said.

"I haven't been since me and you went *last* spring."

With the river just over the ridge, fishing should have been a regular pastime for me and Patrick. But the terrain was so rough that all the close-by fishing spots were hard to get to, and the easy-access places were too far for us to walk.

Samson ran alongside the bike as Patrick propelled us forward, anxious to get a line in the water.

When we made our way down the dusty driveway of Nelson Farm, Mr. Nelson was waiting for us on his front porch.

"Could there be a better day for fishing?" he called out.

"I don't think so!" I said. "Mr. Nelson, this is my best friend, Patrick."

"Oh, yes, I believe I've seen you and Nate out playing in his yard before." Mr. Nelson stuck out his hand to Patrick. "Nice to meet you, son. Now listen, I want both you boys to call me Dell."

"Nice to meet you, too, sir."

We didn't waste time with any more pleasantries. The three of us climbed into the cab of Dell's farm truck, instead of the shiny one he drove to town, and Samson jumped into the truck's bed as he was instructed. We didn't head for the road, though. Dell surprised us by driving through the grass around the house and into his backyard, which made for a fun and bumpy ride. We rode down the edge of one field, then down the outside length of the apple orchard. The Nelsons' land kept going and going, but eventually, we reached a wooded area and the truck could go no further. Dell turned off the engine.

"Okay, now we have to walk just a little ways," Dell said.

Patrick and I got out of the truck. There was no river to be seen.

Dell retrieved two rods and a tacklebox from the bed of the truck, and he handed one of the rods to me.

"C'mon, Samson," I called, and he jumped down and followed the three of us into the woods.

Dell led the way, then came me and Samson, then Patrick, through the woods, up and down over rocks and ravines. It was a short walk, but rough. As soon as Dell said, "Watch out for snakes," I saw a copperhead sunning itself on a rock near my feet, where the sunlight had found a hole in the canopy of trees. I had heard somewhere that Copper Creek didn't get its name for the mineral, like they use in making pennies, but instead, somebody named it for the color of that snake's head. I didn't know if it was true or not.

I heard the river before I saw it; its music called to me through the trees. The wild forest opened up all at once to a wide clearing, a tamed piece of flat ground where the grass was freshly mowed. Thirty feet of river bank was ours to claim.

"Whoa! This is awesome!" Patrick exclaimed. He ran over to the river's edge to take it in.

The bank didn't slope gradually down, but instead, the land dropped off about three feet above the water line. Two long benches sat close to the drop-off and a good distance from each other. In the middle of the clearing was a big, sturdy gazebo with birdhouses of different shapes and sizes hanging all around from the eave.

"I don't use this place as often as I'd like, but it's special to me and Opal. I come out here most of the time just to keep the grass cut. I leave that old cylinder mower in the gazebo there, so I don't have to cart it back and forth. But it's a job bringing the weed-eater through those woods."

Patrick and I walked to the gazebo and stepped inside. Patrick moved in a circle, admiring the setting from all directions.

"We call this spot The Hideaway. And I reckon there's no other place I'd like to hide away to than here."

It was the perfect place—cleared and flat with plenty of room to cast and sit for hours.

"I know it takes a little effort to get here," Dell said, "but you're welcome to come use this place anytime, Patrick. But just you and Nate. And as long as you clean up after yourself. Don't leave drink bottles or old fishing line laying around."

"Yes, sir!" Patrick exclaimed. "Thank you!" He looked like he'd found a secret treasure, better than the one from Tom Sawyer. "And we can help cut the grass and look after it for you, too."

"Well, now, that sounds like a deal."

The benches were long enough for the three of us to sit on one of them together comfortably. Dell helped me rig a line with a split shot sinker and a hook, then I took a still-wiggly half of a live earthworm and threaded it onto the hook.

"That was an expert cast," Dell said when I let the line fly. It was certainly luck because my experience was limited.

Ten minutes passed with no bites and little words. We enjoyed the peaceful sounds of flowing water and chirping birds. Hedged in by the forest on three sides and the river on the other, the clearing felt like a private oasis, a fortress of safety.

"So, boys, what can you tell me about yourselves that I don't know. Like, what do you both want to do for a living when you get grown?"

I didn't have to think about my answer. "I've decided I'm going to join the army," I replied. "Or maybe the air force."

"I didn't know that!" Patrick said. "That's what I plan to do, too." He thought he knew every thought in my head, but we had never talked much about our grown-up futures.

"Just started thinking about it lately. I haven't had the idea long at all." I turned to Mr. Nelson. "Do you think they'll let me in? Even being so little?"

"Well, you've got a lot of growing left to do, Nate. You might sprout up to be six feet tall. You never know. But even if you stay little compared to most, I think you'd pass the bar."

My enlistment was a long time away, but I was happy as could be that Dell thought I could get in.

"I was a navy man myself," Dell said. "Most of my time was spent aboard the *U.S.S. Texas*. In the first World War, we were stationed in the North Sea."

Patrick fired off questions left and right, asking about how big the ship was and what Dell's job was in the navy and anything else he could think to ask about Dell's service. Ever since he had watched a movie about Audie Murphy in World War Two, he had been hooked on anything to do with war and the military.

I focused again on the job at hand. The river was fast and strong, and I was afraid I wouldn't be able to feel a bite if I got one. The more I wished for a catch, the more doubtful I was that it would happen. But while Patrick and Dell talked back and forth across me, there was a new kind of resistance on the other end of the line, more than the pull of the flowing water.

"I've got a bite!" I yelled. I stood up to better manage the reel, and Dell and Patrick stood to watch and encourage me. Patrick cheered when the fish broke the surface of the water; and Samson, who had been sunning himself near my feet, stood and barked at the commotion. My heart sped up when I got my first look at the fish's smooth body and long whiskers.

"That's a nice catfish." Dell praised me without raising his volume. "You might want to take that one home and let Mr. Dooley cook it up for dinner. I bet he could make a tasty meal out of it."

The fish was out of the water, but it wasn't off the hook yet; and I let the poor thing hang there, swinging itself with the momentum of his tail. I planted the end of the rod on the ground, and I looked at Dell with utter confusion.

Why would he assume Bert can cook? I thought.

He read my face and offered more. "I'm sure he cooks good meals all the time when he's not working at the diner. Or maybe he's sick of cooking and needs a break."

So that's what he does, I thought. So many of the smells I remembered made sense.

"He usually keeps it simple," I said nonchalantly, taking the fish finally by the lip and pulling out the hook.

"Well, I know he's a busy man, since he works two jobs."

Again, I felt confused, but I pretended to know what Dell was talking about. "How do you know about that?" I asked.

"Oh, I stop in at the County Line Diner about once a month when I have to be on that side of the county to tend to business. Your father prefers to keep to himself most of the time. He's a very quiet man, but he mentioned it in passing not too long ago. Didn't say where else he worked, though."

"Oh, okay," I said as casually as I could. "Do you want him?" I held the fish up toward Dell, trying to change the subject before he asked me what Bert's other job was, since I had no idea.

"No, that's okay. I have lots of things to do when we get done here. I won't have time to clean him. You can let him go."

I tossed the catfish back into the river as gently as I could. I felt guilty for keeping him out of the water for so long, but he swam away without a care. I envied him.

Patrick stared at me, and it felt like his eyes burned a hole in the side of my head. *What else do you think he knows about Bert? Don't you want to finally know about him?* I sensed Patrick thinking. Or they might have been my own thoughts. I wasn't sure.

"I know your father is gone a lot, so you're welcomed over at our house any time. That goes for you, too, Patrick."

Like, for the next three weeks? I thought. I wondered if Dell's sentiment would hold true when Miss Gentry asked him to let me stay there until Smithy could take me to Aunt Miriam.

I looked over at Patrick. He gave me a big, goofy smile. In one look, he congratulated me on finding a friend like Dell, on learning something I didn't know about my father, and on getting the first catch of the day.

After fishing, Patrick and I both stripped down to our underwear and climbed down the face of the bank. I washed away my cares in the cold river, letting it shock my brain blank with its chill. We played for more than an hour, while Dell looked on. We pretended to be giant catfish, diving under and popping out, hitting the bank and flopping around with every muscle until we slid ourselves back into the murky water, over and over again.

Chapter Seventeen
A BRAND-NEW LETTER

"PATRICK, I NEED TO TELL you something," I said. We stood side-by-side in the Nelsons' barn, our sneakers dirty with riverbank mud and ordinary barn muck. We took turns poking our pitchforks into a fresh pile of hay and shoveling the dried grass into the goat stalls. "I'm probably going to be leaving soon," I announced. It was harder to say than I had imagined.

It had been my idea to help Mr. Nelson with his chores in return for taking us fishing. But Patrick was the most enthusiastic about helping. He worked like he was getting paid, and he didn't stop when I made my announcement.

Patrick spread out the hay neatly, making a nice, clean bed for the goats to have when Dell's helper brought them in from the pasture. "Where're you going?" he asked. His voice was low and sad.

"Remember me telling you I have an aunt in Tennessee?"

"Yeah."

"I'm going to go see her." I paused, feeling unsure of my plan. "I think so, I mean. I haven't written to her yet. But I will; and if she wants me to come, I'll leave when school is out. Smithy's going to take me."

"That's only three weeks," he said somberly.

"I know. But if I don't go to Tennessee, someone from the County will come get me; and I'll have to leave anyway."

I told Patrick about the conference with Miss Gentry and Smithy, about what a disaster it was. He and I had been so excited about fishing that we hadn't talked about it before.

"Will you come back?"

I waited a long time before answering. I didn't know the answer to his question, and it made me ache inside.

"The truth is, I don't know what will happen. But I need to see her. She's all alone out there, somewhere across the mountain, just like I'm alone here. And she's family that I didn't even know I had!"

"You're not alone here, Nate." He rested the handle-end of the pitchfork on the barn floor and turned toward me. "You've got people now. You've got the Nelsons, and Miss Gentry, and that fella who brought you groceries . . . and you've got me. Maybe I could talk to Mama. She likes you a heap, Nate. I bet my mama would want to take you in."

He was insistent, and my heart broke hearing Patrick's voice crack. We were too big to cry, but not too big to hurt, and I felt the hurt in his words.

"I wish it was as easy as that. And I really hope I get to come back. I just don't know. Miss Gentry is going to talk to the Nelsons tomorrow about me staying here until I leave." That was all I could think to say, so we both went back to shoveling hay.

"What if she's not a nice aunt? What if you don't like it there with her? What will you do?" Patrick asked me after a few moments.

I thought about it. "I guess me and Samson will run away. Either come back here, or do like I was thinking about and head out somewhere else."

We finished our job without any more words, then walked up the hill to the Nelsons' house. Dell was out on the farm somewhere working, but Opal was expecting to see us before we left. Patrick had decided to keep three of our catch, and she was kind enough to wrap the fish in paper and store them in the crisper drawer of her refrigerator while he and I worked in the barn. It had been a successful morning at the river. Between the three of us, we caught five catfish and three trout.

Just seconds after I knocked, Mrs. Nelson came to the door with the package and handed it over to Patrick. "I hope you boys had a good time today."

"Yes, ma'am, we did," I said, and Patrick nodded in agreement.

She held the screen door with one hand and patted me on the head with the other; then she looked at Patrick. "You come back and see us real soon, Patrick."

"Okay, Mrs. Nelson. Thank you."

We hopped off the front porch, disregarding the steps. Patrick picked up his bike near the oak tree with the tire swing, and we started up the dusty driveway.

"You get those home quick before they spoil now!" Mrs. Nelson called out to Patrick in a chipper voice. "Nate, we'll see you in the morning!" She had invited Patrick to join us at church, but he had said no, thank you. At the urging of his grandmother, during their time in Ohio, Patrick's mother had decided to take him to the Methodist church in town on Sunday.

We were a strange mix of tired and happy and somber as we left the Nelsons' farm. Even Samson dragged his tail on the ground. The morning sunshine had turned to clouds, and the overcast sky foretold of an afternoon rain.

Patrick walked with his bike in between us until we reached my mailbox, then hopped on and pedaled away. "Bye, buddy!" I yelled. He threw his hand up to say goodbye but didn't look back.

I opened the door of the metal mailbox and looked inside to find one piece of mail. It was an envelope addressed to Bert in swirly handwriting with a Tennessee postmark on the front. I wanted to open it right then and there, but it felt so important that I decided to wait until I was inside the house to give it the attention it deserved.

Samson and I had just put our muddy feet on the first front step when I heard car tires on gravel. Smithy pulled in the drive, and his old car announced its arrival with a loud sputter of the engine. He was out of the car quick, and I motioned for him to follow me inside the house.

"Hey! Whatcha been into today, Nate?"

"I caught a catfish this big this morning!" I stretched my hands wide to show him. "My neighbor Dell has a great place on the river."

"Oh, is that the neighbor who takes you to church? The one you're gonna go stay with?"

"Yeah, that's Mr. Nelson. I've been with them to church only once, though." I didn't understand his tone. "They're good people."

"Well, I like fishing, too. Why didn't you invite me?"

"Because I don't have a telephone. You know that!"

"I am just messing with you, Nate." He made himself comfortable on my couch. "Say, what's that you got in your hand there? Somethin' important?"

"It looks like another letter from Miriam." The edges of the envelope vibrated with the nervousness of my hands.

"Why don't you open it?"

With Smithy sitting there, it wasn't the ceremony I had planned, but I tore into the envelope, letting a few little pieces of ripped paper fall to the floor. I immediately reached down to pick them up and took them to the kitchen trashcan.

"Come on, Nate," Smithy urged. "Get on with it."

I ran my fingertips over the smoothness of the envelope before reaching inside without looking. The first thing I pulled out wasn't a letter.

"That's a twenty-dollar bill!" Smithy exclaimed. I held the crisp, green paper money up high between me and Smithy. My jaw felt heavy, and the weight pulled my mouth to an open position. I couldn't remember ever holding a twenty before. It was a welcome surprise to have it, but the words in the letter I pulled out next were even more valuable than the cash. After putting the money in my jeans' pocket, I read the letter out loud.

"Dear Bert, please wish my nephew a happy birthday from me. I know his special day is coming up soon. I hope he is well and happy. As every year, it would be nice to know that this birthday gift actually reaches him. Please send me a postcard to let me know. If you'll agree, I'd like to write to him directly. Miriam."

"Every year? You didn't even know about her 'til just the other day. Ole' Bert musta been pocketing your birthday money all this time," Smithy said. I gave him a sideways smirk that made him think about what he had said. "Aww, I know I ain't got no room to talk. But that's behind me now, Nate. You know that."

I read the letter to myself again. *I know his special day is coming up soon.*

She thinks about me on my birthday every year, I thought. *She's never met me, but she does care about me. She might even love me, for real. Surely, she does.*

"Hey, why haven't you told me your birthday is soon?" Smithy asked.

"I guess I haven't thought about it much," I responded, playing it cool. The truth was, I *had* thought about it. I thought about my birthday every year, for weeks before; but the excitement was secret, and the celebration was mine alone. Turning older didn't come with any fuss or fanfare.

"Well, is there anything you want for a present?"

Smithy had bought me groceries, and checked in on me, and had volunteered to go with me to Miriam's. I hated to ask him for anything else, but there was something on my mind. He stared at me, waiting for an answer. I tried to decide if there was a different way to say what I was already planning to ask Smithy.

"I want you to do something for me, Smithy," I said.

"Well, what is it?"

"Think of it as a birthday gift, if you want."

"What do you want, kid?"

I sat down in a kitchen chair, my knees pointed toward the couch where Smithy sat. "I want you to go to church tomorrow," I said resolutely.

"Awe, c'mon, Nate." He stood quickly and turned his back to me. "You sound like my sister now."

"What do you mean?"

He threw his hand up. "She's been on my case for years about going with her."

"Well, then, why don't you go with her?"

"I ain't got no use for it, Nate. I just don't. It's all fine and dandy, but it ain't for me."

"Look, I want you to be there when Miss Gentry talks to the Nelsons about me. I need you to help me get things worked out."

I didn't like to admit that I needed help, especially after all Smithy had already done, but it worked. He paced back and forth, wanting to say *no*, but he couldn't.

"You can kill two birds with one stone," I continued. "Make Regina happy and help me out at the same time." He stopped pacing.

"All right, Nate. It's just one Sunday morning. I don't guess it'll kill me." I smiled. "But just remember . . . " He pointed his finger at me like I was guilty of something, and I held my breath. "If it does kill me, you ain't got nobody to drive you to Tennessee."

I let my breath out, and a laugh came out with it.

Smithy hung out for a while, then took inventory of my refrigerator before telling me and Samson goodbye. "I'm meeting some fellas at the pool hall," he explained.

"Stay out of trouble," I called out to him.

He poked his head around the door and smiled. "There you go talkin' like a grown-up agin!" I saw a blur of teeth and ears as he ducked outside and closed the door behind him.

It was time for my radio show, and I was ready to let my brain leave Copper Creek for a while. Samson joined me on the couch.

Around Dodge City and in the territory on West, there's just one way to handle the killers and the spoilers, and that's with a U.S. Marshal and the smell of . . . GUNSMOKE.

The introduction tickled my ears. It was comforting, never changing. I mimed the words that followed, along with Marshal Dillon.

It's a chancy job, and it makes a man watchful. And a little lonely.

I ate my pork and beans out on the prairie that night, under the stars, pretending Samson was my horse, and I thought about what it would be like when it was time to head west for real.

Just after nine o'clock, I laid in bed and studied the maps on my walls. I wondered if my journey would end in Topknot, Tennessee, if it would ever bring me back to Copper Creek, and if my little legs would ever walk the soil of foreign lands on grand adventures.

Then I picked up the Bible that Dell had given me and thumbed around in the New Testament. The book of Colossians caught my attention. I read the first chapter, then started the second, and a single word jumped right off the page and smacked my brain.

"As ye have therefore received Christ Jesus the Lord, so walk ye in him: Rooted and built up in him, and established in the faith, as ye have been taught, abounding therein with thanksgiving."[2]

Rooted.

---

2 Colossians 2:6-7

Chapter Eighteen

THE TRUTH COMES OUT

SITTING ON THE SAME HARD pew as the week before, between Opal and Dell, the preacher had my stomach tied up in knots.

"Don't wait until it's too late!" he cried. "Make a decision today!" His voice was pleading.

What is there to decide? I thought.

I had heard lines like his from other preachers on the radio, but his statements were different. Every syllable he spoke oozed with equal parts love and damnation. It was a combination I couldn't wrap my brain around, but the words left a mark on my heart.

I listened intently, trying to sort things out, until a latecomer distracted me. Fifteen minutes into the sermon, Smithy strolled in like it was the most normal thing in the world. He wore the bowler hat that I hadn't seen in a while, and he didn't even bother to take it off as he scooted into a pew near the front beside Regina. I smiled seeing him sitting next to his sister. I was excited to meet her.

"God is your Father!" the young preacher yelled, and it shocked me back to attention. "He loves you, and He wants you to bring Him every care and every burden." He raised his Bible above his head and waved it, as if to draw more attention to his words. "He is a good Father, and He is never too busy for you." His volume ebbed and flowed, and it pushed me away, then pulled me in with each line. "You are important to Him!"

Loud amens popped up throughout the congregation like gophers in a cabbage patch. Even Dell managed to summon some emotion and encourage the pastor with an even-toned outburst of, "That's good preachin'."

I observed everything around me like a detective. No one else seemed concerned by the preacher's plea to decide about something. All the faces around me looked happy or, at least, unalarmed. One man even stood up and cheered for the preacher by pumping his fist up and down in the air three times; then he sat back down. I figured that either what the preacher was saying was true and good, or everyone in the building had lost their minds. But the latter didn't seem probable.

The end of the sermon was followed by two more songs, after which most people filed outside quickly to do their meeting and greeting in the open. I stayed put, though, and waited for Miss Gentry.

Smithy and Miss Gentry were off to the side by themselves, near the front of the church. They looked deep in conversation. *Has she forgotten she's supposed to speak to the Nelsons for me?* I wondered.

She held her purse against her chest, as if she were guarding it from being snatched away. *We're in church!* I thought. *What on earth is he doing?* Then I figured out what was going on.

She touched his shoulder, like she often did mine, but she wasn't congratulating him on a math score or asking him to clean the blackboard erasers.

"Nate, I'm right outside," Dell came back in to tell me. I got up and followed him out, going over to sit on the tailgate of his pickup while I waited for Miss Gentry to talk to the Nelsons like she had promised.

Maybe I should just talk to them myself, I thought. *I don't really need Miss Gentry to speak for me.* But soon she came out with Smithy, gave me a subtle thumbs-up from a distance, and went over to where Opal was talking with the preacher's wife and another lady. When Miss Gentry whispered in Opal's ear, Opal motioned for Dell to join them.

Miss Gentry, Smithy, Dell, and Opal grouped up together under a tree in the side yard of the church. Smithy shook hands with the Nelsons as Miss Gentry introduced them. I watched, hoping they wouldn't notice I was watching, and I tried to read what was going on.

As Miss Gentry spoke, Dell had the same expressionless face as usual, so it wasn't any help. But I read everything on Opal's face. Her brow furrowed, and she looked like she might break down in tears. Opal talked for a while; then Miss Gentry responded; next was Opal again. Miss Gentry placed her hand on Opal's forearm and continued talking. Opal's face melted into the same mile-wide grin that had greeted me when I opened the front door the Sunday morning before. *That's a good sign,* I thought.

I was still watching them when someone hopped up next to me on the tailgate, startling me.

"So, you're the kid my brother has been telling me about," Regina asked. "I think you've been good for him."

"Um, yeah, I'm Nate."

Regina had dark hair like Smithy. She had a pleasant face; but her skin was weathered, and her eyes had a tiredness to them.

"I'm Regina." She shook my hand with a grasp stronger than most men. "Thank you for getting him here today. You accomplished something I've been trying to do for years."

I smiled, but I also felt sad for her, even though I didn't know why.

"So, you and Rodney are taking a little trip soon, I hear."

"Rodney? Oh, yeah, Smithy. Um . . . yeah, that's the plan. I just need to write to my aunt and let her know we're coming."

"He's told me a lot about you, Nate, and so has my friend Kate. She thinks you're very special. I really hope things work out like you want out there." Her words hit on my confusion. I didn't know how I wanted it to work out. I knew I wanted to meet Miriam. I knew I didn't want child services or whoever they were to take me away. But that's all I knew.

"You'll watch out for him, won't you? For me?" Regina asked.

I looked up at her, squinting in the sun, then shielded my eyes so I could see her better.

"Huh?"

"When you're traveling with my brother. Take care of him for me."

"Me? Take care of him?" I forgot about the important conversation going on thirty feet away from us.

"Yes, and of course, I have every confidence he'll be taking care of you, too. But he needs somebody to look after him. It's been my job for a long time, and I need you to take it over for a while when y'all leave." She looked wistfully at Smithy. "My baby brother's not always had it easy, and he needs a little extra tending to, on account of things he couldn't help. *You* know sorta what I mean, don't you?"

"Yes, ma'am."

Only a handful of cars remained in the dirt lot around the church. Miss Gentry and Smithy finished talking to the Nelsons, and Regina saw them coming toward us. She patted my knee to say goodbye. Before I could say anything, she hopped down from the tailgate and scurried to her car, trotting through the dirt on the toes of her white Sunday shoes.

Miss Gentry walked slowly and smiled gently as she approached. The rest of the grown-ups followed her with the same overly-cautious manner that made me feel like a stray cat fixing to get thrown in a sack.

"Nate, I've told the Nelsons about your situation at home, and they would like to help you. They've agreed to let you stay with them for a while, until we can get you to your aunt."

I never doubted that the Nelsons would let me stay with them. But when it became real, I felt more anxious to get to Miriam.

"And Samson, too?" I asked.

Opal and Dell looked at each other, and Opal said something without words that Dell understood. "Yes, Samson is welcome, too," Dell assured me.

"Nate, I've known Mr. and Mrs. Nelson since I was a little girl," Miss Gentry continued. "Their daughter is . . . well, was a good friend of mine. And I know I won't have to worry about you while you're staying with them."

You didn't have to worry about me before, I thought.

I looked behind her at the Nelsons. Dell had his arm around Opal's shoulder, and she had her hands clasped together underneath her chin. I didn't know what anyone wanted me to say. I was grateful to them, and I liked the Nelsons; but I thought I was doing fine on my own, and that option was being taken away from me. Smithy sensed it and gave me a nod. His look settled me.

"Okay," I said.

They all stood around looking at me, like I wasn't just Nate anymore. I had to say something, since nobody else was talking.

"Smithy, I guess you're off the hook for a while. You won't be having to look in on me until we set out across the mountain."

"Well, now, just because you're staying with us doesn't mean he can't come by and check on you," Opal interjected. She put her hand on Smithy's back like they were old friends; then she winked at me and smiled. "You do seem like a handful to take care of, Nate! Having another person to help look after you isn't such a bad idea!" She turned toward Smithy. "Why don't you come over Wednesday evening for dinner? If there's anything you need to start planning for your trip, we can talk about that."

Smithy agreed, then tipped the bowler to me playfully. Miss Gentry hugged me goodbye, and I hoisted myself back into the cab of the Nelsons' truck.

I expected lots of questions from the Nelsons about Bert and how we got along and what I'd been doing by myself. But Dell and Opal were quiet. Opal hummed the refrain of the last song of the service, then began singing it in muted tones as she looked out the window.

Come, Thou Fount of every blessing, tune my heart to sing thy grace; streams of mercy, never ceasing, call for songs of loudest praise.

"When do I get to go back to my house?" I asked, as we drove down the mountain.

"Why do you ask it that way, Nate? We're not taking you prisoner."

"I just mean . . . what's gonna happen now?"

"Ah. Let's talk about that." Dell let out a big, weighty, weary sigh, and I expected the worst. "I think it would be best if you stayed at your house tonight."

I turned to Opal. She was nodding in agreement. "Huh?" I said, to the windshield. "But I thought you . . . "

"I'll stay at your house with you tonight," Dell explained. "Opal's got a little bit of work to do at home to get a room fixed up for you.

But we don't want you to be by yourself anymore." He spit out the last word like it tasted bad.

"We know you get along fine, Nate," Opal said. "We're very impressed that a boy your age can do so well on his own." She knew I needed to hear it. "But you shouldn't have to do it. Nobody should have to be alone if it can be helped."

I thought of Miriam. *I need to write to her soon,* I thought. *I need to let her know she won't have to be alone much longer.*

Chapter Nineteen

MAKING CHOICES

THAT SUNDAY NIGHT WAS THE first time since my mama died that anyone, other than just me and Bert, had slept under my roof—the first time in over six years. Dell didn't pack an overnight bag to stay. He would head back to his house early the next morning as soon as I left for school. The only thing he brought inside with him was the Bible from his truck.

I enjoyed playing host. I got the softest blanket I could find in the closet and a pillow off Bert's bed and laid them out on the couch for him to have at bedtime. Before it got too late, Dell and I sat together, and I showed him my collection of *National Geographic*, the same way I had shown Smithy. Some of the places reminded Dell of his time in the navy, and he told me stories about visiting far-off lands.

I showed Dell everything in the box I kept under my bed, which included the Bible he gave me and even the shoe box from Bert's dresser.

"Have you read all the letters yet?" he asked me.

"Not all of them. But most. A lot of them just talk about the weather where she is and how much she misses Bert and wishes he would come see her."

"It's interesting, isn't it? She has your address, but she never came here." I hadn't thought about that, and I looked up at him, worried. I wished he hadn't said it because it was just another thing for me to try to work out in my head. Dell realized his mistake.

"Well, I'm sure she had a good reason. And I'm sure she's going to be so happy to finally meet you," he encouraged.

"Dell?"

"Uh-huh?"

"Should I pack up all my things tonight? To bring 'em to your house tomorrow?"

"We can worry about that after school tomorrow. Is that okay?"

"Uh-huh."

Samson kept a close watch on Dell, and his brown eyes cut up at me several times to let me know he was on guard. He seemed happy when Dell rubbed his head but went back to distrusting when the attention was over.

"I believe he thinks I'm going to take him away from you," Dell said.

"Yeah, it's strange. He was fine with Patrick and Smithy." I crossed the room in about three steps and sat down in a chair at the old, cherry-stained secretary desk in the corner, leaving Dell to stretch out on the couch whenever he wanted.

Samson laid down with his back half on the linoleum in the kitchen and his front half on the softness of the shag carpet in the living room, where he could keep an eye on us both.

"He doesn't have anything to worry about, though," Dell said. "I don't think I could take that dog away from you, even if I wanted to. I don't think there's anything that could make him leave you; he's so loyal."

"Yeah, I'm glad Smithy doesn't mind him riding with us to Tennessee." I glanced admiringly at my furry friend. "I just hope my aunt Miriam is okay with dogs. I wonder if I should mention Samson in my letter to her?"

Dell didn't answer, and when I turned to him, his face was twisted up into a look I didn't understand at first.

"Nathaniel . . . " he started, then took a deep breath. "I need to tell you . . . I'm sorry."

"You're sorry? What do you have to be sorry about?"

He hung his head down, so I saw the bald dome. "We should have checked in on you sooner, Opal and me," he said, looking up again. "We knew you spent a lot of time here by yourself. For a long while, I've thought about it. Every time I drove by your place, his car was hardly ever here. But it was easier for me just to imagine that you were both out together, instead of you here alone." His head dropped again. "I shoulda checked."

"But I didn't expect you to, Dell."

"Of course, you didn't. You didn't expect anyone to care, because that's what you're used to. But we shoulda. We shoulda checked in. And I shoulda cared about Bert, too, trying to raise his boy without a mama."

The regret poured out of him until I thought he might cry. Dell, whose perpetual poker face I had come to appreciate, laid it all out on the table.

"I'm ashamed we didn't reach out, see if he needed help, or if you needed something."

"Don't be so hard on yourself, Dell." I wanted to cry, too, seeing how broken he was. It was strange, seeing a grown man on the verge of tears, especially over me. I didn't quite know how to respond.

"You've been raising yourself here in this house, and we were over there just letting it happen. Wrapped up in our own lives and in our own problems and in our own day-to-day. Too wrapped up in *self*. But I've learned a lesson from this, Nate."

I let it be quiet for a little bit, then asked, "What's that?" with genuine curiosity.

"That we should never let ourselves get so blind that we miss our chance—our chance to do good for somebody."

I let his words soak in. "Can I tell you a secret?" I asked.

"Of course you can." His mood was immediately lighter.

"I've been making some plans to do good for somebody. My plans have had to change, though." He looked at me and smiled, his eyes urging me to continue. "These last few weeks since Bert left, and even a little before then, I've been trying to decide what I should do." Dell hung on every word. "I figured without him here, I could just head out on my own, wherever I wanted to go."

"And where did you decide you wanted to go?"

"East. Before this whole business of going to my aunt Miriam's, I planned to start out east right after school was out for the summer."

"How far east did you want to go? This great state has lots of pretty places to see."

"All the way to the beach."

"Wanted to see the ocean, huh?"

"No, sir." I twisted my hands in my lap. "Well, that would be nice, but that's not the reason." I was looking forward to seeing the Atlantic in person someday, and the thought of it made me smile. "I saw in a newspaper at school about all the damage this hurricane did last September. Hurricane Donna. Did you hear about it?" He nodded yes. "I read that some people down at the coast are still building back from it, after all this time. I thought me and Samson would try to get down there, and maybe I could help. I can swing a hammer. Or push wheelbarrows. Something."

The lines around Dell's eyes were crinkled up tight. And as sad as he had looked before, he looked just as happy then. "You have a good heart, son," he said. "And I just believe that the Lord is going to give you a big job to do."

"I hope I can do good for my aunt Miriam. I surely want to. From the sound of her letters, she needs somebody. She surely does."

"Then I bet that's the job God has for you now, to be there for her." He pointed to my special box on the floor near the end of the couch. "Your book there. The one from your mama. Do you mind if I read it to you before we get some shut-eye?"

I got up and retrieved the book, then held it out toward Dell, but with hesitation.

"Nobody else has ever held this book before, since it was bought— besides me and Mama, I reckon'."

He kept his hands down, waiting patiently for me to be ready to hand it over.

"It's very special, then," he said softly.

I handed Dell the book, then sat back down at the desk, ready to hear the words I knew so well spoken aloud. He read the same story I had read a few nights before about Joseph and his brothers. The story felt so different, hearing it in someone else's voice.

"See, Nate," he said when he had finished. "What those brothers meant for harm, God used for good. Look where Joseph ended up! The Bible says that all things work out for good if you love God."

I thought about all the good things that had happened since Bert left.

"Dell, what did the preacher mean this morning about *decidin'*?" I asked. "I decide to read my Bible book, and I decide to be good. But he was talkin' about something else, wasn't he?"

"It's pretty simple, really. Some people know about God in their head, but they choose not to give Him their heart. It's a choice everybody has to make."

Dell taught me a lot of things—things I had never had a chance to hear before. He explained to me how all the stories in my book fit together like pieces of a puzzle. He explained God's big plan to make things right after Adam and Eve messed up from the beginning and how it was just as simple as choosing to believe it. That night, I made my choice, and I rested with a peaceful feeling way down on the inside, even though I knew it might be the last night I would sleep in my own bed.

Samson curled up beside me. His ears perked up at the sound of Dell snoring in the other room. Before I drifted off to sleep, I thought about how my life was changing and what might be in store for me, and I thought about my hero, Captain Kittinger. In the article he wrote for my magazine, there was a line that stuck in my mind like a cocklebur to a shoelace. That night, it had new meaning, and I decided to make it mine.

But here in the eerie silence of space, I knew that my life depended entirely upon my equipment, my own actions, and the presence of God.

Chapter Twenty

SETTLING IN

DELL'S TRUCK SAT IN MY driveway when I got home from school on Monday. He sat on the front step of the house, waiting for me and whistling to the birds in the dogwood tree as if he spoke their language. A couple of cardboard boxes were on the ground near his feet, and he held a burlap sack in his hand.

"Hey, friend," he said, as he met me in the yard. "Let me take that for you." Dell took my satchel and put it into the bed of the pickup. "How was school?"

"Normal," I said, meaning nothing out of the ordinary had happened, and that was all to report.

"Well, I hope *normal* is good." He chuckled. "Now, let's get you packed up and back to our house for a special dinner this evening. Whaddaya say?"

I shrugged my shoulders in response. I wasn't unhappy about going to stay with the Nelsons, but I wasn't excited about the change either.

We made quick work of packing, as there wasn't a whole lot to be done. Dell stood back, for the most part, and did whatever I asked him to do. He didn't try to pack anything on his own, and I appreciated that.

"Do you want me to put your clothes in this sack, Nate?"

"That's fine. They're in that drawer there," I said, pointing to my dresser. I hoped he would keep them folded, so I wouldn't have to re-fold them later, but I didn't say that.

One-by-one, for each of my maps and articles, I took the pushpins out of the wall and laid the posters neatly on my bed. Then I laid the stack of stories and maps of countries, regions, and continents carefully in the bottom of one of the boxes. The pushpins went into a little wooden box with a clasp on it to make sure they didn't hurt anybody.

I set the shoebox of letters from Miriam on top of my box of special things.

"Dell, will you please get Samson's dog food in the kitchen? It's a heavy bag."

"Sure, I'll take that out to the truck now," he answered.

I used the time Dell was gone to reassure Samson about our new living arrangements.

"It's gonna be okay, boy. They have a really nice house. It's bigger than ours, and I bet we can still listen to the radio whenever we want. Maybe they'll let me and Patrick come back over here to play under my hammock, too. I would take it with me, but I don't know if they have two trees close enough together like we do."

Samson didn't seem the least bit worried.

I wonder if Aunt Miriam has two trees close enough together? I pondered. Dell came back in and found me standing in the middle of my room in a daze. Most everything I had was sitting on the bed in front of me.

"Nate, what can I help you do next?" he asked gently, trying not to startle me.

"Um . . . I'd like to take the radio. Do you think that's okay?"

"Well, I don't see why not."

"It's in the kitchen, too," I said. Dell left to fetch it for me.

I went to the bathroom and got my toothbrush, leaving the holder completely empty on the counter. I put the brush into a plastic case from under the sink; then I put the case in the sack with my clothes. Besides the sneakers on my feet, with the almost worn-out bottoms, I had a pair of snow boots. Those were already in the other box, the one without the maps. Dell came back and put the radio with the boots.

Seeing that I had plenty of room, I put the box of letters and my special box down on top of the maps. I decided to leave the few knick-knacks on top of my dresser. I took the key to the front door of the house out of my top dresser drawer for the first time in as long as I could remember. Dell carried both boxes, and I slung the burlap sack over my shoulder. I checked to make sure all the lights were off, and it occurred to me that my plan to stay until the power went out hadn't worked. My bargain with God hadn't worked. But after my talk with Dell, I knew His plan was good, even if I didn't understand it.

I shut the door behind us, put the key in the lock, and turned it. The unfamiliar click of the lock from the outside of the house echoed in my brain.

Dell let Samson ride in the cab of the truck on the short drive to his house. He sat in the floorboard in front of me, with his tongue hanging out and his head turning from side to side with excitement. After we both jumped down from the truck, Samson stayed lock step with me as we walked toward the farmhouse.

The windows on the front of the house were open; and from the porch, I could hear Opal singing a lively tune. The melody flowed out through the window screens and welcomed me into the newness of my temporary home.

We followed Dell through the front door that led into the parlor. Of all the rooms in the house that I had seen so far, it was the only one that had a fancy feel to it—wooden chairs with curvy arms and backs and seats covered in velvety material. The rest of the rooms in the Nelsons' house felt more relaxing, but the parlor had a special feel about it. Opal appeared in the doorway of the room. She looked so happy, like she could jump right out of her skin, but she didn't come any closer than two steps away. Her hands were clasped together tightly, next to her body, just under her bosom.

"Nate! We're so glad to have you. And Samson, too," she said. "Why don't you set your things down for now and come on in here?"

Dell hung his hat on the rack in the parlor, and we all followed her to the main living room.

"Have a seat." She motioned to the couch. I sat down, and Samson laid down on the floor at my feet, as if he knew he was a guest and shouldn't get on the furniture. Opal picked something up from the side table.

"We have a little welcome gift for you. After you open it, I'll show you where you'll be sleeping."

My eyes were like fifty-cent pieces, fixed on the wide rectangle-shaped package in her hands. It was wrapped in brown paper with a stiff blue ribbon tied around it in a perfect bow. I took it from her excitedly, then froze, feeling awkward about accepting the gift.

"Go ahead. Open it," she urged.

I carefully slipped off the ribbon and pulled at the tape, not wanting to rip the paper. Dell and Opal looked amused by my method.

The paper fell away to reveal a stiff, green, cardboard tray with four compartments, two big ones and two little ones. The compartments held a stack of fancy paper, a pen, a stack of envelopes, and some round, gold foil seals. I admired it, while Opal spoke.

"I know a stationery set may seem like a strange gift for a young boy, but I thought it might be useful to you." She hesitated. "After you leave here, I hope you'll write to me and Dell and tell us all about your adventures."

"It's perfect," I said, with sincerity. "Thank you both."

"You're welcome, Nate. Now, you can follow me up the stairs here, and Dell can bring your things."

"No, I can help," I said, and I went back to the parlor and retrieved the burlap sack I had carried in. Opal patted me on the back, and I saw her give Dell a wink before she and I started up the stairs.

"There are two bedrooms and a bath up here. One of the rooms is just collecting junk right now." There were little pauses between her words, as her knees pulled her body up each new stair. "But the other one is fixed up nicely, just for our special guests." I liked that she acknowledged Samson, who was on our heels.

She opened the door at the end of a short hallway. "Here we go!"

It was a nice room with beige walls and a window seat. It had a bed that was bigger than mine at my house, a desk with a lamp on it, and a tall wardrobe. I put the burlap sack on the bed, covered with a patchwork quilt made of mostly pink, purple, and green swatches.

"Was this Jenny's room?" I asked.

"Yes, dear. And I hope you'll find it comfortable."

"It's very nice, Opal."

Dell managed to get all my things up the stairs in one trip, but he was a little winded when he entered the room. He placed them on the floor near the bed. "We'll leave you to get settled in for a bit," he said.

"We'll call you when supper is ready," she added.

"Make yourself at home," came out of both of their mouths at the same time, and they looked at one another and giggled like high school sweethearts.

As soon as Opal left the room, she poked her head back in again. "Is there anything you need?"

"Maybe just one thing. But not right now. Do you have any stamps?" I asked.

"I believe we do. I'll find one for you before dinner!"

"Thank you. I really appreciate all you're doing." She smiled and ducked back out again.

I left all my things on the floor where Dell had set them, took my welcome gift from the Nelsons, and sat down at the desk. I didn't want to waste any more time—I needed to get my message to Miriam soon.

Dear Miriam,

Thank you for my birthday present. I would have written to you sooner, but . . .

But I didn't know she existed, I thought. I couldn't tell her that. I thought it might hurt her feelings to know that Bert never talked about her, even more than the fact that he never came to see her. I needed to keep it simple in my letter. *It will be better to tell her everything about Bert in person.*

I had to start again on a new page, and I cringed at wasting a sheet of my new stationery.

Dear Miriam,

Thank you very much for my birthday present. I would very much like to meet you. A friend is bringing me to see you in three weeks. We'll be there on Saturday, May 27. Please write me back and let me know it is okay to visit.

Your nephew,

Nate Dooley

I sealed the letter in an envelope and set about putting my things away. I put everything I had brought with me into the drawers of the wardrobe, except my radio and my posters. I hesitated to put *Bible Stories for Children* and my magazine collection in the drawer instead of under the bed like I was used to doing; but it was a large piece of furniture, and it made sense to keep all my things in one place, since I wouldn't be staying long.

The radio went on top of the dresser, and the posters went on two walls of the room in the same order they had been in at my house: United States, Sahara Desert, Mongolia, Swiss Alps, Sinai Peninsula, Asia Minor, and then the articles. I stood back and admired how the sunlight flooded through the window like a spotlight on some of my maps. On other parts of the wall, the sun and the branches of a tree close to the house created a pattern of highlights and shadows that looked like a map.

"Dinner will be ready soon, Nate," Opal called.

With the letter in my hand, Samson and I made our way downstairs. The wonderful aroma and the sizzling sound of chicken frying met our noses and ears.

"I found your stamp, Nate," Opal said as I came in. She wore a flowered apron and used a fork to poke at the chicken legs in the pan of popping oil. She left the stove to get it for me, but I didn't take it from her.

"Um . . . do you mind if I just leave the letter with you?"

I couldn't explain my reasoning, but I didn't have to for Opal.

"I'll take care of it," she said gently. She patted my hand before she took the letter from it.

Dinner felt different than the Sunday lunch I'd had with the Nelsons. It was nice, but sitting down at the table with them felt like more of a ceremony, since we would all be sleeping under the same roof.

The food was as good as it smelled, and my belly was still full at bed time. Opal followed me upstairs and stood outside my door while I took off my jeans, laid them across the end of the bed, and climbed under the covers.

"Okay," I called out, to let her know I was in bed. I didn't understand why she wanted to come with me; but it was her house, and she could do as she liked.

"All cozy?" she asked, entering the room.

"Yes, ma'am."

"Good. If you need anything, you just come downstairs and knock on our door."

Why would I need something? I wondered. The thought was silly to me, because I had managed quite well on my own for so many nights; then thinking back to my sickness a couple weeks prior, I remembered that there are times when not having anyone else in the house is a disadvantage.

Opal walked uncomfortably close to the bed and pulled the covers up closer to my chin. "I didn't think I'd ever be able to tuck a child in bed in this room again," she said, and I thought I saw a tiny tear glimmering in the light behind the round lenses of her glasses.

My cheeks felt flushed from embarrassment, and my stomach felt a twinge of pity for Opal. I wasn't sure why she had done what she just did or why she wanted to do it; but the corners of my mouth turned up despite my confusion, and warmth rushed through my chest.

"Good night, Nate. Sleep well." She was out the door before I could finish saying good night back to her.

At the latch of the door, I got out of bed and went to the dresser. The picture of Bert, Mama, me, and Colleen was face-down on the top of the box of letters from Miriam. I didn't flip it over to look at it, but I took it from the box and slipped it under my pillow.

Chapter Twenty-One

TABLE FOR FOUR

"OPAL, THIS IS JUST ABOUT the best meal I've had in ages," Smithy gushed. His fork pounded the plate and brought back a new piece of juicy pot roast to his mouth over and over, until the plate was clean. Opal served seconds before Smithy could even ask.

"Hey, Nate," Smithy said, holding a fork full of meat in the air, "this sure beats those franks and wieners, don't it?"

"Yeah, you're right about that," I agreed.

The story of how Smithy and I met fascinated Dell and Opal during dinner. Listening to Smithy tell parts of it made me feel like it was somebody else's life I was hearing about.

"And here this little kid, this teeny-tiny kid, who looks like he's about six years old, walks in, and he's there to ask about his power bill!" Smithy said, laughing with mashed potatoes in his mouth. "Sorry, Nate." He leaned toward me.

He meant no harm by his comments about my size, and I didn't take offense. I enjoyed watching Smithy charm an audience with his storytelling skills, despite his lack of table manners.

"And how brave and clever of you to do that, Nate. I don't think many boys your age would have thought to check with the electric company," Opal said.

"He's a sharp one!" Dell agreed.

I told the part about seeing Smithy at the fair, and they laughed when I described the one-man band.

"All Smithy had to do to make the melody was hum into the kazoo," I said, "but I don't know what song he was trying to play!"

"It was 'Dixie'!" Smithy shot back, sounding incensed.

"'Dixie'? It sounded more like 'Happy Birthday,'" I replied, laughing.

Smithy put his fork down for the first time since the meal had started and slapped both his open palms on the table so hard it made ripples in the milk in our glasses. "Hey!" he said, and he wiped the gravy off his mouth with the back of his hand and then off his hand with a napkin. "I'm glad you said that, Nate. It reminds me." He looked at our hosts. "Did Nate tell you it's his birthday next week?"

"Why, no! He didn't!" She looked excited.

"So, you'll be eleven then, right?" Dell asked.

"Yes, sir," I answered, dropping my head. The attention made me want to crawl under the table.

"What day is it?" Opal asked.

"The eighteenth," I mumbled.

"Okay, that's a Thursday then, I think. How would you like to plan a little party?"

A party. She's asking about a birthday party, I thought. *Is she really talking to me? She wants to have a birthday party for me?*

All the grown-ups looked at me, expecting me to be excited and to say yes right away. I wanted to say yes so badly, but it wouldn't come out of my mouth. Parties were for people with families like Susie Pennywell's—not for me.

I scanned their happy faces. Time felt frozen in the awkward quiet of the room. Smithy's eyebrows were raised. Opal leaned forward, anticipating my answer. But Dell, in his quiet, unassuming way, sent me a message. Dell's eyes said, *Go ahead, Nate. Accept a party. You deserve it.*

I started softly. "Can we invite Patrick?" I asked.

"Of course," Opal said.

"I'd like to invite Susie, from my class. And Hershel, too. Is that okay?" I asked, with more excitement.

"Whoever you want to invite is fine with me, Nate," she answered. "The more, the merrier! I just need to decide if I'm serving a meal or just party food." Her voice trailed as she started planning in her mind.

"Am I invited?" Smithy asked playfully.

"Well . . . let me think about it." The idea was sinking in, and I felt like I could enjoy the conversation again. Opal and Dell laughed, and Smithy kicked me gently underneath the table as payback for my joke.

We passed the smiles and laughter around the table like the bowl of mashed potatoes, and it was the closest thing to having a family I had ever known. For not much more than a moment, it was picture-perfect.

"Oh, I want Miss Gentry to come, too!"

"She'll be there!" Smithy said confidently. "She'll be coming as my date!"

The blood in my veins stopped cold. "Your date?"

"That's right!" The grin took up half the space on his face. "After treating me like a thorn in her side for as long as I've known her, Miss Kate Gentry has finally seen me for the prize that I am."

Dell and Opal chuckled at his feigned arrogance, but I didn't see the humor in it.

"But she wouldn't dare think of . . . " I blurted out.

"Wouldn't what?" Smithy said after a moment. He leaned forward, daring me to finish the thought.

"Smithy, you're just not good enough for her!" I spat out.

He looked as if my words had sprouted hands and had reached across the table and slapped him in the face. Dell and Opal both sat up like a lady with a tight corset on, and they looked back and forth at the both of us, wondering who was going to speak next.

"Nate, you think I'm not good enough for her?" His voice was nine-tenths hurt and one-tenth anger. But as soon as the words were out of his mouth, the equation flipped. "So, I'm good enough to bring you food, and to check on you, and mow your grass, and to show up at a conference when you get yourself in trouble, and to offer to take you across the mountain to see your aunt, but you don't think I'm fit to date your teacher?"

I couldn't respond. I already knew it was a rotten thing I'd said to Smithy, but I still felt it was the truth. Miss Gentry was wise and gentle. She was thoughtful and tender. Smithy was a hillbilly with a criminal history. No matter how good he had been to me, the idea of him bringing *my* Miss Gentry to *my* birthday party as *his* date just felt wrong in every way.

I wanted to cry, but I couldn't make such a scene in front of everybody; so, I just clenched my jaw and begged the tears not to fall, staring straight back at Smithy. His angry face softened, and he scooted his chair back. The chair legs rubbing against the floor made an irritating squeaking sound. Smithy stood up.

"Opal, thank you for a delicious dinner. Dell," he said, reaching to shake Dell's hand, "nice to see you again. Thank you for having me."

"Won't you stay for dessert?" Opal asked.

"No, I think I should go." He choked back being mad at me enough to be polite to his hosts.

"Well, you are welcome to visit any time, Smithy," Opal said. He nodded at her in appreciation.

"Let me walk you out," Dell said to him.

I gripped the seat of my chair and stared down at my plate as Smithy left the room. The screen door banged when they went out; and Smithy and Dell talked on the porch for a while, but I couldn't hear what they were saying. Samson left his spot under the table and started licking the taste of beef gravy off my fingers, but I didn't move.

Opal sat with me quietly and kept on eating her vegetables. After the last green bean, she asked gently, "Nate, do you want pie tonight, or should we save it for tomorrow?"

"Tomorrow," I said.

"Okay." She reached to get my plate. She rose to take the dishes to the kitchen. I couldn't believe she hadn't called me out for being rude to Smithy.

"I'm sorry I spoiled it," I said. Opal sat back down with the stack of dirty dishes in front of her.

"What do you think you spoiled, Nate?" I thought she was acting aloof, but Opal had a way of getting me to think about things.

"We were planning my birthday party and laughing, and it felt nice. But I messed it up. It's all gone wrong now because I couldn't hold my tongue."

"Nate, dear, you didn't spoil the nice time. It already happened. And you can't erase something that already happened. The good moments can still be good in your memory." She scooted over into the chair next to mine. "Your words may have changed the outcome of the evening, but they didn't erase everything that came before them."

I let go of the chair seat, and my muscles began to relax.

"I think I need to tell him I'm sorry. Do you think he has a telephone? I never asked him." I tensed again at the sound of Smithy's car coughing as it backed down the driveway and the screen door knocking as Dell came back in.

"I don't know, dear," Opal said, "but maybe you can ask Miss Gentry at school tomorrow." She didn't mean to rub salt in the wound, but it stung nonetheless.

"No. I don't want to talk to her about it."

Then another matter more important than my birthday party hit me.

"I bet he's so mad he won't take me to Aunt Miriam now! How will I get there? And we've already mailed the letter! Haven't we? I can't take it back now!"

"Yes, the letter's mailed. Herbert, the postman, picked it up from the box yesterday, Nate. But try not to fret. It will work out fine."

I dismissed her advice and let my head fall hard against the edge of the table in despair. She left me to wallow and went about clearing the table.

Dell came through the dining room on his way to his easy chair. He carried a piece of the pie on a saucer, the pie that Opal said we would save for the next day. He patted me on the back as he passed, and the unfamiliar weight of it, the strangeness of a manly hand offering comfort, made me sit up. The smell of chocolate wafted near my face, but I was too upset, even for pie.

Chapter Twenty-Two

BEDTIME KISSES

SAMSON LAY SIDEWAYS ON THE bed on top of the covers, with his front paws across my belly. His fur was long already, though not much time had passed since his haircut on the porch at my house.

Every day that week, I passed my house after school, but I hadn't stepped foot inside since Monday—the day I packed my things, locked the door, and left the place where I had slept every night of my almost eleven years. I missed my square little house, but not nearly as much as I expected I would.

For five nights, Opal had come into Jenny's old room at bedtime and tucked me in. On the second night, she asked if she could read me a story, and we decided together on an article from one of my magazines. On the third night, after I had gotten so upset by the idea of Smithy bringing Miss Gentry to my party as his date, she read a story from my Bible book, even though I didn't feel like listening. The fourth night, she told me a story about Jenny, just from her bank of sweet memories from when her daughter was a little girl. She talked about how Jenny had snuck out of her classroom on the first day of school, determined to walk all the way home because she wanted her mama. We talked for an hour that night, and I thought of things that I had never thought about before—like how Bert always put a box of school supplies on my bed at the start of every school year. He never said anything about them; they were just there. And how, when he was home and he cooked, he dipped out a plate for me and left it on the counter, even if he went to his room and shut the door to eat his dinner by himself. Since Bert left, I could see a lot of things about him that I couldn't see before.

It was Friday night, and Opal sat in the desk chair across the room from my bed, reading aloud another article from one of my magazines. Her ankles were crossed, and her elbows rested on the wooden arms of the chair. She held the magazine close to her face. The article was about bats and how they use sound to hunt. Every few lines, she stopped to comment.

"Isn't this interesting, Nate?" She dropped the magazine to smile at me.

"Oh, my, I learned something new." She slapped her knee.

"How fascinating!" She held onto her cheek and shook her head from side to side in wonder.

It made me happy, how much she seemed to enjoy the article.

"Well, good night, Nate," she said when she finished. She put the magazine back in the box inside the dresser drawer.

"Good night, Opal."

As she headed for the door, she hummed with a bouncy cadence, a tune that sounded familiar.

"Opal?" I called to her. She turned and leaned against the doorframe. "What's that song?" I asked. "It's the same one I heard you singing on Monday when I got here, I think. I like it." She came and stood beside the bed to answer.

"Oh, hmm . . . " She hummed a piece of it again as she searched for the words in her mind. "Oh! That's an old one. It's a little ditty I learned when I lived in London." She began to sing.

"Over the hills, and o'er the main,
To Flanders, Portugal and Spain,
The queen commands and we'll obey
Over the hills and far away."

"You lived in London?" I asked, and I sat up in the bed, wide-eyed. "What did you do there? Why did you go?" I envisioned Big Ben and the River Thames, and I couldn't believe I was in the company of someone who had visited those grand places.

She sat down on the edge of the bed near my feet. "I studied there for a little while," she said happily. "It was my final year of university, and I transferred from a college in Virginia to King's College there. They had an excellent women's department."

"I knew you didn't talk like everyone else in Copper Creek, Opal! You talk too fancy, like someone who went to college and lived in London for a year! All proper. I knew there was something different!"

She threw her head back and let out the trademark giddy laugh that I had grown fond of. "Well, actually, Nate, you speak differently than most children. Your reading has benefited you."

She wasn't the first to say it. Miss Gentry complimented me a lot on my vocabulary, and Patrick was forever frustrated with me for using big words that he didn't know.

"I can't believe you went to college in London! What did you study?" I asked.

"I earned a degree in history," she said rather proudly. My face squished up in surprise at the fact. She went on without me having to ask more questions. "When I was a little girl, my parents took me to visit the Smithsonian in Washington, DC. I was absolutely captivated by all the treasures from the past that had been placed there together, all in one space—much how you seem captivated by your magazines and their wonderful stories. I knew very early that I wanted to be a student of history, and I had big dreams of becoming a museum curator one day."

"Well, what happened?"

"I took a different path. I met Dell, and I wanted to be with him, and well . . . there are no museums in Copper Creek." There was not even a hint of sadness or longing in her voice. I studied her face, searching for regret hiding there, but it didn't exist.

"But, all that hard work you did, going to school. Didn't you feel like it was a waste of time?"

"Oh, no, dear. Education is never a waste." Then matter-of-factly, she added, "Neither is a kind thing you do for someone else or a moment spent in prayer. Remember that, please, Nate. Those are three things that always pay off in some way."

I laid my head back on the pillow and fidgeted with my clasped hands across my chest. "Do you ever feel like . . . maybe you belong somewhere else, though?" I asked. "Like you're missing something out there?"

"No, not really. These mountains have a way of sorting people out. Some run away from them, feeling like there's more to see. Some people just feel too hemmed in by them. And there are some who are drawn here by their mysterious beauty, by the air, by the people. The mountains just seem to call out to them. That's how it was for me."

I settled deeper into the fluffy softness of the pillow while her words sunk into my mind.

"Could a person be both?" I asked.

She smiled at the curious question, but she gave a thoughtful reply.

"It's a hard thing, but yes. Some settle here but keep a wandering spirit, and some venture away and still keep this place close to their hearts. But you have to remember, Nate—just like there are spring, summer, fall, and winter, life has different seasons, too. Sometimes, the Lord moves us where He wants us for just a season."

I wasn't thinking about myself. I thought of Smithy and his ideas about traveling—how when he talked about it, he sounded desperate for somewhere other than where he was. Opal seemed to see straight through my skull and cipher the thoughts inside my brain.

"Want to hear something interesting?" she asked.

"Sure."

"The Smithsonian that inspired me so much was founded by a man who very well could be an ancestor of your friend, Smithy." I squirmed at the word *friend*. I wasn't sure it was still an accurate description, although I wanted it to be. "There was an Englishman by the name of Smithson. He left his entire estate to our government for the purpose of creating the institution, even though he never even visited this country."

"I think I've read about him," I said. "Do you really think Smithy could be related to this Smithson that started the Smithsonian?"

"It's certainly possible. Would that change your view of him? Do you think you would consider him worthy of Miss Gentry's affection then?"

"I don't know." I turned my eyes downward.

"Well, you think on that, Nate. I've enjoyed our talks this week."

She bent down and placed a quick, gentle kiss on my forehead. Other than Susie Pennywell's kiss on the day I punched Peter at school, I couldn't remember ever being kissed by anyone else. I wanted to remember my mama doing that. I knew in my heart that she had done it often. But the memory was gone.

"Opal, I hope my aunt Miriam is nice like you."

"I'm sure she will be, dear."

Chapter Twenty-Three

THINKING ON GOOD THINGS

ON SATURDAY, THE SUN SHINED down on me like my own personal spotlight. I soaked in its warmth while sitting on a picnic blanket at The Hideaway with Opal, Dell, and my dog after a wonderful picnic lunch. I lay there listening to the river tumble over rocks and eating a second piece of chocolate chess pie for dessert.

From close-by in the woods, a three-syllable bird call rang out, making Samson's ears perk up.

"Well, now. That's a treat to hear," Dell said.

I looked at him curiously, wondering why the birdcall was special.

"We don't get many whippoorwills up here," he said, anticipating my question. "They prefer the lowlands. Plus, they're night birds." He cupped his hands together and pressed his thumbs against either side of his mouth and perfectly mimicked the bird's call.

"You know, there's an old wives' tale about those birds," Opal added. "They say when a single woman hears a whippoorwill for the first time in spring, she'll remain single for another year unless she hears it call for a second time. If the bird does call again, she'll be single for life unless she remembers to make a wish, but she has to keep it a secret."

The bird answered Dell.

Opal's story reminded me of a question that had been on my mind.

"I wonder why my aunt Miriam never married," I told them. "I mean . . . I guess she didn't, anyway, since her letters say she's alone."

"Lots of possible reasons, Nate," Dell said. "I'm sure you'll find out when you go to stay with her."

All along, everyone around me had been talking about me going to *see* Aunt Miriam, not *stay*. I knew that staying would most likely be the outcome, but I preferred to pretend that the meeting was just a trial run and that I could come back and live in Copper Creek again if I wanted or take off to see the world if things didn't work out. I didn't like the sound of it when Dell said *stay with her*.

"You know," I said, looking out at the water, "sometimes, I almost wish I hadn't even found that box with the letters from Miriam." Dell and Opal both looked at me with surprise, and I felt guilty for confessing it. "Things might be simpler if I still didn't know about her."

"Don't you want to meet your family, dear?" Opal asked.

"I do want to see her. I have to see her. I feel like she's a missing piece of me. And I feel like I need to go help her, since she's all alone and her letters sound so sad. But I still think it would have been easier to not know about her. Maybe if I didn't know about her, I could stay here with the two of you."

"That's a lovely idea, Nate." Opal had a longing look in her eye. "But we don't know if the county would let that happen or not."

Dell chimed in. "I hope you know that if'n they did, you'd be more than welcome."

"It's just hard to think about leaving sometimes," I said. My heart was heavy.

"I imagine it is hard to think about, son," Dell said. "In the navy, I spent a fair share of time away. It's not easy. We just have to focus on the good, so that it makes the bad easier to deal with."

A helicopter seed caught my eye, and I stayed quiet as I watched its long, swirly descent through the air. The seed landed in the middle of a crop of rocks near the bank, and for some reason, it made me sad. Any kind of weed might be able to sprout up from there, but a red maple was different.

"Well, like when I was in the service," Dell continued, "I had to keep reminding myself why I was there. That I was helping my family back home by being there to stand up to the bad guys." He leaned back, putting his palms on the ground behind him to prop himself up and let the picnic digest.

Dell could see I understood in theory, but it was a big thought that needed to simmer in my mind a little longer. "Like that report you're working on for school. The one you told me about yesterday, about turning parts of these here mountains into a park. It wasn't very long ago, the government came in and bought up a lot of land near here, and they forced people out." I knew about the logging companies that had devastated the forests, but I hadn't thought about it the way Dell talked. That wasn't in the books I had read. "And then after the park was made, when the hydroelectric dam was built and a whole town was flooded on account of it . . . well, people had to relocate, and some have relatives buried on land that was taken from them, and . . . well, some of them are still pretty bitter." He looked up at the sky as far as the bright sun would allow. "And I can't say as I blame them. But what's done is done. All that we can do now is focus on the good. Because there's always some good. Like how these mountains and these forests will go on forever and stay here for people to enjoy because the trees can't be cut down, and the mountain can't ever be blasted anymore to make room for more buildings and roads. Not to mention how the power from that dam played a part in putting an end to the Second World War. That's the good out of that, and we have to choose to focus the more on that part of it now."

"I think she needs me," I said. I realized I had subconsciously ripped several handfuls of grass from the earth and dropped the blades on the blanket while Dell spoke. I brushed the grass away in a bit of a panic, smoothing the wrinkles out in the fabric as I did it.

"It sure sounds like she needs somebody, Nate," Opal agreed. "And you're a good somebody to have."

"But what if I can't get to her? I really do miss Smithy. Not because I need him to take me. Just because he was such a good friend to me. But I don't know whether or not he'll still want to take me after what I said." My words came out faster and faster. "It's only two weeks away. I'm just not sure he'll cool off enough by then, even if I do tell him how sorry I am. And even though I'm sorry I said it, I still don't like the idea of him and Miss Gentry, anyway."

"Nate, I could take you to your aunt Miriam," Dell said gently. "I'm sure Opal could take over the work on the farm for a day without me here. But . . . I wouldn't be able to stay and make sure you get settled in all right. I'd have to come right back the same day. Maybe if we wait a few weeks, I can go with you and stay a couple of nights to make sure you're okay there."

"I'll have to write her back and tell her I'm coming later, I guess," I said.

"Don't worry, Nate. Things are going to work out just fine," Opal said. Her words felt like the truest truth I could hear. I never questioned anything Opal said because she was as genuine as the mountains were tall, and I suddenly felt better.

"Well, we'd better go. It's almost time to go pick up your friends!"

Opal packed the basket, and I helped Dell fold the blanket. I tucked it under my arm, and we made our way back through the rough patch to where the truck was waiting.

I rode in the back with Samson; and when we went to Patrick's house, and then to Susie's, they got to ride in the back with us, too— one of us in each corner of the bed, the kids with their arms stretched out on the sides, partly relaxing, partly bracing.

Patrick and Susie came over to the Nelsons that afternoon for two reasons—to work on our end-of-year school projects together and to help Opal make plans for my birthday party, and both helped me forget about my cares, for just a little while.

"Nate, I don't understand why you're having to write that paper, and all we have to do is draw our family trees real neatly and color them in," Susie said. The three of us sat at the kitchen table, which was covered with plain white paper, lined paper, colored pencils, and plain black, lead Dixons. Samson, who had only recently gotten comfortable with leaving my side for even a little while, enjoyed the sunshine on the front porch but watched me through the window. "Ours seems a lot easier to do," she added. "But Miss Gentry is usually so fair."

I liked that she was concerned about me and whether I received fair treatment or not.

"Nah, this assignment was my choice," I said. "I've been doing some reading about the National Park and Fontana Dam."

"When are you not reading, Nate?" Patrick jabbed. I kicked his shin under the table, but not hard enough to hurt.

"Well, Miss Gentry told me I could write about something I'm interested in, like those things, instead of doing the family tree project y'all are working on."

"But how come? Why wouldn't you want to do the easiest one?"

"'Cause it would be too easy," I admitted. Susie knew I was staying with the Nelsons because Bert had disappeared, but neither she, or even Patrick, realized how little I knew about my family. Susie looked at me with a mixture of confusion and a knowing sadness.

"I've got only two branches, just four people. Well . . . I've got more, I guess. I just wouldn't know how to fill in the blanks."

Opal came in at the right time to change the conversation, so I would avoid feeling sorry for myself. She took a bowl of fruit from the counter and set it in the middle of the table and took the empty seat. "I hate to interrupt young geniuses at work, but I really need to get your ideas for the party next week."

We all dropped our pencils. Opal reached over and picked up the one Patrick had just dropped, then took a piece of lined paper and wrote across the top: Nate's Birthday Party Ideas.

Chapter Twenty-Four
THE PARTY

JUST BEFORE SEVEN, I STOOD in the Nelsons' kitchen, looking out the window, waiting for the guests to arrive for my party. Patrick was already there, playing with Samson in the living room. He had been there with me since right after school, and he was almost as excited as I was.

"It's almost time!" Opal sang as she entered the kitchen. She took the last tray of dessert off the counter to carry into the parlor. "I hope you're ready to party, Nathaniel James!" I smiled at her new way to address me. Most kids were called by both names when they were in trouble. Opal called me by my first and middle names when she was very happy or excited, which was often.

I had been given strict instructions to not enter the parlor, to not see the party all set up before it was time. Patrick being there helped keep me occupied, so I didn't go crazy waiting. He came into the kitchen with Samson, just as a car came down the driveway and passed the old oak tree with the tire swing. I recognized the Buick that had taken me back home after Susie's birthday party, only a lady was driving.

"Opal! Opal! Susie and Mrs. Pennywell are here!" I called, not leaving the window.

"Okay, Nate. Come in and greet your guests," she said.

Patrick and Samson led me into the parlor. Patrick covered my eyes with his hands until I was in the middle of the room. It was even greater than I had imagined. While Susie and her mother made their way from the car to the porch, I surveyed the room and the smiling faces of Patrick, Opal, and Dell. A pointed, striped party hat covered Dell's shiny head, and the sight made me chuckle.

My party was bright and cheerful, and it had an overwhelmingly delicious theme—candy and dessert. Two tables were set up on either side of the parlor, far enough away from the walls so that guests could walk on around either side. Sweets and confections of all kinds covered both tables. Opal purchased some of the treats, and others she worked on all day. Aside from food, there were special plates and napkins and blue, red, green, and yellow balloons and streamers.

"Thank you so much," I said to the Nelsons. "This is wonderful!"

Opal opened the front door just as Susie was about to knock on it. She wore a Sunday dress, not a school dress. It was bright yellow with ruffled sleeves, perfect to match my party colors.

"Come on in," Opal said.

"Hey, Susie! Hi, Mrs. Pennywell!" I spoke up from behind Opal. I was so giddy, it was hard to formulate words.

Mrs. Pennywell sported the same giant hair and kind eyes I remembered from Susie's party, when she had handed me the Kool-Aid.

"Thank you for coming and bringing Susie, Martha. It's so nice to see you." Opal greeted Mrs. Pennywell.

I didn't notice Hershel's grandfather drop him off in front of the house. Hershel came in right behind the first guests, and other classmates soon followed—kids whom I had worked up the courage to invite. Anna, John, and Spencer accepted the invitation without hesitation, and I was glad Opal and Dell were so popular around Copper Creek. Parents were happy to bring their kids to a party at their house.

I introduced my friends to Samson, and I couldn't remember ever feeling prouder.

"I wish I had a dog like this!" Anna said.

"My pa makes me keep mine outside. He wouldn't be as well-behaved as yours," John said.

"Ween . . . I mean, Nate, you sure are lucky," Hershel said.

Samson soaked up the attention, slapping his tail against the floor as the kids rubbed his ears and scratched his head.

The adults sat around the room, including my friend Mr. Jones, Dell's farmhand, who had snuck in through the back door after finishing the evening milking. Mr. Jones, who still smelled of cows, sat next to Mrs. Pennywell, who engaged him in friendly conversation.

The kids settled in the floor in the middle of the room, playing with Samson. As we played, a sweet, tender voice came floating through the screen door.

"Knock, knock," Miss Gentry called. "Am I in the right place for a birthday party for a very special boy?"

My heart jumped, then the rest of my body followed up from the floor. I ran to the door to open it and invite her in, but she wasn't alone. I looked back in the house at Opal and Dell, who were watching me, and I could tell they already knew what to expect.

"Smithy! You came!"

Smithy stood one step behind Miss Gentry on the porch, his lanky frame a silhouette in the twilight. "Of course I came, silly," he said, as if he didn't think there was any reason for me to doubt he would. I stepped out onto the porch, out of view of my other guests.

"I ain't mad no more, Nate," Smithy said tenderly.

I wrapped my arms around his thin waist and pressed the side of my head to his belly for half a second; then I turned to Miss Gentry. Her hand was on Smithy's elbow as he stood with his hands shoved deep into his pockets.

"I'm glad you're here, Miss Gentry," I said. Her brown eyes twinkled in the light coming from the parlor. She reached out with the hand not touching Smithy and put her arm around my shoulder, pulling me close.

"I wouldn't be anywhere else," she responded brightly.

We said nothing else about the way I had hurt Smithy's feelings or about Miss Gentry being Smithy's date. Things were back to how they were before, and it felt like a cool rain shower on the hottest day of the year.

Inside the house, Opal lit candles. She finished dressing the clean, white wick of the final one with a dancing, fiery top hat, just as I re-entered the parlor with Smithy and Miss Gentry following behind me.

As soon as I stepped inside, a familiar song rang out.

"Happy Birthday, dear Nate. Happy Birthday to you!" Some sang off key, others too loud, but my ears heard an angel choir.

Not a single person sang, "Happy birthday, dear Weenie."

I didn't want to blow the candles out because I wanted the moment to go on forever. The wax began to drop slowly underneath the dancing flames. Dell placed a comforting hand on my back. "Go ahead, son. Make a wish."

I closed my eyes and held my breath. The room felt tense with anticipation. I opened my eyes again and blew the candles out without making the wish. I whispered a prayer instead.

Everyone clapped as the smoke of eleven candles drifted off toward the screen door and out onto the porch with the spring breeze.

Opal served me the first piece of chocolate cake, a piece almost as big as my face. By the time I was half-finished, I was nearly full—a fact that didn't stop me from serving myself a sample of four other desserts. A fruit tart with fresh cream, peanut butter and chocolate balls, a piece of apple pie, and a bouncy slab of lime gelatin covered my blue party plate, along with the remaining half piece of chocolate cake.

My friends went on and on about the food. Patrick said three times it was the best cake he'd ever had. Susie started to agree, but she kept quiet to avoid hurting her mother's feelings.

"Okay, Mister Nate," Dell said when everyone finished their food. "I think you've got some gifts here to open."

With all the splendor in the room and all the special friends gathered there, I hadn't even noticed the presents stacked in the corner. Dell handed them to me one by one, and I sat in the straight-back chair, my feet swinging just above the floor. There was a yo-yo from Spencer, and Patrick gave me a matchbox car from his personal collection. It was my favorite one from our games in the backyard at home; and even with all the new things, I suddenly missed my bedsheet hammock.

The biggest present was a suitcase from Dell and Opal. It was a silver-colored metal one with wheels, and it looked top of the line. I loved it, but I was glad no one pointed out how soon I would be needing it. The Nelsons also gave me a brand-new pair of sneakers to replace my worn-out ones. I put on the black high-top PF Flyers before moving on to the next gift, thanking Dell and Opal over and over as I laced them.

Miss Gentry gave me my very own subscription to *National Geographic*. When I saw the card and the Tennessee mailing address printed on it, I felt confused.

"I wanted to make sure you are still able to get them while you're away," she said. "Plus, this way, you don't have to wait on me to finish with them. And I'll put my volumes in the classroom. Maybe my other students will enjoy them as much as you do, Nate." She nodded toward my classmates.

Away. I would be leaving soon. Leaving all the people gathered there to celebrate me.

I perked up when Susie handed me a homemade card, signed from *a friend*. On the outside was a picture of a rainbow and birds. On the inside, Susie had drawn me with an enormous birthday cake—either that, or she had drawn me really small next to a regular-size cake.

The card read, "Dear Nate, you are a very nice boy, and you have a very nice smile."

Her mother sat across the room watching us with a big grin, and I wondered if she knew about the kiss Susie placed on my cheek at school.

"Here's the last one," Dell said. He handed me a small, green box. There was no note, but when I opened it, I knew who it was from.

"A pocket watch!" I could hardly believe it. It was gold-colored and had a long chain. I mashed the winding knob to release the latch, so I could examine the inside. The black lines that represented digits stood out against the crisp whiteness of the watch face.

"It's not like the kind you get for working the railroad," Smithy said mischievously, "but at least you won't have to worry about this one falling off your wrist." No one else understood, but it didn't matter.

"Thank you, Smithy. It's perfect. All of this is perfect. Thank you, everybody!"

The party was even more wonderful than I had imagined it would be. I stayed hyper from the thrill of it all, combined with the substantial amount of sugar I had eaten, until long after my friends were gone and Opal and I had packed up the leftover treats.

"You know, you were really great with your guests tonight, Nate," Opal said as she tucked me into bed.

"What do you mean?"

"Well, you have such good manners. And you're a very good host. And you help clean up without being asked. It just amazes me."

Opal stood beside the bed with a hand on one hip, still aglow from the excitement of the evening, too. She suddenly didn't look nearly as old to me as I had thought she was. She had a light in her eyes that erased years.

"But why?" I asked.

She paused, trying to figure out how to answer my questions the right way. "You've spent so much time alone, just you and the radio in that house, from what you've told me. And, it's just that . . . you had so little influence from a mother or a father." Her voice was full of admiration, but carried a hint of pain. "It's remarkable that you've turned out so well, Nate. It just goes against the odds, I guess." She smiled and searched my eyes, trying to see if her words had hurt me, or if I had accepted them the way she meant them.

"It's funny. I never really felt alone. I got lonely sometimes, but I didn't feel alone. I guess that doesn't make much sense, does it?"

"It doesn't have to, I suppose."

"Well, I had lots of company—from my magazines and books, but mostly from my Bible book." I stopped, still afraid she might think it was strange. But the look on her face urged me to keep going. "Daniel, and Solomon, and Jesus, and lots more people—the real people from the stories—they kept me company. And it was like my mama gave them to me, to keep me company. Well, that's how I felt, anyway. She left them to take care of me."

"You had some great company then, Nate. And I'm glad that's how you see them. They taught you well."

She tucked me into bed; and after coming down from my sugar high, I finally fell asleep, only to dream about having birthday cake with Shadrach, Meshach, and Abednego. I dreamed they brought me strange gifts that I thought were the greatest ever—a catfish wrapped in newspaper, a toy train, and a handful of dandelions.

The next day, on the nineteenth of May, I received another birthday present—a real one; it wasn't a dream. In the mailbox at my house, for the first time, was a letter addressed to me.

Dear Nate,

I can hardly find the words to write. I am overjoyed to hear from you and beyond excited that you plan to visit me. This is the long-awaited answer to my prayers.

You are welcome to stay here as long as you like, or as long as your father will let you. You didn't mention him in your letter, so I don't know if he's bringing you or how you plan to get to me. To have you both here would mean so much, but however you can get here safely, please get here.

The letter provided landmarks to help find her house, in more detail than I thought was needed. The handwriting in her letter changed from neat and loopy at the beginning, to scribbly and tight toward the end, as if she were writing furiously as she finished.

P.S. I would have addressed you as Nathaniel if you hadn't signed your letter as Nate. I didn't know that's the name you go by, so it may be hard for me to get used to. For years, I've referred to you as Nathaniel in my prayers.

In just one week, I would meet my aunt for the first time.

Chapter Twenty-Five

GOODBYE

"I CAN'T BELIEVE TOMORROW IS the last day of fifth grade," I said.

"I can't believe you're leaving in two days," Patrick responded.

We tossed a kickball back and forth underhanded near the playground fence.

"I know. But I'll write to you and tell you what's going on. Once I figure out if I'm staying there or not, I mean." The other kids on the playground were carefree and excited for summer, a stark contrast to the two of us. "And . . . I know you don't like to write much, but . . . you have to promise me you'll write me back. Like, right away. Don't wait a week and then do it. As soon as you get a letter from me, start one back."

"I promise, Nate."

"And another thing, Patrick. I want you to write to me if Bert comes back. If you see his car at our house, will you write to me as soon as you can and let me know?"

"I will, Nate."

We didn't talk about me leaving anymore, that day or the next. When we got to his house from the bus stop on Friday afternoon, after our final day as fifth graders, we pretended it was just like any other day of the school year.

"See ya, Nate," he said as he turned toward his driveway.

"See ya, Patrick."

It may have been an unusual goodbye, but it was how it needed to be.

When I got to the Nelsons' house, Samson didn't come running out of the house to meet me in the driveway. There was no singing or humming coming from the kitchen or the garden like normal. It was quiet.

I went inside, carrying my nearly empty school satchel across my shoulder; and I found my shiny new suitcase, packed with all my things, waiting in the parlor where I had left it that morning. I stopped at the threshold between the parlor and the living room, surprised by what I saw. Opal sat on the couch with Samson, rubbing his head and talking to him softly. She held a white handkerchief with eyelet trim in her free hand.

"Oh, you caught us," she said when she realized I was standing there staring. "After we worked so hard to keep him off the furniture, I go and give in on his last day here. Isn't that silly?"

I smiled and crossed the room to sit on the other side of Samson.

"So, how does it feel to be finished with the fifth grade, young man?" she asked.

I shrugged my shoulders.

"Well, there's a snack for you in the kitchen if you're hungry," she said. "Dell will be in from the field soon. He wants to spend some time with you before you leave."

I went to the kitchen in search of the oatmeal cookies Opal made for me. I thought she would come sit with me like she usually did in the afternoon, but she and Samson both stayed on the couch. I poured myself a glass of milk and sat down to eat my two cookies, savoring each bite more than the last.

Dell came in just as I finished and sat down across from me with the same snack.

"It was nice of Miss Gentry to plan to cook dinner for you and Smithy before you leave," he said. "Opal tells me you're supposed to be back at your house at six. Is that right?"

"Yes, sir."

"Very good then."

"I really like my room here," I said, "but I *am* sorta glad to have one more night in my old house . . . you know . . . before I leave. Plus, this way, I won't have to wake you up tomorrow. I think Smithy and I will head out pretty early."

"Well, you know I'm up with the sun, Nate. It wouldn't have bothered me. But we understand you wantin' to see your own house again. It's okay."

"Dell, I hope you don't mind, but my posters looked so good hanging up in Jenny's old room . . . the way the sun came through and landed on the maps . . . I didn't want to take them down. Is it all right with you if I leave them here?"

"Yes, it's okay, son. If you're sure you want to do that. We'll take good care of them for you."

The afternoon passed too quickly. Dell and I walked around the farm with Samson, and I said goodbye to the cows and chickens and to Mr. Jones. He surprised me with a silver half dollar, which he said was his good luck coin, and he hoped it brought me luck on my journey. I put it down inside my new left shoe and promised to take care of it.

On the way back to the house, I stopped and looked out on the white lavender hill, so fresh-looking and beautiful. *They might have been started in rocky ground, but they sure did turn out to be something special,* I thought.

I looked up to see Opal standing on the back porch, just watching me quietly. She turned and went back inside the house, and the rest of us followed.

It was almost time for me to meet Smithy and Miss Gentry at my house. But Dell and Opal had lots to say to me first. We stood in the parlor, two arm-lengths from the door. I gripped the handle of my suitcase, and Samson sat down at my feet.

Being small, I was used to looking way up to most grown-ups, and having clothes and furniture swallow me up was a normal thing. But in that moment, I noticed my smallness in a different way. Getting ready to leave the comfort of the Nelsons' home and embark into the unknown made the world around me—the room, the chandelier, the trees I could see through the window, even Dell and Opal—somehow bigger.

"This is our phone number." Opal handed me a slip of paper. "If you can find a phone out there, you call us any time, day or night. Just dial zero for the operator and tell them you want to make a collect call, okay? I've written it on three other pieces of paper and put them in different pockets of your suitcase."

"Yes, ma'am."

"We'll look in on your place. I'll get your mail, and I'll keep the grass cut. You don't have to worry about those things anymore, Nate," Dell said. "And if your father comes back, we'll let him know where you are."

I nodded.

"And, Nate, I've put a little money in your bag, too. Just in case," Opal said.

"Aw, Opal. You didn't have to do that.'

"Now, I understand you don't like charity. But we wanted to do it."

"Thank you. I appreciate everything y'all have done for me. And I won't ever forget it."

"Well, I'd be lying if I said we're not sad to see you go, Nate," Opal said. "You haven't been here long at all, but you've become very special to us."

She fought to hold back tears, and I felt sorry for leaving her like Jenny had done. Dell wrapped an arm around her shoulder.

"I want you to know something," Opal said. "The struggle I had with my faith . . . well, it turned out to be a blessing. I've learned how to really pray now, more than I ever did before. And . . . well, I've been praying for you a lot, Nate. And I just want you to know—things are going to turn out so well for you! Greater than you can imagine. So, don't be scared. Even if it seems like things aren't working out. Because they will. In His timing, it will all work out like it's supposed to."

Dell and Opal grabbed me in a hug at the same time, and we stood there like that for a long while.

"I've got a verse of Scripture for you, Nate," Dell said. "I hope you'll remember it." He put his hands on my shoulders and looked me in the eye. "It comes from Isaiah, chapter forty-one. The tenth verse. 'Fear thou not; for I *am* with thee: be not dismayed; for I *am* thy God: I will strengthen thee; yea, I will help thee; yea, I will uphold thee with the right hand of my righteousness.'" I let every word soak in, and I memorized the sound of Dell's voice saying them.

"Nate, are you ready for me to drive you over to your house?" he asked.

"Actually, I think I'll just walk," I answered. "The suitcase isn't too heavy."

"All right, son. If that's what you want," he said. They followed me and Samson out onto the porch.

From the first step down I said, "Tell the preacher bye for me. And tell 'im thank you for helping me think the right way about things. I really enjoyed his sermons."

"We'll tell him, Nate," Opal said.

When my feet hit the grass of the front yard, in between the stone slabs that made a path to the driveway, I thought of something else.

"Hey, Opal?"

"What is it, dear?"

"Can you sing me that song? The one about the soldiers leavin'?"

Dell looked at her quizzically, but she didn't hesitate to fulfill my request. I turned my back as she started singing. Samson followed me as I half-walked and half-marched down the driveway.

"Over the hills and o'er the main,

To Flanders, Portugal and Spain,

The queen commands and we'll obey

Over the hills and far away."

She sang the chorus at least five times, louder each time so I could still hear her, until I was out of sight.

Chapter Twenty-Six

THE PICTURE OF FAMILY

I CHECKED THE MAILBOX AT the end of my driveway. The only thing inside the black metal box was another power bill, earlier than I expected it. I set the suitcase down halfway between the road and the house, eager to open it. There was a lot more money on the account than I thought there would be, but then I remembered I hadn't been at home to use any electricity in a while.

Samson chased a bird in the front yard while I hoisted my suitcase up the porch steps and dug the house key out of my jeans pocket. He bounded up the steps to make sure I didn't go in and leave him behind.

I unlocked the front door of my little house and stepped one foot over the threshold. I paused to breathe in the familiar smell of my house. It didn't have any particular scent that I could distinguish. It was neither good nor bad. It was just the smell of home—home, mixed with the staleness of my absence.

I drew my other foot slowly into the house, and Samson followed it. Fully inside, something overwhelmingly strange happened. I saw my mother.

As plain as day, she lay there stretched out on the couch in front of me. I wanted to run to her, but I was frozen where I stood. *I'm losing my mind*, I thought. Samson had no reaction to this new person in the house; so, I knew she wasn't really there, and I couldn't help but cry.

The vision was short, and I didn't see only my mother. My four-year-old self ran to her side, took her pale, bony hand and ran it through his stumpy fingers. My Bible storybook lay on her chest. She stroked my hair, then with great effort opened the book to read to me. I hoped to hear the story, but the vision faded as the sound of tires on gravel startled me to reality. I wiped my eyes quickly and tried to act as if I hadn't just seen a ghost.

Samson barked at the two cars in the driveway—Miss Gentry's shiny, cream-colored Volkswagen Beetle and Smithy's bucket of bolts we would take across the mountain. He got out of the car in a hurry and ran to help her with the bag of groceries she carried. I waited for them at the door.

Miss Gentry wore a white dress, much fancier than what she had worn to school that day. Smithy had on his trademark suspenders and bowler hat, and I could smell his cologne before he had even made it to the porch.

"Hiya, Nate!" he said cheerfully.

I had been so excited to have Miss Gentry as a guest in my home, but having to say good-bye to the Nelsons and seeing a vision of my mama overshadowed the feeling. I just hoped the evening would be happy and calm.

"Hey, Smithy! Hey, Miss Gentry!" I called to them, as if everything were normal.

I moved my suitcase aside and stepped back out onto the porch to hold the door open for them.

"Isn't he always such a gentleman!" Miss Gentry praised, her eyes bright.

"Yeah, he makes me look bad, doesn't he, Kate?" Smithy joked.

Miss Gentry giggled in a way I hadn't heard before.

"Nate, thank you for letting me come visit with you," she said. "Your home is lovely."

I looked down at my sneakers. "Thanks. But I'm not sure if I can really call it home anymore." There was a moment of awkward silence.

"Well, it's still your home for tonight, kid," Smithy said. "And we're going to enjoy the evening!"

"Okay," I said, determined not to spoil things. My friend and my favorite teacher were both in my house, and my teacher was going to cook us dinner. That was something to be happy about. I remembered what Dell taught me about focusing on the good and what Opal said about everything working out all right.

Smithy and Miss Gentry were already in the kitchen, emptying the grocery bags out onto the counter.

"Nate, are you hungry?" she asked.

"Yes, ma'am!"

"Well, good. I hope you don't mind showing me where all the dishes are. Then if it's okay with you, I'll just get to work."

"Why don't we all help?" I asked. "What do you need first?"

"Well, just a pot for the noodles to start. And a pan for the hamburger."

I set about finding what she needed to start cooking. Smithy washed his hands in the kitchen sink, then said, "I'll find some plates to set the table."

"Hey, I have an idea!" I ran to my suitcase, opened it, and pulled out the old radio that used to live in the kitchen. I plugged it in, set it on the counter, and tuned it to a rock n' roll station.

"Good idea, Nate!" Miss Gentry seemed so happy and vibrant.

Samson barked at the music like he was singing along, then at Smithy when he started dancing from the cabinets to the table with three plates. I laughed and went to dance with my dog, grabbing his front paws. Samson seemed to enjoy it.

Before long, Miss Gentry had the noodles and the hamburger cooking on the stove, and I found a pan to broil the garlic bread in the oven. Smithy sat down on the couch with Samson, tapping his feet to the lively tunes coming from the radio.

When Miss Gentry added the sauce to the pan, it splattered.

"I don't know what possessed me to wear a white dress to cook spaghetti," she said matter-of-factly. Smithy rushed to help by grabbing a dish towel and wetting it for her. She scrubbed at the stain. Not prone to vanity, Miss Gentry stayed calm even though her white dress was decorated with tiny red polka dots. "Oh, look at me. I'm a mess, aren't I?"

"You still look pretty," Smithy and I said in perfect unison. He laughed; Miss Gentry blushed; and I wanted to crawl underneath the table. I couldn't believe I had said it, and at the same time as Smithy, no less. That made the embarrassment worse.

"Well, thank you, gentlemen," she said sincerely. "You are both too kind."

Her sweet words eased my humiliation, but only slightly.

"Okay, now. Go ahead and take a seat. Dinner is almost ready," she said.

She took the bread out of the oven, then mixed the meat sauce into the drained noodles. Miss Gentry brought the pot from the stove to the table and dipped big servings onto each of the plates—first mine, then Smithy's, then her own. After she brought the bread to the table, she sat down with us.

"I hope you enjoy!" she said.

Smithy picked up his fork and began to twirl noodles around it.

"Wait!" I cried. "We need to give thanks."

"Oh, you're right, Nate. How could I forget?" Miss Gentry said. "Would you like to do it?"

I nodded, and I saw Smithy roll his eyes out of the corner of my own.

"Dear Lord," I began. "Thank You for this food and the hands that made it. Please bless it. Amen."

Miss Gentry smiled approvingly.

"Oh, and God," I added, "thank You for my friends, and for Aunt Miriam, and please give us a safe journey tomorrow. In Jesus' name. Amen."

Miss Gentry's face glowed with approval. Smithy sat perfectly still, waiting to make sure I was done, so he could eat.

The meal was delicious. Not quite as good as Opal's cooking, but better than pork and beans by a mile.

"Oh, Kate," Smithy said, "this really is wonderful." She batted her eyelashes. I could tell she didn't do it on purpose; it just happened.

"I'm sorry I didn't get dessert," she said. "But I probably need to leave soon after dinner anyway, to let you two get to bed early."

"Smithy said it should take only about three or four hours. So, we shouldn't have to get up too early. Isn't that right, Smithy?"

"That's right. We're not in a big hurry," he said.

"I bet you're getting very excited to meet your aunt, Nate," Miss Gentry said. "Tomorrow is a big day."

"Yes, ma'am," I said, and I meant it. The sad feelings of leaving and the excited feelings of seeing Miriam kept running all over top of each other, but the excitement was building.

I looked from Miss Gentry to Smithy and back again. They were much too young to be my parents, but I wondered if it were the kind of scene that happened regularly before my mama died—a man, a woman, and a boy sitting there having dinner. I looked over at the couch, half expecting to have the vision of her again, but there was nothing there.

When we finished the meal, Smithy and Miss Gentry stood side-by-side at the sink and washed the dishes. I offered to help, but they told me just to relax with Samson.

When the kitchen was clean, we sat around and talked for a while—mostly about the wonder of *National Geographic*, and Miss Gentry and I compared our favorite articles. She talked to Smithy about how well I had done on the last test in her class, and we talked about Opal and Dell and what sweet people they were. It was the perfect way to curb any anxiety I might have had about the trip I would take the next day.

An hour after sundown, Miss Gentry insisted she had to go, and Smithy insisted on walking her to her car. She hugged me tightly; I promised to write to her; and we both said we hoped to see each other again one day soon. Then she was out the door.

Alone inside the house, I pulled the stationery set out of my suitcase, sat down at the kitchen table again, and started writing. It wasn't something I had planned to do, but the idea came to me like a power switch flipped in my brain.

Dear Bert,

A lot has changed since you went away. I've made some good friends who helped look after me, but I did a lot on my own, too. I kept the house clean, like always. And I even got a job to make some money. It was just for a day, but I earned $6.50.

I wasn't going to tell him about Samson, so I didn't mention that I needed money in part to buy dog food.

I wonder sometimes where you went. I hope it was a good trip. I've been doing some thinking, and I want to tell you that I forgive you for leaving me. I'm not sure what it is, but I figured out that you have some kind of problem that makes it hard to talk to me and do things with me. I've had to go away for now, and I don't know for how long. I'm not even sure if I will come back. Maybe I will write more letters—in case you do come home and in case you read them.

Signed,

Nate

I crumpled the paper into a ball, sad to waste yet another piece. On a fresh piece of paper, I wrote a new letter, then sealed it in an envelope and left it on the kitchen counter.

Dear Bert,

I hope to see you again.

Nate

I decided to go on to bed before Smithy came back inside. He would sleep on the couch like Dell had done. On the way to my room, I turned toward Bert's room and blew a kiss to my mama's picture. Then I blew a kiss to Bert, too.

Samson followed me to our old place. He seemed happy to be back where he had first found me. I took off my jeans and laid them across the end of the bed for the next day, then crawled under the familiar old sheets. I looked around at the bare walls, missing my posters but glad they were safe at the Nelsons' house.

I had my Bible storybook and my Bible from Dell with me. Lying there with Samson across my feet, I read—first from the storybook and then from the book of Exodus. I read about the children of Israel fleeing Egypt—how God parted the Red Sea, and they made it through safely. It was a fitting story because it was time for my own exodus. I just couldn't be sure if I was headed to the promised land or if I was leaving it behind.

Chapter Twenty-Seven
A NEW JOURNEY

"WELL, BOY, IT LOOKS LIKE we're leaving before they turn out the lights after all."

My electricity *fleece* hadn't turned out like I thought it would.

Samson ate the last bites of his breakfast in the kitchen. I checked my new watch chained securely to my belt loop, then I dropped it back into my pants pocket. I hadn't slept well; my bed wasn't as comfortable as I remembered it being. Samson and I were both up before Smithy. He lay with his feet hung over the arm of the couch. The faintest of snores came from his cavernous open mouth. The sun was barely up; but I was anxious to get on the road, so I gently woke him.

Within a half hour, we had all our things loaded into his old car, and I took out my key to lock up the house again, this time for no telling how long. I put the key in the lock but paused before I turned it. It felt like I was forgetting something. I opened the door and peeked back inside to make sure I had put the radio back in my suitcase. It wasn't in the kitchen, so I assumed I packed it. Then it hit me.

"Do you think it's okay to leave the porch light on?" I asked Smithy, who was standing in the yard waiting. I didn't look at him when I said it. "I want to leave it on, just in case . . . just in case . . . well, in case Bert comes back. I don't know why. I just want to."

"That's no problem, Nate," Smithy said. He spoke uncharacteristically slowly. "You do whatever you want. It's your house." He understood what I wasn't able to explain.

I reached inside the house and felt around on the wall. I flipped the switch for the porch light, then closed the door and locked it.

Samson jumped in the backseat of Smithy's car, ready to ride, and I went around and hopped in the front with Smithy, excited for the surprise I had planned.

"Here, take this," I said nonchalantly as the car engine roared to life. I pretended there was something interesting to see out the window.

"What's that?" he said. I turned to see that he looked almost repulsed by the bill in my hand.

"It's called money, Smithy." I smiled at my own cleverness.

"Don't get smart with me, boy. Why are you givin' that to me?"

"For gas. Since you're drivin' me to Tennessee to see Miriam, I want you to have the birthday money she sent me."

"Nate, I don't want your money."

"Don't you know the sayin', 'Never look a gift horse in the mouth'?"

"Look at ya, usin' my own words back on me. And talkin' like a grown-up agin." He pretended to be surprised. "Seriously, Nate, this is about fifteen dollars too much for gas money. I should be able to get across the mountain and back on one tank."

"I want you to have it anyway, Smithy," I said. "I appreciate all you've done for me. If you don't need it all for gas on this trip, save it for your next trip."

We hemmed and hawed over it a bit more, but eventually I convinced him to take the money. It felt good, paying Smithy back for his kindness and charity—it added a little sweetness to help cut all the bitter, the hurt of leaving my house. But then I caught a glimpse of my bedsheet hammock tied between the sourwood trees as we backed out of the driveway, and I went back to longing for the impossible, to be in two places at one time.

We made our way to the highway, listening to the radio as the car bumped over the gravel road—first an Elvis song, then Brenda Lee, then Fats Domino. Samson didn't whine or bark, but he kept repositioning himself in the backseat. He stood, turned in a circle, and sat back down again about every half mile, and it almost looked like dancing.

Just outside of Copper Creek, I turned down the radio.

"Smithy, I still feel bad about you giving up your trip for me."

"Aww, ain't nothing."

"But I know how much you were looking forward to it," I insisted.

"I'm on vacation *now*; what are you talkin' 'bout?"

He looked toward me and grinned but saw that I was serious and changed his tone.

"Listen, kid," he said, "I'll still get to go on a vacation. Don't you worry 'bout it."

"But you've been thinking about it for a while, and now I'm afraid you'll have to wait a long time to get the chance, just because of me."

"It won't be that long, Nate, if things work out like I hope." It felt like he had more to say, so I kept my mouth shut and waited. "Nate, I know you aren't too keen on me and your Miss Gentry," he said, "but . . . when I get back from Tennessee, I'm going to ask her to marry me. If I had my druthers, I'd marry her tomorrow."

He paused to make sure I was okay with the news. It surprised me, but I wasn't upset. After seeing how happy Miss Gentry looked during dinner at my house, after hearing her laughter, I knew that Smithy was good enough for her. He was even better than good enough.

"If she says yes, I'll take her on a honeymoon clear to California, if that's what she wants. I know it's soon, Nate, but something happened in the last couple weeks that I sure weren't expectin'. I didn't think I'd ever be ready to settle down, but now it's what I want more than anything."

"I'm really happy for you, Smithy," I said.

"You mean it?"

"Of course I mean it."

I turned the radio back on at the right time to hear Sonny James crooning about "Young Love," and Smithy and I both had a good chuckle.

Near the county line, he stopped for breakfast like he had promised me.

"I can count on one hand how many times I've been inside a restaurant!" I jumped out of the car. I could already smell the sausage and bacon. The early morning air was cool, and we left the windows rolled down partway for Samson while we went inside.

We took a seat in a booth but had no sooner started looking at menus when a voice boomed from across the room. "Well, well, well. Look who it is!"

Smithy looked up. "Big Lou?"

My head spun around at the name, and I recognized the man from the pool hall. Smithy's watch chain hung out of his pocket.

"I plumb forgot that you run this place," Smithy said. Lou stood uncomfortably close to the booth on my side.

Before Smithy could say anything else, Lou put his hand on my shoulder; and leaning on the table with the knuckles of his other hand, he leaned forward and looked at him intently.

"Hey, Smithy, I want to apologize for being a jerk at the pool hall. Especially in front of the kid. I had a few too many, plus it had been a bad day, and, well . . . I'm sorry." Smithy had a blank stare as if he hadn't quite understood what Lou said, so I spoke up for him, and me, too.

"Thanks, Lou. We forgive you," I said. Smithy nodded in agreement.

"Good. Good. Well, what will it be, fellas? Breakfast is on me today," he said.

Smithy grinned from ear to ear and hurriedly checked the menu. I already knew I wanted biscuits and gravy with a side of bacon and some orange juice. Big Lou took a notepad from his apron pocket to write down our order.

"Son, what was your name again?" he asked me. "I'm bad with names."

"I'm Nate, sir," I said.

"Yeah, this here's Bert's kid." Smithy waved a hand toward me as he looked up from his menu momentarily.

"Wait! *You're Bert's* Nate?" Big Lou's eyes got big, and I suddenly realized where I was.

The diner! The one Dell told me about!

"Your pa talked about you all the time," Big Lou said. I could hardly believe my ears. "He always talked about how smart you are."

"He did?"

"Yeah, I mean, that is . . . when he talked at all. He stayed shut up like a clam most of the time, but if he said anything at all it was about his boy."

I felt like I had suddenly been warped to another dimension, where Bert was more like Mr. Pennywell than the Bert I knew.

"Yeah, I hated to see him go." He slid into the booth beside me like we were old friends. "He was the best cook I ever had. Kept the kitchen neat as a pin. And he was a hard worker, too. Do you know what you want yet, Smithy?"

While Smithy gave Big Lou his order, I sat on my hands, rocking back and forth ever so slightly in my seat. It was almost more than I could handle, waiting to hear more about Bert. Big Lou got up and carried our ticket over to the window.

"Yeah, that Bert sure was a hard worker," he said. "Never missed a shift, even when he had worked a double for the railroad."

The second job! That's it! I thought. *He did something for the railroad! He worked two jobs, and that's why he was always gone. Maybe he was just too tired to talk to me.*

"Do you know where he went?" I blurted out anxiously. Big Lou looked confused.

"Naw, just said he was takin' another job. That was it."

Disappointment consumed me. I had found a big piece of the puzzle, but there were still too many pieces missing.

Our food came, and we ate hurriedly to get back to Samson and back on the road. My belly was full, and my mind was racing as Smithy steered the car back onto the highway. *Next stop, Aunt Miriam,* I thought.

"Do you need me to help navigate?" I asked about half an hour into the trip. The engine pulled hard against gravity as we went further still up and across the Smokies. "I can read a map pretty well."

"Not for a while. This is the only way to go until we start heading back down the other side. It's a long way yet."

"Okay. Just let me know." I laid my head back against the seat and closed my eyes. I wasn't tired, just trying to settle myself. I was already the furthest away from home I had ever been.

Without warning, Smithy's arm slapped me hard on the chest, and the car jolted to the right. At the same time, Smithy gave a sort of shriek—the tone of it blended in with the sound of the Patsy Cline song on the radio. Samson, who had been napping in the back seat, barked at the sudden movement.

Smithy had jerked the wheel just slightly enough to miss the semi-truck that had crossed the center line, but enough to miss steering us into the rock face where the mountain had been dynamited to build the road. I barely saw the eighteen-wheeler at all, but I got a glimpse of Smithy's face before the car straightened back out. Genuine panic was plastered all over it. He breathed out hard.

Smithy didn't stop the car, but he slowed down, way below the speed limit as he tried to calm himself. I didn't say anything, but my face was pinched up in panic like his. I looked back to make sure Samson was okay. He was sitting up in the seat, on full alert. I reached back and let him lick my hand.

As soon as it looked like Smithy was finally calm, he got riled up. "That son of a . . . !" he fumed. He smacked the top of the steering wheel hard with his palms.

I sat back in my seat and whispered a prayer of thanks that we made it through the danger safely; then a heaviness settled in my gut, and my limbs went tingly. I felt something pulling at me from every direction. After about a mile, I gave in.

"Smithy, what do you think would have happened if we woulda hit that truck?" I asked.

"I *know* what woulda happened. We wouldn't be here anymore."

"Yeah, I know *that*. But don't you think . . . we'd still be *somewhere*? Even if we weren't *here*?" I tried to make my words gentle, like a soap bubble landing on a sponge.

He was confused only briefly. "Oh, don't start that with me, Nate. I don't want to hear it."

I didn't say any more, but I prayed that he wouldn't forget the question.

The scenery on the journey helped me get over the near-crash quickly. I didn't close my eyes anymore, but rather studied the landscape as we journeyed further up the mountain. I spotted two deer through the woods, not far off the highway. Even more interesting, I saw straight ahead of us in the distance, where the road curved sharply to the left, a tree that grew nearly perpendicular to the ground, in the middle of a giant wall of stone. *That's not just a little weed in that rock!* I thought. "Hey, look at that tree, Smithy!" I said. "Look how it's growing out of the mountain like that!"

"Yes, sir! That's something!" he said. "It's gotta have mighty strong roots to do that."

We rounded the curve, and I turned in my seat to get a last look at the tree.

"So, you gettin' excited?" Smithy asked. "We're about halfway there."

"Yeah. And just a little nervous."

"What do you think she's going to be like? How do you picture her?"

"Well, in my head, her voice sounds like Miss Gentry's," I admitted. "And the only way I can picture her is lookin' like my mama. And she sings like Opal."

"I bet she'll cook for you, just like Opal. I bet she makes a good apple pie. Whaddaya bet?"

"Yeah, but not as good as Opal's."

"Of course not. But real close."

"Do you think you'll have a bedroom just to yourself? Like, what if she's got these pet goats that stay inside, and she wants you to bunk with them?" Smithy knew how I needed to handle the uncertainty—with humor and imagination.

"What if there is no Aunt Miriam?" I countered. "What if that box of letters was planted there by the Russians! I bet it's all a conspiracy to lure me away from Copper Creek because there's going to be a big railroad heist, and they needed me far enough away from the train depot not to bust the bad guys."

Smithy laughed, and I knew I had outdone him in the imagination game.

"Well, I guess we'll find out soon enough," he said.

Chapter Twenty-Eight

THE MEETING

THE HILLS BEGAN TO CHANGE around us. I couldn't feel the car going downward anymore, and the land around continued to get noticeably flatter. Not flat, but flatter. My stomach felt queasy from the windy descent, like I imagined a roller coaster would do, but with less excitement.

There was no "Welcome to Topknot" sign to greet us, but the atlas told us we were there by the names of the roads we passed. I checked every fine line on the map, making sure the names matched the signs. Had we blinked, we would have surely missed the town altogether. We'd been in the car for nearly four hours and hadn't seen a gas station or a business of any other kind for at least thirty miles. Then Smithy spotted the road that would lead us just a couple miles further through the rolling countryside and to Miriam. My stomach tightened more and more as we got closer. I recognized landmarks that Miriam had described in her letter, and I felt sicker still, even more than from the winding roads.

The mailbox at the end of the driveway was white, but curly pieces of peeling paint clung all around the box, letting the gray wood underneath peek through. The car turned onto the gravel drive, which had its own road sign. *Dooley Trail.*

Ornamental trees dotted one side of the long, private road. An open field of tall grass was to the other side. Vegetation sprouted up here and there in the driveway, too strong to be held down by the weight of the sparse gravel. I felt a strange kinship with each stubborn plant that found itself for a split-second in the car's shadow.

The sights didn't change for a quarter of a mile, until we drove across a little wooden bridge over a narrow creek, and the house came into view.

The white farmhouse was bigger than almost all the houses I had ever seen in Copper Creek. *Much too big for one person*, I thought, baffled. The covered porch went down two full sides of the house and had ornately carved brackets that hugged every post. There weren't any pretty hanging baskets of flowers like on the Nelsons' porch, though.

The house was hidden away from view of any neighbors, tucked between two giant hills. The front yard sloped downward until it met the creek.

Smithy pulled the car right up close to the house and turned off the engine. I took a deep breath, stepped out of the car, stretched my limbs which had been still and confined for too long, then I opened the back door on my side to let Samson out. He jumped down and made straight for a crepe myrtle to relieve himself, then came back to my side, waiting patiently for my next move.

My feet were frozen within a foot of the car. I tilted my head backward to inspect the gables and windows of the second story. The place looked like something from a painting, a rugged beauty that managed to hold to most of its original grandeur, despite the abuse of weather and time.

"Would you look at this place!" Smithy said as we both surveyed the house. "I'd say you've got it made, Nate!"

"It sure is pretty," I agreed.

I moved at last, reaching to get my suitcase out of the car, but Smithy stopped me. "Let's just go in. I'll get it later."

There wasn't a soul around to greet us, as far as we could tell. The whole place was still. Not even a breeze stirred.

"Come on," Smithy said. "Let's do this." He seemed anxious himself, but he placed his hand gently on my back and led me to the house and up the front steps. I reached into the pocket of my blue jeans and felt for the car Patrick gave me for my birthday. Nervously, I rolled one of the car's back wheels under my thumb.

The house was dark inside, but the front door stood open. Through the wooden framed screen door, we saw a figure in the shadows of the front hallway.

"Please come in." The figure's tiny voice called to us before we had a chance to knock or say hello.

Smithy went first, opening the screen and taking two steps inside. He made me feel safe, even though I knew there was no reason to feel otherwise.

Samson and I stepped in behind Smithy, and the voice spoke again.

"Oh, Nathaniel! Is it really you?" the woman squeaked out. "I mean . . . Nate."

From the shadows, she rolled herself into the patch of light that edged into the house from the door.

A wheelchair. She's in a wheelchair.

She was a tiny woman. One of the first things I noticed, other than the surprise of her handicap, was her wrists. Lying limp across the armrest of the chair, they were impossibly small, even smaller than mine. And I could tell that if she were able to stand, she wouldn't have been much taller than me. She looked like a little porcelain doll seated on a shelf, with a mop of curly fire-red hair piled up on her head and fancy, but outdated, clothes. She was like a doll that had been put up just to be looked at, instead of taken down and held.

"I've waited so long for you." Her voice was breathy and weak.

I barely managed to reply hello. My heartbeat was a rapidly repeating, uncomfortable thud that made my chest hurt. All I had imagined about or planned for the moment was wiped out of my mind, and it was as if I had just learned I had an aunt for the first time all over again.

Miriam seemed in a trance. Her eyes fixed on mine until I had to look away, overwhelmed by the intensity of her stare.

"Hi, ma'am." Smithy spoke in his most charming voice. "I'm Nate's friend, Rodney Smithson. Most people call me Smithy. It's a pleasure to meet you."

She was shaken from her stupor and politely accepted Smithy's extended hand in greeting. She turned to me again, and I worked up the courage to approach the chair. Samson let out a concerned whine.

I put both of my arms around the stranger's shoulders, and I put the side of my face close to hers, instinctively. She reached both her arms around me in return, and she wept. She wept long and loud and without shame. And I stayed there in her embrace, surprised, but not embarrassed, until she quieted. When I pulled back, I saw the same eyes as Bert's staring back at me with something in them I couldn't remember ever seeing in his before.

"Eleven years old," she said, looking me up and down. "I've been waiting eleven years to meet you. Longer, counting the time that we knew your mother was expecting." A warm smile crept across her pale face, as if a sweet memory had been unlocked. "You're even more handsome than I imagined." Her tears had dried, and she wore a smile.

"I'm glad to finally meet you," I said. "Should I call you Aunt Miriam? Or something else?"

"Aunt Miriam is perfect."

She looked at Samson and beamed. "And you brought a dog!"

Her level of excitement to have Samson in her home surprised me, and I was relieved that she didn't mind. I introduced them, and she reached a shaky arm out toward him. Samson came to sniff at her hand.

"He's magnificent!" she said. "The three of you, follow me, please."

She turned the wheelchair around and rolled down the wide hallway to the first room on the right. To the left side of the hallway, in the very middle of the house, was a set of stairs that looked to be as wide as Smithy's boat of a car.

We went through the double doorway and entered a room that reminded me of Dell and Opal's parlor, only much bigger. It was a formal sitting room with fancy furniture. She pointed for me and Smithy to have a seat on a funny-looking, velvety red couch with only one arm, and we did as she instructed. Samson laid down in front of me and Smithy, between us and Miriam, with his head resting on my shoes.

"Nate, I'm so glad you came." She reached her hands toward mine and grabbed them both firmly. "I've missed my brother for so long, and I see a lot of him in you." I could only smile and let her study my face while I searched hers as well, looking for traits other than small stature that might bear proof to the bond we shared.

She was older than Smithy, but younger than Dell and Opal. Her skin was much lighter than mine, but I couldn't tell if she was naturally pale or just preferred to stay out of the sun. I didn't find much at all that was familiar in her features, but the piercing gray eyes so much like Bert's and our shared smallness were proof enough of our kinship. Had it not been for the years of loneliness, Miriam would have been beautiful.

"I have always dreamed of meeting my only nephew!" She took her hands back and clasped them together tightly, her voice much stronger than when she greeted us. "I have to know everything about you!"

I was ready to answer, to tell her the first few things that came to mind, things I thought she would be interested to know. But she changed the subject before I could speak.

"How is my Bertram?" she asked. "What can you tell me about him?"

"Bertram?" I stumbled on the unfamiliar name.

"I think she means Bert," Smithy helped out.

"Oh . . . " I didn't know how to answer.

"Mr. Smithson, thank you so much for bringing him to me," she said, changing the subject again. "I truly am grateful." Miriam seemed to fill with life each second we sat there, but her hands still trembled.

"It was my pleasure, ma'am," he said.

The meeting wasn't like anything I had pictured in my head. But I felt drawn to the fragile woman.

"You have a very lovely home. Do you live alone here?" Smithy asked.

"Yes. Ever since my housekeeper died. Well, she was more like a nurse. And she was my best friend. Augusta looked after Bertram and me when we were children. And she looked after me until she died, the day after Thanksgiving last year."

"I'm sorry to hear that, ma'am," Smithy said.

"Before then, my father lived here with us, too, until he died. But a very, very long time ago, it was the five of us—Mother, Father, Bertram, me, and Augusta."

I suddenly realized I had no plan for explaining to Aunt Miriam why I had decided to visit when I did. I had no idea how to tell her that Bert had left me. But Smithy was there to handle all the hard things. Just like at the conference with Miss Gentry, I marveled at his charisma. He was so much more than the former thieving one-man-band I knew him to be.

"Miss Dooley, I know you and Nate have a lot to learn about one another," Smithy said.

"We certainly do," she said, and she reached out and gently patted my knee.

"I . . . I guess you're wondering why I drove the boy out here to visit."

"Well, I'm so happy to see him, I'm not too worried about the whys and hows. But will you be staying here for a while, too, Mr. Smithson? With Nate and me?"

"I'd like to, if that's okay with you. Nate is a good friend, and he has really been looking forward to coming to visit you. I'd like to stay with him to make sure he . . . well, to make sure he feels comfortable here in a new place."

It made me feel like a baby, needing Smithy there. But I did need him. I couldn't imagine being dropped off there and left, not knowing what to expect.

"I understand. And it's more than fine. He's lucky to have a friend to look after him," she said. "You're both welcomed to stay here as long as you want. I have my groceries delivered every week. There's plenty to eat; and as you can see, there's more than enough room."

Hope flooded her eyes, probably for the first time in years, and I heard it in her voice, too. "Nate, I think you will really like it here. I believe you will."

I wanted to like it. I wanted to like her. It was just much too early to tell about either.

"Why don't I show you around," she said. "We can talk about how long you'll be staying later." Her voice was equal parts happy and desperate, with a distinct southern sweetness, and every word she spoke carried the slightest hint that she might fall to sobbing again at any moment.

Each room in the house was large and lavishly decorated, at least by my standards. She wheeled, and we followed, room after room. She showed us the galley kitchen that took up half of the back side of the ground floor, and the screened porch that occupied most of the other half except the little room with an electric washing machine in it. Next, we saw the two downstairs bedrooms—hers and the other one across the hall that had been Augusta's.

Miriam's room was the smaller of the two. The four-poster bed in the center of the room was close to the floor and covered with a colorful patchwork quilt. We only peeked inside, but I noticed two framed photographs on the dresser. One was a portrait of a dark-skinned woman with a round face and smiling eyes. The other was of a man and a woman and a little girl and a little boy, standing in front of a church with a tall, skinny steeple.

Samson followed close behind as we continued the tour. He sniffed the floors and walls, like a hound on the hunt, inspecting his new surroundings. He let out a loud sneeze and shook his head from side to side.

Miriam's voice turned sheepishly quiet again. "I'm sorry for all the dust," she said. "I haven't had anyone to come in and just do a good clean-up in a while."

"It's okay," I whispered. "We don't mind it."

She led us to a den that had three matching sofas positioned in a semi-circle in front of a large color console television. I hadn't imagined that my new home, at least temporarily, might have a television.

"Does it work?" I asked excitedly.

She laughed. "Yes, of course, it works. And to be honest, it is a great company to me. I think I might have just gone crazy here alone without my shows to watch. Augusta and I used to love to watch our stories together. Now all those characters keep me company by themselves." It was another thing we had in common—our most-kept company wasn't really there.

When she left the room, my eyes were still fixed on the television. I itched to turn it on. Smithy chuckled quietly, knowing how excited I was about the set. I followed Aunt Miriam out of the room reluctantly.

We had made a circle of the downstairs of the house and came back to where we started, to the staircase that led to the second floor.

"Well, you'll be sleeping up there, and I'm sorry I can't help you get settled in. I know it will be dusty, and you are sure to find some spiderwebs in the corners; but I hope that, otherwise, it's comfortable. It should be just as Augusta left it."

"So, you never go up there?" I asked.

"Not much since I was a little girl. My father used to carry me up there sometimes, to look out the windows with better views. But, no, I've not been up there very many times at all. You'll have it all to yourselves."

"Nate, I'll go get our things from the car," Smithy said. "Then we'll go find our rooms. You can stay here."

Miriam, Samson, and I waited there alone, and she fixed her eyes on me intently as she had done before, as if she were not just seeing *me* for the first time, but as if she had never seen a little boy at all. It made me uncomfortable, and I tried to avoid meeting her gaze.

Smithy came back with our things, and we headed upstairs. "Just pick whatever room you want, and come back down whenever you have settled in," she called up the stairs. Her breathing was fast, and I wondered if her health could handle the excitement of guests.

Smithy and I found rooms beside one another, just as fancy as the downstairs. We didn't pay much attention to how each of the rooms was different from the others or which one was the best. We just took the rooms closest to the stairs, out of the four available. The other two rooms were on the opposite side. The wall that connected the two sides had a doorway to a bathroom with a clawfoot tub in it. Opposite the bathroom, a balcony with black iron railings overlooked the dining room.

I didn't unpack anything. While Smithy checked out his room, I spent my time sitting on the edge of the bed, praying. I had finally come to the right understanding about talking to God—He wasn't too busy for me, and He actually listened.

"Show me where I belong, Lord," I prayed. "Is it here? Help me figure out where You want me."

Smithy and I rejoined Miriam, who was in the middle of making us lunch. I was impressed by her ability to get around in the kitchen, despite her chair. While Smithy helped her finish the sandwiches, I called Opal and Dell, with Miriam's permission. The telephone was in the living room, the same room as the television. I spoke to them both, only briefly, just to let them know I was safe. And I promised to call again before a week had passed.

I retrieved Samson's food and bowls from the car, so he could eat with us on the screened back porch. After the initial awkwardness of the meeting, it felt good to relax and enjoy a meal together—my first ever meal with both a family member and a friend. The beauty and warmth of May surrounded us.

My aching for answers that didn't come soon overshadowed the pleasantness of lunch. All afternoon and evening, the subjects of why I was there without Bert and the box of letters that led me there didn't come up. As if there was no reason at all to talk about why Miriam and I had never laid eyes on one another until I was eleven, the conversation was ordinary and unproductive.

Miriam did most of the talking about things like the architecture of the house, her favorite television shows, the weather, and Augusta. And she asked Smithy lots of questions. I learned more about him than I did about Miriam or the rest of my family. I felt like the donkey chasing a carrot dangling from a string right in front of him, never able to catch it.

The missing pieces of my story were still missing at bedtime. As we split off at the top of the stairs to go to our separate rooms, Smithy seemed to know what I was thinking.

"Give it time, Nate," he said. "We just got here."

I laid down in bed, leaving the door open, and Samson jumped up beside me. I squeezed him tightly, and he nuzzled my neck. In his canine wisdom, he understood my heart.

I missed Opal's voice, and her company, and having the blankets pulled up close to my chin. I couldn't remember much about the love of a mother, except what I had experienced for just a few weeks in her care. And now it was gone.

I couldn't help but be sad. *If I stay here with Aunt Miriam, she'll never be able to tuck me into bed like Opal did,* I thought. Then I felt guilty. *It's not just about me,* I reminded myself.

Chapter Twenty-Nine

ENLIGHTENMENT

I SLEPT SOUNDLY UNDER AUNT Miriam's roof; and when I woke up on Sunday morning, for a moment, I didn't know where I was. The sun flooded through the window and washed the whole room in a radiant glow, from the dusty wooden floorboards to the sharp angle of the vaulted ceiling. I blinked and rubbed the long slumber from my eyes, feeling for Samson in the pillowy bedspread that covered the large expanse of bed. I found him beside me, still sleeping. The brightness of the light, plus a faint call coming from downstairs, meant I wouldn't be going back to sleep. But illumination was coming in more ways than a late May daybreak.

"Nate, come on down, please!" Miriam's voice bounced off the wooden stairs. "Nate?"

Samson jumped at the sound of her quiet urgency, and he waited for me to dress. I slid my hand down the banister as I went down the stairs, suddenly wide awake with curiosity.

"Good morning, Aunt Miriam."

"Good morning, Nate. Oh, how I do love hearing you call me that. Child, listen," she lowered her voice even more. "I want to talk to you. Why don't we let Samson out back, and we can talk on the porch before breakfast? How does that sound?" She was more focused than the day before—steadier and confident.

"Yes, ma'am."

I walked outside with Samson while she waited on the long porch, never taking her eyes off me. Samson didn't seem the least bit skittish in his new environment, just excited. There were plenty of new sounds and smells for him to discover, which meant his morning constitutional took longer than normal. "Hurry up, boy," I said under my breath, anxious to hear what Miriam had to say.

Samson finally finished, and we came back inside, where I gave him his breakfast.

"You take such good care of your pet," Miriam said.

"Well, he's been taking good care of me, too, so it's only fair."

"Come here and sit down, Nathaniel." She motioned to the cushion-covered wicker chair next to her wheelchair.

"I'm sorry if I acted strangely yesterday," she said. "I know there is a lot we should talk about, but I just wanted to enjoy your company on our first day together before we talked about . . . the difficult things."

Relief washed over me. She did understand. She had only been procrastinating. At last, I would have answers. But both of us had to feel our way around first to figure out the questions.

"I guess you know that your father and I haven't spoken very often over the years," she said.

"Yes, ma'am."

"Although I've tried . . . "

"I know."

"What *do* you know, Nate?" she said. "Maybe that will help me."

"Aunt Miriam, I know Bert is sick." It wasn't what I had wanted to say, but it spilled out before I knew it. "He's got something wrong with him that won't let him be like other fathers. I don't know what it is, but he's always been that way. And whatever it is, I guess that's why he won't come visit you or answer your letters."

"You know about my letters?"

"Yes, ma'am." I dropped my head. "Your letters are how I found out about you. I didn't know I had an aunt until just a few weeks ago. I've never known anything at all about my family, or where I came from, until I found a box of letters in his room."

It came out then—how Bert had left me and how I had found the box of letters when I was looking for medicine after having been so sick for several days, about how my teacher found out I was alone.

"Oh, you poor dear," she said, sounding as if her heart could break. "And that's why you're here. You need a place to stay? You need to live here with me?" She seemed hopeful.

"That's part of it. If I don't have family to stay with, I'll have to let the county decide what happens to me. But it's also because I want to know about my parents. About you and my grandparents. I want to know why Bert is the way he is."

"You call your father Bert?" she asked, surprised.

I nodded, hoping she understood it wasn't disrespect, but just how things had always been.

"Okay, Nate," she said softly. "I understand you need answers. And so do I. I've lost many years with my baby brother, and my sweet sister-in-law, and you. Maybe we can help each other put together the pieces."

She relaxed back in her chair, smoothing out the crocheted blanket she kept draped across her lap, despite the heat. I leaned forward in my chair with my elbows on my knees and my chin resting on my fists. Her words flowed out, slow and smooth, as she told me everything she thought I might want or need to know, and I drank it in like water in the desert.

"You're right about your father. He has some challenges. He always has. I'm not sure what to call it. I don't know if it has a name. Our father was a doctor; and he treated Bertram with medication when he lived at home, and it helped him cope. You see, Nate . . . your father is a very, very smart person. Some might say too smart. Smart in a way that makes it hard for him to relate to people of average intelligence, like me. He could have gone to college wherever he wanted, but there were some things that stopped him."

"What were they?"

"Well, his challenges for one—the trouble he has with people. And he could never stand for things to be out of order. It nearly drove him mad to walk in and see a dirty dish in the kitchen sink." My mind swirled as I thought about my own habits, how I couldn't stand for my clothes to get too dirty and how I liked things to be just a certain way. *Am I like Bert?* I thought.

"And going away to college seemed it would be too much for him to handle," she continued. "Plus, he hated schoolwork. As smart as he was, he hated putting pen to paper. But mostly, it was because he fell helplessly in love with your mother and didn't want to be anywhere but with her." I thought of Opal's story, about giving up her dream of working in a museum to be a mountain farmer's wife.

"He and Deborah wanted to marry, but Father was against it. He wanted Bertram here, where he could protect him. But Bertram made up his mind that he didn't need medication or our parents or me. He thought your mama was the only medicine he needed." She lost her thoughts for a moment, staring through the screen on the porch at the waving branches of a willow tree. I had to say her name to reset her.

"Then the war started," she picked back up. "He was still too young to serve, and he wasn't fit anyway. But when he heard they needed workers to build the big hydroelectric dam over in Carolina, he saw his chance to marry and to help the country. He and Deborah left Topknot together just before he turned eighteen."

My parents moved away for love, I thought. *I wasn't planted in Copper Creek for no good reason. I didn't wind up there just because.*

"I know that place, where he worked! It's not too far from Copper Creek. I did a report on it for school! I made an 'A' on it," I said. I felt embarrassed that I'd said the last part, but she smiled and made her eyes wide to say she was proud of me.

"He wrote to us all the time at first." Miriam sighed deeply. "He seemed happy. The company housed the both of them in Fontana Village, and he made a good living and didn't even have to do the hard labor. No, he showed them he had the mind of an engineer, even if he didn't have the degree for it. After the dam was finished, they bought a house somewhere in the next county from a friend he had met on the job. Bert found other work, but not as an engineer. He did a little of this and that, and your mother did odd jobs for money, too. It was a much harder life than he was used to, but I believe he was happy. Truly happy. And I couldn't blame him for leaving. He still wrote to us after they moved to Copper Creek, and I wrote to him, too, of course. But Father refused to even read his letters. He never forgave him for leaving. They weren't very far away at all, just over the mountain. But we never made plans to visit."

For the first time since she began recounting our family's story, Miriam looked as if she might cry. Samson heard her sadness and got up from in front of the screen door and came to sit beside her, resting his head in her lap. The surprise of his gesture kept the tears from falling, and she stroked his fur as she continued the tale.

"Eventually, the letters came only to me, and we didn't talk about Bertram much here at home anymore. The day he sent me your baby picture in the mail, I cried. I wanted so much to go to you. But I couldn't drive, and I was afraid to ask Father to take me."

"What about my mother? Does my mother have family here?"

"Deborah didn't have much family to speak of, and what family she did have didn't treat the poor thing very well. Your mother came from nothing. And that's another reason Father wasn't pleased about their marriage. But, oh, she was such a good girl! She had the most peaceful spirit. And the most amazing faith of anyone I ever knew. She prayed all the time, about everything. I never understood where she got that kind of faith. But I understood why Bertram was drawn to her. Something about her settled him. It was like he was a different person when he was with her."

It was my favorite moment of all since getting to Topknot—hearing Aunt Miriam, someone who had seen my mama in the flesh and knew her, actually knew her, talk about her so glowingly and to have proof that she was every bit as good as my memories told me she was.

Smithy stirred around upstairs, and Miriam tensed up, like she didn't want to share our family's story with someone who wasn't part of it. And she looked tired from the energy spent recalling and reliving the past. The talking and the feeling had taken a toll.

"Are you okay?" I asked.

"Yes, I'll be fine, sweet Nathaniel. But I should probably share with you that I have challenges of my own." She paused for a long time, a mix of worry and shame on her face.

"I haven't left this house in seven years," she forced out quickly. "Not been further than the porches. Not even into my own yard."

"Miriam, that's terrible!"

"Maybe. But it's really how I've wanted it. I used to go out; but about two years before my father passed, he turned very frail and couldn't help me into the car anymore. Then I got used to not going out; and over time, I've preferred it. I want it this way. Do you understand? The thought of leaving now just makes me ill. Like I said, I have some challenges of my own. I suppose we all do."

"But, Aunt Miriam, Bert should have come back for you, to help you. Maybe y'all could have helped each other. Aren't you mad at him, that he stopped writing? That he didn't come back when your father died?"

"Oh, he does write. Once a year. On my birthday. It's the only thing about growing older that I enjoy." Her voice trailed off into a whisper of self-pity, and her eyes looked at me but didn't see me.

After a moment, she came back to me. "Of course, I'm still hurt," she said, "and I'm sad that I lost him, but I'm not mad. I understood a long time ago that it's part of his illness, part of the same abominable thing that kept me here in this house instead of going to him!" She dropped her head and fiddled with the blanket. "I'm sorry, Nate." She pulled a breath all the way up from her lifeless toes. "I'm actually mad at myself . . . that I couldn't get over it. I'm mad for not hiring someone to drive me across that mountain and get me to you and to him. If I had gone right after your mama died, maybe you'd still have your sister."

"You know about Colleen?" I was overjoyed. Having someone else that knew she existed made her more real, and Aunt Miriam and I had another thing in common. I stood up and leaned on the windowsill, letting the tip of my nose brush against the screen.

"Yes, he told me about her. Right after he gave her away was when he stopped writing, except the once per year. Nate, please understand. He was already a damaged man; but after your mama died, he broke. The sickness has always been in his mind, but now it's in his heart, too, and I don't know which one of them is worse."

So much made sense to me, and I felt the most grown-up I had ever felt in my eleven years, figuring out such grown-up things. For a long time, I thought the world was made of three groups of people—the mean ones, the ones that didn't care, and the nice ones. But I was wrong. There was a fourth group of people—the ones that wanted to care but just couldn't. That's where Bert fell in.

"What about your mother and father, my grandparents? What were they like?"

"Nate, like you, my mother died when I was young. The same polio that crippled me took her life. But I know she was a good mother. My daddy's name was John Thomas Dooley. Everyone called him Doctor John Thomas, no matter where he went."

He had two disciple names like me, I thought.

"He was a good man, even though he held such resentment toward Bertram. And he did love us very much. But when we were young, he was away much of the time. He worked hard to make sure his children had a comfortable home and an easy future. He succeeded in that, Nate. I have plenty of money in the bank, which means I have everything I need here. Everything except the things that matter the most."

Smithy's big boots clip-clopped on the staircase. It was about an hour after sunrise, and he followed his nose to the pot of coffee that Miriam had put on to brew in the kitchen. He helped himself to a large, porcelain mug from the cabinet and filled it with the steamy coffee, then found Miriam, Samson, and me on the porch.

He leaned against the doorframe and watched us while he sipped the coffee. Miriam and I sat, each holding a side of the large, leather-bound album she had me retrieve from the coffee table in the living room, and we admired the pictures together. She flipped through the pages, naming people and events I'd only ever imagined. I saw that I had my Grandpa Dooley's chin, and that I looked a whole like Bert did when he was a kid. My Grandma Dooley, whose name I learned was Roseanna, was a tiny woman like Miriam. The gene for small stature had skipped Bert but had obviously been passed on to me.

Why did he make me wonder about it all this time? Make me feel like there was something wrong with me because I'm little? Why couldn't he have just told me? Told me that it runs in the family? Told me something? Told me anything?

There were pictures of my grandparents' brothers and sisters, most of which Miriam said were dead. But I was still glad to know about them. Every person in the world that's living and breathing knows they came from somewhere, but seeing just a few of the people who were part of my story made me walk a little taller.

The answers were a long time coming; and after getting most of what I needed from Aunt Miriam, I could finally say that I was happy to be in Topknot, Tennessee, at least for a while. I was happy to be with family.

Chapter Thirty

JUST US TWO

MIRIAM SHUT DOWN LIKE AN engine out of gas, as if sharing our family's story in such detail had left her devoid of any more words to use. The woman who had greeted me at the bottom of the stairs, anxious to talk on Sunday morning, was gone, and a different Miriam sat quietly in front of the television set in the glow of flashing lights, transfixed by a reality that wasn't her own.

I watched television with her all of Sunday afternoon and evening, then half of the next day. She even ate her meals in front of the television. For a while, I forgot about everything else, too. I marveled at the stories played out in pictures right in front of me, stories that made me laugh and made me excited.

I recognized the plots in *Lassie* from stories I had heard from kids at school. *Bonanza* turned out to be my favorite. Aunt Miriam's was *Perry Mason*. Smithy watched with us, too, because there wasn't much else to do indoors and because all three of us really enjoyed the game shows. It was nice to be there together, all relaxed and entertained. Smithy and I stretched out on our own couches, and Miriam didn't mind that Samson joined me on the furniture. But after a while, I grew bored of the screen. I missed the familiarity and comfort of my books. The *National Geographic* articles, that I had read over and over, still held my interest.

I went to my room upstairs and read about the lochs of Scotland and the splendor of Venice. Then I turned to the heroes in my Bible storybook. I read about Abraham, Isaac, Jacob, and more old friends. They were there to keep me company, just like they had done for years.

Late Monday afternoon, I took Samson outside, and we explored the eight acres of land that surrounded the house and belonged to Miriam, the land that she had told me would most likely belong to me one day. It was hard to believe. From my square little house and tiny parcel to all this? Samson and I romped around in the bright sunshine to escape the stuffy house, and I imagined how I might plant potatoes on my very own land one day, like Dell.

We were just out of sight of the house when Smithy's twangy voice rang out across the hills.

"Nate! Where are you? Nate?"

Samson and I looked at one another, then raced back toward the house to see what he wanted. We crested the hill and spotted Smithy standing behind the house, looking around in all directions for us. He waved his arm back and forth high in the air in greeting when he saw us. It didn't seem to be an emergency, so I slowed my pace and waved back, out of breath.

"Listen," Smithy said when I was close enough to hear, "I've decided . . . I . . . um . . . I'm going to head out for a couple days."

"You're leaving me here already? But I'm not ready for you to go!"

"Nate, I've stayed just long enough to make sure it's safe here. At the very least, you're safer here than you were back in Copper Creek living by yourself." He put his hand on my shoulder. "She seems nice, buddy. And I think you and your aunt need time to get to know one another without me around. I'm just gettin' in the way."

I looked down at my feet. I had tried not to think about how hard it would be when Smithy left, and it came sooner than I expected. "Nate, I'll be back in two days. I promise," he said. "I'm just going to go take in a few sights, see what kind of trouble I can get into; then I'll come back." He squeezed my shoulders and flashed the big, mischievous smile.

"How do I know you'll be back?" I asked, my voice cracking.

"Nate, look at me. I didn't drive across the Smoky Mountains just to dump you off and leave you here. I want you to have some say in this, and I won't make you stay if this ain't where you belong. But I think Miriam's a swell lady, and I think you probably ought to plan to stay here. But I'll come back to make sure before I head home."

He stood bent-kneed, ducking from side to side near my face, trying to look me in the eye. "Two days. That's all. Just two days. I'll be back Wednesday evening."

"Okay." I looked up at Smithy and nodded. Staying with Miriam made sense, and I was happy to have found her; but the place was still so new, and having family other than Bert was strange.

"Look, I already packed up and explained what I was doing to Miriam. So, I'll guess I'll just head on out now," Smithy said.

There in the shadow of the big farmhouse, as my eyes were fixed on a dandelion in the ground between my shoes, Smithy got down on his knees and wrapped his lanky arms around my chest. It was just as hard for him to leave me as it was for me to be left. He went from total stranger to loyal, irreplaceable friend so quickly, I knew it was something only God could have done. The way Smithy and I crossed paths seemed a feat no less miraculous than the parting of the Red Sea. And it reminded me just how much God loved me. He would take

care of me, whether I was in Topknot, Tennessee; Copper Creek, North
Carolina; or Kathmandu, Nepal. I wouldn't worry anymore.

Smithy made a fast exit, patting Samson on the head as he left.
"Look after him, boy," he said to my dog, just before the front door
closed. The heavy wooden door made an echoing sound, like the
signal to the start of a new chapter—a new house in a new town
with new family.

Miriam had come out of her television trance and sensed my sadness to see Smithy leave.

"Nate, I know you're going to miss your friend, but, I'm so glad
you're here with me. It's a pretty day. Would you like to sit outside
for a while?"

I agreed and offered to help her push her chair outside. She was
able to get around just fine by herself, but taking the handles of the
chair and guiding it to the porch felt good, like a new sense of purpose.

"Oh, it is nice out here," she said, and she let out a long, peaceful sigh.

"Aunt Miriam?"

"Yes?"

"Do you want me to stay here with you? To live here?" I took a seat
in the white, wooden rocker beside her chair, eye-level with the top
of the porch railing.

"I would like that very much, Nate. We're family. We should be
together."

"I think so, too," I said. We sat in silence for a long time. Samson
ran down the front porch steps and snapped at a butterfly, unfazed
by the talk of big changes.

"Where will I go to school, Aunt Miriam?"

"Oh, school? Well . . . there's a fine little school, not terribly far. Maybe thirty minutes by bus. But, there's no hurry, is there? You can take some time off from your studies. Maybe just stay here with me for a few months; then we can enroll you. I'm sure you'd catch up real fast."

"I'm not sure I can do that. Don't I have to go to school?" I said.

"Well, you know, Nate, children can be very cruel sometimes. Especially to new kids. Did they ever pick on you at your school, you know, for being smaller than the others?"

"Yeah, they did, but it wasn't that . . . "

"Oh, you poor dear. How sad!" she interrupted. Her concern was exaggerated. "Maybe I could hire a private teacher to come here, and you could avoid all that. Wouldn't that be better? I can afford it."

"I still think I might like to meet some kids my age."

"I don't know any children your age, Nate," she said matter-of-factly, "but I bet you'll love to meet our delivery boy. The young man who brings my groceries and medicines and household supplies, he's barely seventeen. Maybe you'll be able to get to know him." Then her eyes got like grapefruits, and she quickly changed the subject. "I know what we should do! Right away! I'll buy you a bicycle. How would you like that? That would be so fun for you! A bicycle will give you a way to explore these hills."

"That might be nice . . . "

I wanted to ask her about going to church, too, but she didn't give me a chance.

"Well, it's settled. That will be your welcome gift. I'll arrange for it right away. And maybe you'd like to have a rifle? Every little boy needs a good rifle. So you can go plinking and hunting?"

"I always wanted to learn how to shoot . . . "

"I haven't cooked venison in a very long time! It would be nice to have some again. I'll even make rabbit stew if you get one. That used to be your father's favorite, believe it or not." She looked out at the yard, letting herself be transported in her memory. "I can't wait to make it for him again." She whispered it faintly, but there was no mistaking what I had heard.

"What do you mean, you're going to cook for Bert again?" I asked.

She tensed up in her chair and grimaced like a child caught stealing a cookie from the jar right before dinner.

"I mean . . . I'll make him rabbit stew when . . . when he comes here looking for you."

"Miriam, I don't know where Bert is or if he will ever go home to Copper Creek. What makes you think he would come looking for me here?"

She looked away and twisted the blanket on her lap. "He wrote to me, Nate."

I turned my head sideways in confusion. "You already knew Bert was gone? The whole time I was telling you about it, you already knew?" I felt betrayed.

"He wrote to me near the end of March and told me his plan. I couldn't believe I actually had a letter from him, and it wasn't even my birthday. He wanted me to know he was leaving the state for a while. He told me he was doing it for you."

"Doing it for me? Doing what?"

"He's been working two jobs and saving money for a long time because he wants you to go to college one day, Nate. His letter talked about how smart you are and how he wants to make sure you get a good education." She took a long pause. "He's on an oil rig down in the

Gulf of Mexico. At least . . . that's what he told me. He said it pays real good money. I know it's hard to understand. But he said he's planning on coming back. I don't know exactly when."

The power bill. The food. It made sense. He had planned ahead, to provide for me for as long as he would be gone. It meant that soon, Bert would return to Copper Creek.

"I need to go back, Aunt Miriam."

"But don't you see, you can have your friend, Smithy, keep an eye out for Bert. Once Bert is home, we'll get a message to him, and he'll come out here to get you. And I . . . I'll finally be able to see my brother again. And maybe, I can convince him to stay here with me, with you and me. And our family can be together! What's left of it . . . "

I got up and paced back and forth, pounding the wooden planks as the urgency in my heart grew.

"No, Aunt Miriam, he won't come for me. You told me yourself, he's sick. He needs help. If he comes home and I'm not there . . . well, I just can't be sure of what he'll do. I just need to go back. I need to be home when Bert comes back. And I bet it won't be long. He paid up the power bill through the end of next month, but he could be coming home sooner than that."

"So, you won't stay with me? When Smithy comes back, you'll leave me here?"

"You can come with us back to Copper Creek! You don't have to stay here alone in this house. There's no reason for both of us to be alone." I got down in her face, my eyes begging her to agree with me.

"But I told you! I haven't left this house in seven years! I can't do it. If I could have ventured that far away from Topknot, I would have done it a long time ago."

"Miriam, I think you can do it. I'll be with you! I'll help you! We can both go back and see Bert."

"I don't know . . . " she said between sobs.

"Miriam, before Mama died, she bought me a book full of Bible stories for children. I've read it over and over, for as long as I've been able to read anything. Do you believe in God?

"Well, yes, I do. But . . . "

"Do you know about Abraham?" She nodded, but the look on her face didn't convince me.

"Listen to me for a minute, please, Aunt Miriam. God sent Abraham on a journey, but He didn't tell him where he was going or what it was going to be like. He just told him to go. And Abraham had faith. He trusted God. You're going to have be like that. I need you to be like Abraham now."

"I can't promise anything, Nate. What I want to do and what I'm able to do are often not the same thing. But for my family, I'll try. I'll try to go back to Copper Creek with you, so we can both be there for Bert when he comes back."

Chapter Thirty-One
THE PAIN OF LOSS

JUST BEFORE DUSK, I TOOK Samson outside. A bat swooped down too close to me, and I jumped. The air was still, and except for the occasional, faint flapping of bat wings, it was quiet out.

Samson sniffed around the yard, searching for a suitable spot to do his business. He hadn't yet found his regular place at Aunt Miriam's house. Back in Copper Creek, he had much less yard to consider and had made the left corner near the wood line his normal spot to visit.

I talked to him while he searched. "We're headed home soon, Samson," I said. "I bet you'll be so happy to see Opal, and Dell, and Patrick. And I know they'll be happy to see you."

He finally settled on a spot near a wild little tree that had sprouted up from a squirrel's forgotten acorn, and I placed my hand on the banister of the back-porch steps to head back inside. I was anxious to get to my room and jump into stories of faraway places and times.

From across the long yard, at the edge of the woods, came a faint sound. I thought at first that it was another dog. I froze, listening carefully, and Samson went on point. It started as a low-pitched whine, then changed to a guttural, spine-chilling growl. I couldn't see the animal in the shadows, but Samson suddenly charged toward the trees to fend off whatever had made the growl. My heart plummeted into my stomach at the sound of eight paws pounding leaves as one animal pursued another.

I yelled, knowing there was no one to help me; then I ran, calling out to Samson to come back. I ran as fast as my short legs would take me, all the way into the woods, but I stopped before the lights from the house were out of view. It was no use. The sky had just melted from gray into black, and I could no longer hear them running. I had no idea which way Samson might have gone. I sat down on the forest floor and cried in fear and panic. Not too much at first, because I had hope that Samson would bound toward me any minute, wagging his tail proudly and waiting for praise for having banished the threat. I sat there waiting, with my knees hugged up to my chest, rocking back and forth. But he didn't come.

I stayed on the ground in those woods for half an hour or more, waiting, listening, calling his name over and over. I wondered if Miriam could hear my yells over the sound of the television. When she finally came out to the porch and called my name, I had no choice but to go back to the house without my dog, and it made me cry harder than I could remember ever crying before, the kind of sobbing that leaves you exhausted and achy in the chest.

Miriam's face melted into pity and reflected a measure of my pain when I told her what had happened.

"It must have been a coyote," I said. "He was trying to protect me. That's the only reason Samson would run away. He wouldn't just leave me."

She tried to reassure me that Samson would be back soon, but I didn't want to talk. I made my way up the stairs and lay down alone, a heavy weight upon my chest and a kind of emptiness I had never felt. When Mama died, I was too little to understand what I had lost.

When Bert left, there was too much resentment standing in the way of me being very sad. But seeing Samson run off into the dark night and not knowing when or if he would come back, it wrecked me worse than the loss of my parents.

"God, I don't ask you for a whole lot of things!" I yelled within myself. "But I need my dog back! I need to know that he's okay. You gave him to me! Please don't take him away." I remembered the story of Job and all he had. *The Lord gave, and the Lord hath taken away; blessed be the name of the Lord.* Then I didn't know anything else. I had cried myself to sleep.

The next morning was a gully washer. The rain came down in sheets that couldn't make up their mind what direction they wanted to blow in. I put on my boots, and Miriam found an old umbrella for me. Along with a motherly word of caution to not go too far, she wished me good luck as I went out the door. At least in the daylight, I had a chance of finding him.

My feet pounded the muddy ground on a mission, in the direction of where I thought Samson had gone. I recalled a picture from my Bible storybook. It was a beautiful image of the Good Shepherd, the One who left his ninety-nine sheep in the fold and went out in search of the one who was lost.

The one who is lost. Lord, help me find the one who is lost.

Deeper into the woods I went. The canopy of the trees shielded me from the soaking rain only in small measure. The rain wasn't cold, but it stung as it blew underneath the umbrella and bounced off my cheeks.

Bert is like a lost sheep, too, isn't he? I thought. Then I prayed. *He's just lost. Find him, Lord. Please find him.*

I picked my knees up high with each step to avoid getting stuck in the mud. There wasn't much distance between my feet and knees, so I couldn't afford to sink far. My movement reminded me of a march, and I pushed myself forward by singing Opal's marching song.

"Over the hills and o'er the main,

To Flanders, Portugal and Spain,

The queen commands and we'll obey

Over the hills and far away."

I walked for what seemed like hours. Over hills and into valleys, across open fields of tall grasses, and into thick woods. I tried my best to keep my bearings, to remember the way I had come. But when my legs were so tired I thought they wouldn't carry me anymore, I feared I had gotten too turned around to find my way back.

I prayed again. It hadn't worked for finding Samson. God hadn't brought me my dog. But I hoped it would at least work to get me back to Aunt Miriam's house. "I need You to lead me the right way, God," I said out loud.

The rain stopped; and as if waiting for its cue, the sun rolled out from behind a cloud almost immediately. I was soaked to the bone, despite the umbrella, and the warmth of the sun gave a small amount of relief.

My walk back to Aunt Miriam's house took half as long as my search for Samson had taken. For the whole time I was gone, Miriam stayed put in the same spot on the screened porch, watching and waiting and, as I would later find out, praying.

Chapter Thirty-Two
HEADED HOME

THE WHOLE TIME SMITHY WAS away, I searched, prayed, and mourned. Miriam was sympathetic one moment, trying to comfort me with kind words and food, and distant the next, retreating from the emotion of it all into her make-believe television world. We didn't talk about her going to Copper Creek anymore, but I couldn't talk about leaving Tennessee knowing it would mean leaving Samson behind.

When Smithy came home from his short getaway, I was there to greet him as soon as I heard the car door shut, to tell him about the turn of events.

"Smithy, Samson's gone, and Bert's coming back!" I half screamed. "And Miriam is going back to Copper Creek with us, only we can't leave until we find Samson!"

"Whoa, now. Hold on," Smithy said, meeting me halfway between his car and the house. "Sit down here on the porch, and tell me what's goin' on."

I explained everything as best as I could, more than once, trying to make sure Smithy understood my dilemma. I was torn between staying until I could find my dog and leaving to make sure I was home when Bert got there.

"Nate, I know you love that dog, but you have to face the possibility that he may not be coming back. He's in a place he don't know. He may not be able to get back. It looks like y'all have had lots of rain here, and that means the smells he mighta used to find his way back has all been washed away. And what if he fought with that coyote and lost?"

"But I promised him I would take care of him! It's my job!" I buried my face in Smithy's shirt, sitting there on the steps of the porch, and I let years of hurt spill out with the new pain.

"Nate, I'm so sorry. I really am sorry." He let me cry, and he held me tightly. Then he spoke gently. "But Nate . . . I'm planning on heading back in the morning. I have to go back to work next week; and to tell you the truth, I miss Kate somethin' terrible. If you want to stay here and keep looking for Samson, maybe I can come back and get you next weekend. It's not all that far of a drive. You've got a phone here. You can call me at work and let me know what's goin' on; or you can call Dell and Opal, and they can get a hold of me."

"But what if Bert comes back, and I'm not there? I don't want him to think I gave up on him, and I don't want him to be mad that I left."

"Nate, listen. I wouldn't put so much stock in whether or not Bert comes home. You can't even know for sure that he will. Even if he did write to Miriam and tell her that's what he plans to do, he seems pretty . . . unpredictable. I just want what's best for you. You're my buddy. And you have to admit, you've got a really nice place here."

"I just don't know what to do!" I cried. And then it hit me. "The fleece!"

"The what?"

I explained to Smithy the story of Gideon; and for the first time, he seemed inclined to hear about the Bible. He didn't shut me down. I told him about my deal with God over the power bill and how it hadn't worked out like I thought it would.

"If it didn't work about you leavin' Copper Creek, how come you want to try it about goin' back or not?"

"What else *can* I do?"

I left Smithy on the porch and walked around the back of the house, where I found a giant oak to kneel beneath.

"God, if you want me to go back to Copper Creek with Smithy, please let Samson come home before Smithy leaves. If I can't find my dog, I'll take that as my sign to stay put right here. I hope this bargain is okay with You. And I'll trust You, either way You work it out."

What I prayed would take a lot of faith, the Abraham kind of faith I had pushed Miriam to have—faith enough to believe Him, even if things didn't work out the way I thought they should. Just as hard was explaining it to Miriam and convincing her to be ready to leave the next day, even though we might not be going anywhere. I started helping her pack a bag; but halfway through, she left her room to turn on a show. I finished packing without her, even going to her bathroom and grabbing everything I thought she would need to be comfortable and happy at my house.

She can sleep in Bert's room, until he comes home, I thought. Then after he comes home, I'll sleep on the couch and let Bert and Aunt Miriam figure out who gets which bedroom.

Later, I went to the living room where Miriam sat eating a sandwich and watching Leave it to Beaver. She looked wrapped up in her viewing, so I decided to try to talk with her after the show was over. I turned to leave the room.

"Nate," she called. "I need to tell you something. If you go tomorrow, I intend to go with you. It will probably be the hardest thing I've ever done in my life, and you need to understand that I'm doing it for you and for my brother." Her voice was mechanical, churning out words that were hard to say but necessary.

"I know, Miriam."

"It won't be easy for me, but I'm letting you know now . . . I want you to make sure I go, no matter what I do or say tomorrow, okay?" She never looked away from the television.

I didn't know what to say.

"If you go, tell Smithy to make me go, too. Even if I tell you tomorrow that I've changed my mind. Okay?"

"Okay," I said, and I left the room.

I didn't sleep in the big, comfortable bed that night. I slept on the floor of the screened porch, in case Samson came back in the night and wanted in. I roused several times at the nighttime sounds. Bullfrogs, crickets, and owls joined together in the normal spring symphony, but there was no scratching of paws at the back door.

In the morning, Smithy came to wake me; but I was already up, sitting and staring out the window.

"Nate, I'm almost ready to go."

"Okay, my things are waiting at the front door," I said.

"But Samson hasn't come back yet. Did you change your mind? Are you coming with me anyway?"

"No, but I'm not giving up until you've cranked the engine of that car."

"But Miriam hasn't even come out of her room this morning."

"Then we'll have to get her up."

I tiptoed into Miriam's bedroom, unsure of what I might find. I had played out several possibilities, but I didn't expect to find her in the condition she was in.

Miriam lay on her bed, completely dressed in the clothes she had worn the day before. Her eyes were open, but she didn't speak. She didn't move. She looked frozen with fear, and she looked even more the part of a porcelain doll laying on top of a quilt on a little girl's bed.

"Miriam, Smithy's getting ready to leave. And I have your bag packed, too," I said. "Just in case." Still, she didn't move. Smithy leaned close to her to check her breathing. He gave a quick nod to let me know it was normal.

"Miriam, let's go outside."

I held the wheelchair steady while Smithy scooped her up off the bed and carefully placed her in it.

"It's gonna be okay, Aunt Miriam. You're doing great."

"Nate, there's no reason to have her outside if y'all ain't goin'," Smithy said.

"She and I are going outside."

"Like I told you, you can call me this week and let me know how you're doin', okay?" Smithy said. "I can come back next weekend." I ignored him.

I parked Miriam's chair near the door. The thought of leaving had left her nearly catatonic, and I felt sorry to have caused her the stress, even if it was for her own good.

"Okay, Nate," Smithy said. "Time for me to go." His Adam's apple bobbed as he choked down sadness.

"Okay, Smithy." He gave me a quick hug goodbye and walked toward the rusty old car parked just a few feet from the house.

"I'll see you soon," he called.

I followed as far as the bottom step, then sat down and looked out over the vast yard and down to the creek. Smithy opened the car door to get in, and I buried my face in my hands. I couldn't bear to watch him leave.

No matter what, just trust Him, I thought. *No matter what.*

"Nate!" Smithy yelled loudly.

My head jerked upward; then I looked to Miriam to make sure she hadn't fallen out of her chair or something else bad. She was exactly how I left her.

"Nate! Look!" Smithy yelled again. I turned around fast, and there was Samson, trotting toward me with an infuriating aloofness, just like when he showed up at my house that first day as if he had always been there. And just like the first time I saw him, he was dirty from head to tail. When he reached me, I buried my face into the fur on his back, and I thanked God.

"Oh, Samson! Samson! I missed you so much! You scared me, boy."

He licked my face to say he was glad to see me, too.

"Where did you go?" I cried, and I prayed that he would never get lost again. "Oh, Samson! I'm so happy you're back. I love you, boy!"

Smithy came over to join us, and he kneeled down to pet Samson, too.

"Well, it looks like your prayer was answered the way you wanted," he said.

"It sure was. Now we can all go home!"

Miriam's fragile voice came from behind me. "Yes, Nate. We can all go."

Smithy and I looked at Miriam, surprised she had spoken. She was still stiff, and she sounded scared; but the corners of her mouth turned up ever so slightly as she watched my reunion with Samson.

"You're going to do great, Aunt Miriam!" I said. "There are friends for you in Copper Creek. Good people, who will be glad to know you." I was reminded of a phone call I needed to make before we left.

Back inside the house, with Samson by my side, I held the shiny black receiver up to the side of my face with both hands.

"I'm coming home, Opal," I said when she answered. "I'm coming back to Copper Creek!" I knelt in the floor and pulled my dog near me, overwhelmed with joy to have him back.

"Oh, Nate! I'm so happy to hear this news! But is everything okay, dear? What about your aunt Miriam?"

"She's coming with me, Opal! And I can't wait for you to meet her. She could really use a friend like you. I'll explain everything when we get back later today."

"Today? That's wonderful!"

"Oh, and . . . I love you, Opal."

The line was silent for a moment.

"I love you, too, Nate," she said tenderly.

Samson and I went back outside to see Smithy push Miriam's chair down the ramp and to the car. He lifted her out of the wheel-chair and placed her gently in the back seat. Before I closed the car door, I leaned in and gave her a soft kiss on the cheek. She turned toward me, and the light in her smoke gray eyes shined. She was back with us.

We packed the trunk, putting Miriam's chair on top of the bags; then we locked the door of the house. We put Samson in the back seat with Miriam and set off.

Miriam closed her eyes tightly and kept them that way for the first half hour. Every breath she took was deep and deliberate. I reached into the backseat and grabbed her bony hand. She squeezed mine tightly, then let go and focused on her breathing again.

"You're doing great," I said.

As we reached the Great Smokies and started our ascent up the western side, Smithy had something to share.

"Nate, I didn't tell you where I went while I was gone, on account of you were busy thinking about Samson."

"Yeah, I'm sorry I didn't ask. Did you see any good places? Have any adventures?" I asked him excitedly. I fiddled with the chain of my pocket watch.

"Well, it was certainly an interesting vacation! I went to visit the Tennessee State Penitentiary." He took his eyes off the road to see my reaction.

"You did what?"

"My daddy's there, Nate. I went to see my daddy! Can you believe it? I drove almost to Nashville. It was a heck of a drive, but I got to see my daddy for the first time since I was fifteen. Nine whole years since I'd seen him!"

I looked into the backseat, where Miriam sat with Samson's head in her lap. Her eyes were open, and the look on her face said she was as intrigued by Smithy's story as I was.

"That's great, Smithy!" I said.

"And guess what he done while he's been in there?"

Smithy didn't expect me to answer, but he paused a long time to build the anticipation.

"He went and found Jesus. I mean, he's locked up like an animal. Ain't seen his family in years. And he says he's the freest and the happiest he's ever been. Don't that beat all?" There was an unmistakable joy in Smithy's voice. Something had changed in him.

"He told me how sorry he was for not being around. And he told me he loved me. For the first time I can remember, he said he loved me."

Smithy took his eyes off the road longer than he should and gave me a serious stare. "It got me convinced, Nate. There's gotta be something to it. If it can change my daddy like it done, if Jesus can turn him around, then I'm a believer, too. I mean it."

The skin on my face drew tight from smiling. "And what you said to me on the way to Tennessee, about what happens after we leave this world . . . well, that's what started me thinkin', Nate. I was thinkin' before I even got there."

Out of everything in my life that I had ever done right or well, helping Smithy think about his eternal soul ranked right up there as number one on the list of things I was proud of. It was a feeling I wanted to experience again, and I hoped there would be more opportunities to share God's plan with people the way Dell had shared it with me.

Looking out the window, feeling so full of life and purpose, and headed back to the place of my roots, I thought of my baby sister, and I wanted the same kind of joy for her. Suddenly, I saw her in my reflection in the car window—the image of a seven-year-old girl, with my eyes and my nose. I would probably never know about Colleen, but I hoped that wherever she was, she was blooming.

Chapter Thirty-Three
BIG PLANS

"DON'T TAKE US HOME, SMITHY. Take us to Dell and Opal's. I want to see them, and I want them to meet Aunt Miriam."

"Well, that's good, 'cause that's where I'm goin' anyway," he said wryly. I didn't ask why.

We pulled into their driveway, right around dinnertime. Two cars, besides Smithy's, shared the driveway with the Nelsons' old farm truck and their Sunday truck.

"Hey! Isn't that Miss Gentry's car?" I asked Smithy. He only smiled like a kid at Christmas.

We left Miriam and Samson in the car together. We first needed to explain Miriam's shyness to Opal and Dell and whoever else was in the house.

I ran up the steps and stopped at the screen door. Familiar faces filled the parlor. Miss Gentry was there, and Regina. I saw Susie and Patrick, and Mrs. Pennywell, too, just like at my birthday party. I felt ten feet tall. It was a party to celebrate my return. Just like the prodigal, I came home to a party.

"Welcome home, Nate!" Opal shouted gleefully when she saw me standing on the porch. Miss Gentry got up and hugged me as I went in, on her way outside to greet Smithy. They stayed on the porch alone as I went in to greet everyone. I hugged Opal and Dell first. Opal cried, and Dell gave me a rough scrub to the top of the head.

"Two parties for me in two weeks' time!" I said. "You guys are the best."

"I can't believe you came back so soon!" Patrick said.

"It's good to see you, Nate!" Susie said.

"Welcome back, Nate," Mrs. Pennywell added. "I hope you had a nice visit with your aunt."

Joy filled my heart to see my friends gathered there again, and I had almost forgotten about Miriam and Samson. I explained the delicate situation as best I could, and everyone agreed to try to help Miriam feel at ease. Once Smithy and Miss Gentry had had long enough to greet one another in private, I went outside to get Miriam and Samson from the car.

"Are you ready?" I asked her.

"Yes, Nate. I'm feeling much better. You've been praying for me, haven't you?"

"For a good part of the trip I was," I told her.

There was no ramp, so Smithy had to carry her inside the house. Everyone was cordial, but reserved, as to not overwhelm her.

Just like I knew she would, Miriam took to Opal. If ever there was a gentle spirit who could pull someone out of their own darkness, it was Opal.

Samson was happy to see all his friends, too, even though some were hesitant to pet him. He was in such a desperate need of a bath after his adventure away from me. "It's a long story," I explained to Opal and Dell.

Opal served dinner in the dining room. Two giant pans of chicken pie and all the usual fixings waited for us there.

Patrick sat next to me at the dinner table. "Hey, Nate. Guess what," he whispered. "I've been staying here with Dell and Opal for the past couple of nights, in the room with all the posters you left. Funny, isn't it?"

"What do you mean? Why?"

"The day after you left, Howard got himself hurt. He got tore up drunk and wrapped his truck around a tree."

"Is he okay?"

"No, but he probably will be eventually. Mama's staying at the hospital with him, but she brought me here. And she's talkin' 'bout leaving him, only after he gets better. She can't take his drinkin' no more. And Opal told her we can both stay here as long as we need."

"That's great, buddy," I said. "You'll love it here."

Halfway through the meal, I wanted to share something important. "I have an announcement to make." The whole room got quiet. "I know I've traveled only as far as one state over, but going to Tennessee helped me figure something out. I know I'm young, but I already know what I'm going to do when I grow up."

"But you've known that for a while, haven't you? You're planning to join the army when you get old enough, right?" Dell said.

"Yes, I still want to do that. But I mean after."

"Let's hear it, Nate," Miss Gentry said. She smiled at me while she clung to Smithy's arm.

"I'm going to travel all around the world and tell people how much God loves them!"

I studied the reactions of my family around the table. Most of them weren't blood kin, but they were all family; and everyone was supportive of my news.

"And I want to go find people who don't have a father, and tell them that they really do," I continued. "We have a Father in Heaven. And I'm gonna be here when Bert . . . when my dad comes home, to help him. And I need your help to convince him to go to church."

"Nate, I knew the Lord had big plans for you," Dell said. "I just knew it. And it sounds like you're figuring them out."

"I'll talk to Bert about coming to church, Nate," Smithy offered. Several heads turned toward him in surprise, and no one looked happier than Miss Gentry.

"In my Bible storybook," I said, "there's a story of a woman who had been sick for a very long time. But she was healed. I know that if we can get Bert to believe, God can help him; and maybe things will be okay with me and him."

I turned to Aunt Miriam, whose chair was parked at the end of the table on my left. "And God can make things good between you and Bert, too," I said.

"I hope so," she said.

"Just have faith."

After the delicious meal, Regina surprised Smithy by bringing out his one-man band suit.

"Why don't you give us a show, baby brother?" she said playfully.

His face turned red, and he shook his head. "Not in front of Kate! Please!" he protested. But Miss Gentry urged him on. Dell brought out his fiddle and joined in. I didn't even know he played fiddle; and, unlike Smithy's just-for-fun music-making, Dell was very skilled.

Smithy put on a heck of a show. He danced around the living room and beat the drum loudly. And when he saw Miriam clapping her hands, he gently spun her chair around in a circle twice. She surprised even herself with a deep belly laugh as she spun.

I sat shoulder-to-shoulder with Susie on the couch, and Samson sat on the floor next to my feet. As the fiddle and drum beats rang in my ears, I thought about how things had come full circle.

So much of life seemed to be about people coming and going—Bert and my mama leaving Tennessee to get married, mama leaving and going to Heaven, Bert leaving and going to Louisiana, me leaving and going to Tennessee, Miriam leaving her home to come to Copper Creek with me. Even Opal, Dell, and Jenny's story had a lot of coming and going—Opal leaving college to marry Dell, and Jenny leaving her parents to find something else. In that moment, I was thankful for the one thing that was sure. God never leaves. He had been there all along.

My roots reached down into shallow soil, but it's where I was planted; and they were strong.

THE END

EPILOGUE

YOU COULD SAY THAT MY life got even better after *The End*.

Bert came back before the next power bill was due. I can't say that he came home a changed man and that he read me bedtime stories every night and made sure I brushed my teeth every morning. That was never Bert. But he did become someone I respected; and with the help of good doctors and the Lord, we built a relationship I didn't think was possible. At the end of his life, I could say with confidence that he loved me—not just because I heard him say it, but because I felt it from him. He figured out ways to show it that didn't cripple him.

Miriam stayed with us a long time; but eventually, she returned to Topknot. She was back every Christmas, though, and I spent at least a month with her every summer.

The idea that anyone could do anything if they worked hard enough never left me. I planned to join the service, then the mission field, but I decided to go to college first. It was my father's dream for me, and he saved up enough money over the years to completely cover the cost.

People often asked me why a preacher studied sociology instead of theology. Some thought it was a waste of time. But as a wise woman once told me, education is never a waste of time or energy.

I studied sociology my whole life. First in the pages of *National Geographic*, which I still read, then in college, then on the mission field. My magazines hadn't taught me as much about foreign lands as it had taught me about people. Not any certain kind of people—just people. All the kinds God made, who are more alike than they are different.

I did go into the service, but not the army. Instead, I became an airman, like my hero Captain Kittinger. And since I learned how to fly planes, when the time came, I was able to visit just about any place on the map and share the Gospel.

When I joined the mission field, my first big donation came from the former Miss Susie Pennywell and her wealthy banker husband. They have been faithful monthly contributors to my work ever since.

I met my wife while ministering in the British West Indies. At nearly six-feet-tall and with perfect cocoa skin and eyes the color of an Irish moor, she was easily the most beautiful woman I had ever seen. I remember the day she approached me like it was yesterday—she came up and introduced herself after a tent meeting in her village. After we married, she left her island home to serve the Lord with me at our next mission in Italy, near the Amalfi Coast.

As for my friends, I was best man at Smithy and Kate's wedding. (I started calling her Kate the day after Smithy proposed.) They have one daughter, Jocelyn Faith, and Smithy is head deacon at Copper Creek Baptist Church.

Patrick lived with Dell and Opal off and on until we were in high school, when his mother got married again to someone more stable. Now, he's married, and he manages the farm for the Nelsons. His three children have always known them as Granny and Pa.

Opal shipped a Christmas pie to every international location I served; and now that we're back in my home state, about two miles from the Atlantic Ocean, I'm able to pick them up in person some years.

The Bible storybook has a special place on the shelf in my study. My favorite thing is seeing the light in my children's eyes when we read the stories together. And each time I cuddle up with Nathaniel, Jr. and Mary Colleen to read, we take out my mama's picture, tucked safely within the pages, and blow her a kiss.

AUTHOR'S NOTE

About the setting:

I have so much fun creating fictional towns that hold true to the unique beauty and undeniable charm of real towns in my state. My first book is set in Springville, North Carolina—an imagined place that bears a strong resemblance to many places in Wilkes, Surry, and Yadkin counties, the greater area in which I was raised. (If you'd like to know what happened to Nate's baby sister, *Grace & Lavender* is a short, contemporary novel, which features Colleen as the main character.)

In this book, Copper Creek is a make-believe place I like to imagine is found in the region of Swain and Haywood Counties of North Carolina. Perhaps Copper Creek is a place that helped shape the borders of the Great Smoky Mountains National Park. Maybe the park referenced in the story is a smaller territory than the beautiful place we know and love in real life, allowing for more towns to have grown up in the region.

My writing has covered the Piedmont and the Mountains, so obviously the next story brewing in my mind is set on our majestic coast. The Coastal Plain of my state is ripe with great story essence.

I hope, first of all, to honor the Lord with my writing and to point people to Him. I also enjoy showcasing my home state and highlighting important issues, while hopefully evoking emotion in the reader and entertaining.

Thank you for reading.

For more information about
Heather Norman Smith
&
Where I Was Planted
please visit:

www.heathernormansmith.com
@HNSblog
www.facebook.com/heathernormansmith
www.instagram.com/heathernormansmith

For more information about
AMBASSADOR INTERNATIONAL
please visit:

www.ambassador-international.com
@AmbassadorIntl
www.facebook.com/AmbassadorIntl

*If you enjoyed this book, please consider leaving us a review on
Amazon, Goodreads, or our website.*